Sam

By

Gabriel Klasing

Printed in the United States of America

First Printing, 2016

ISBN 978-0-9982173-1-4

Gabriel Klasing
915 Thomas J. Drive
Flint, MI. 48506

Dedication

To all of my friends and family. Thank you for your encouragement and always being there to lend me a hand. I love you all. And to my children always believe that you are worth everything. Never forget that mommy loves you!

CHAPTER 1

I became a vampire in July of 1803. That makes me 213ish I think, as my actual age today. It is hard to remember after you get past the first 100 years. In human years, I'm forever frozen at the ripe old age of twenty five.

A woman vampire started the process of my change. I had never seen her before, and in the small sleepy little town where we lived, everyone knew everyone and there had not been any talk of the beautiful women. If the people of the town knew she had been here, we would have heard about the beautiful woman, as all the girls that I knew would have been jealous of her.

I remember it like it was yesterday... Her beauty was unparalleled to anything that I had ever seen before. She had pale skin like the rays of the sun had never kiss her body. Her face was round in shape with the cuties little nose, big full crimson red lips, her eyes a deep sky blue. Her eyes were the kind that either pierce through you like bullets from a gun or the kind that are as soft and gentle as a new born baby. Her eyes that day were the soft and gentle blue. Her hair was long straight and sandy blond in color and it framed her face perfectly, and shimmered in the sunlight. She was thin and was dressed as if she belonged in the dark ages. Her dress was plain and red in color she wore a black cloak over it. Her beauty held my attention as if she was the most beautiful white rose in the world and I was in awe of it. I had never seen someone like that in all of my twenty years. I could not help but just stare at her unmoving, almost as if I was in some kind of trance. My mind only thinking about how beautiful she was and wishing at the same time I could be that beautiful. I guess I should have been more careful about what I wished for.

What I did not know is that she was plotting how she would kill me. Her eyes meet my staring gaze and were instantly locked on her by some unforeseen force. Even if I wanted to, I could not look away. The force was so intense that I had not even noticed her advancement and now she was right in front of me. The force seemed to be blocking my mind from working and comprehending what was going on. She took my hand in hers and twirled me around like a ballerina. After the twirl, I seen her raise my hand and arm to her face. She smiled a wicked smile at me. Then a shock wave of pain hit me as she sunk her teeth into my wrist at first. The pain was unreal. The one and only time that I had felt pain close to this is when I accidently cut myself with a knife, that I had been told not to touch all through childhood. Then she let go and smiled an evil bloody smile at me. Her eyes were not the deep sky blue any more like they had been a seconds ago. Now they were a pale blue almost translucent that seemed to glow in the sunlight. I could not scream I could not move until my eyes left her gaze but it was too late she had already bit my neck. I tried to scream at that point but my body was too weak to make a sound. I remember the pain as her teeth punctured my skin. I could feel my veins collapsing under the pressure of her sucking my blood.

At this point, all I could do now was stare up at the blue sky and watch as it was quickly started to fade away. The blue sky started fading to black around the edges of my vision. The blue sky was getting smaller and smaller with every sucking sound that she made. I was slipping further and further away. Just when the end was near and there was only a pinhole of light coming through she let go. I do not know what frightened her off and at that point, I really did not care. I was moments away from dying, all I could think about was my mother, and how upset she was going to be. As I lay there motionless hearing and seeing nothing I felt a few drops of something on my lips. There was nothing for a long time and I thought I was dead. I could not see, smell, feel or hear anything. However, where was the light at the end of the tunnel? That is what people said you would see when you die. All I could see was blackness.

Then all at once, it began, thousands of needles piercing through my skin ever so slowly. Like when you are sewing and you accidently prick your finger but instead of the needle being pulled out, they are slowly pushed farther and farther into your skin right to your bones. Of course, this did not happen all at once it came in waves. It started with my hands and up my arms, then my feet through my legs this eventually spreading to my chest. When the needles got to my heart it did not feel like little needles anymore it felt more like a dagger that someone had plunged into me.

Through the process, I thought I was dying and I could not help but wonder if this was a part of dying. No wonder no one ever wanted to die if it felt like this. As I lay there slowly, being tortured wishing for it to be over, and wishing I could leave my body I found that I could focus on other things to block out some of the pain. Like the nagging questions that kept repeating over and over again. Was this death? Was it supposed to be this painful or should it be? To which I did not have answer but I mulled it over in my mind repeatedly. I am assuming that days, months maybe even years went by as I lay there hoping for a sign that I could leave my body along with the pain. Eventually as the pain finally started too subsided, I thought I was going to be able to leave this body and do whatever it is you do when you die.

Feeling started coming back to my fingers at first. I could feel the grass, sticks and stones under my fingers as my fingernails scraped the ground like metal rakes. Stones felt like they were made of glass, smooth, soft and very fragile. The grass felt like velvet under my palms and arms. Then like tiny electric shocks, I started feeling other parts of my body. The ground that used to be hard now felt like I was lying on a pillow made from the finest down and feathers. As I thought about those feelings, I noticed that I could hear a bird chirping. Wow the bird was really loud, and I thought it was right by my head. I turned my head towards the noise and forced my eyes open. The sunshine was so bright that it made my eyes hurt and I could just barely make out that there was no bird sitting there. Even though it still sounded like it. As I realized that the bird was not there my sight took me off guard even though my squinting and fluttering eyelids. I could see the definition of every leaf on the trees in great detail. The green was almost transparent when the rays of the sun hit them. I could see all of the veins of the leaf and the tiny hair like structures. It was almost as if I was looking through a magnifying glass at them.

I lay there taking in all the new sights and sounds then I decided it was time to get up and in the same moment that I thought it, my body sprang to life. Standing looking around I was seeing the world in a completely new perspective. The colors of the field and surrounding forest where brighter than I had remembered them ever being. Just as I was getting used to my new senses one more thing started. A burning fire in my throat, it felt like I had swallowed the coals from a fire. I made the decision to move towards a creek that I could hear babbling in the distance. I guess I will go there and get a drink maybe the fire will go away. As I walked, I could hear all of the animals moving in the forest around me. At the same time I was hearing their beating hearts like I had placed my ear right up against them thud, thud, thud.

The next sense that came back to me was my sense of smell. I could smell things that I had never smelt before. I could smell the earth, the cool water running in the creek, the coming rain and the wildflowers that had a very potent sweet smell. I could smell the wild flowers before but they had never been this strong smelling.

At the creek side, I bent down to take a drink. I sucked in a big gulp of water and swallowed it but the fire in my throat was not extinguished and still raging out of control. The water also made my stomach upset and I regurgitated it as quickly has I had drank it. I sat down on the bank of the creek with my mind spinning out of control. Was I sick…should I go see the doctor…is it the cholera?

Sitting there pondering why I felt sick. A deer approached the bank on the other side of the creek. I watched the deer as it drank and saw the blood pumping through its veins and could hear the thudding of its huge heart. My brain reacted and the next thing I remember was draining all of the blood from this deer. I let the carcass go and it fell to the ground with a thud, but all I could think was I need more, and the blood lust began. I drank about three or four more deer and was full for now. The fire in my throat had been extinguished and the feeling of being sick to my stomach was gone for now anyway.

So exhausted from the feast, I sat down on the ground and rested my back against the tree. Although I did not need the support, it was still nice. I yawned and stretched my arms around the back of the tree. I guess that I had been so lost in thought that I had not heard someone approaching me. The next thing I knew someone or something had locked my arms behind the tree. It was not painful but more irritating and scary than anything. I tried to wiggle free but whatever had me pinned there was not letting go without a fight.

"What are you doing out here?" a man's voice asked from behind me. To shocked, to answer right away by the creepiness of his tone I said nothing. Again, he said "What are you doing out here?"

"I…I…I don't know." I said in an almost inaudible voice stumbling over the words.

"Where did you come from?" He asked.

My mind started to struggle even more. Who is this man and why is he holding me here the voice inside my head said. Fear started to swell inside my head and triggered the flight response. I started to physically struggle against the restraints. The tree was making cracking, and groaning sounds as I struggled more, and more against the restraints holding me there. As I struggled, I managed to find my voice again.

"Who are you and what do you want from me?" I yelled at him.

"Wait a minute, I'm asking the questions miss!" He said back to me in a gruff tone.

"Okay, okay, my name is Sam. I don't know how I got here or where I am for that matter." In truth, I knew exactly where I was and how to get home but I was not going to tell him that.

"Ok Sam, so you are telling me that you don't remember anything of how you got like this or how you got here?" He said this time in what seemed to be a normal non-creepy voice.

"That is correct. Could you let me go now?" I asked but something he said stuck out in my head *how I got like this*. What was he talking about? How I got pinned against the tree? The thought was interrupted by his reply.

"No way, how do I know that you are not here to kill me or something?" I wanted to laugh, me kill him. That was funny I am only a small little girl.

"Look I will not hurt you I'm just as confused as you are." I said trying not to laugh still.

"Ok then against my better judgment I'm going to release you." He said

My hands freed, now do I run for it or stay. As I contemplated for a half a second, but before I could do anything the most beautiful man that I had ever seen walked out from behind the tree. Long glowing black hair framed his face. His eyes emerald green color. His face was that of an angel. His skin was very pale almost translucent white, the same color as a porcelain face on a doll. I do not know why my brain did not make the connection that his skin was the same color as the lady's skin that had tried to kill me but it didn't. My eyes followed all of his contours down to his toes, he was muscular but not to muscular. I was mesmerized by his looks. I thought that at least it was someone handsome that was going to kill me. I was now at the point that I did not care if he killed me. Nevertheless, I could not just spread my arms and say go ahead. So I said in a gruff tone.

"Ok I told you my name now it is your turn. What is your name?"

"My name is Jaxson mam." He replied in a completely different tone now with a slight smile on his face.

"Jaxson what was that about pinning me to the tree and all?" I asked with anger in my tone.

"Nothing just having a little fun, I was out hunting when I caught your scent. I followed it here, and when you did not seem to notice me I thought it would be fun to scare you." He said almost laughing.

"Well, (I said with a huff) that was not funny. You should not do that to people sir!" I spat at him.

"How old are you?" Jaxson asked me as he closed the small gap between us.

"I'm 20." I answered thinking, that is an odd question to ask a person that you just meet, especially a lady. That was one of the golden rules of my world; a man did not need to know your age.

"What is your real age?" he asked this time, with a serious look on his face.

Why would he ask me that, does he think I would lie about my age, why would I. "That is my real age. Why how old are you?" I replied with a bit of sarcastic tone.

"I'm 200 years old." He replied with a serious look about his face.

Uncontrollable laughter filled the forest; I just could not stop or help it. Did this man really just say that he was 200 years old? What was he some kind of funny guy now?

"You are not people don't live to be that old." I choked out between giggles.

"I'm not just any person." He said

"Oh, you look like a person to me." I said even though he did look a little different from any human I had ever met before.

"Oh my, he exclaimed you have no idea, do you?" He said with a look of concern on his face.

"No idea of what?" I blurted out getting very irritated by his endless questions.

"Ok, I am a vampire." He said in a slow even tone and flashed those beautiful green eyes at me with a wicked smirk across his lips. I started laughing again.

"They are not real" I got out through the laughter. When this came out of my lips, he grabbed a hold of me and looked straight into my eyes. I looked deep into his eyes and watched as they change color from that beautiful green into translucent glowing blue almost white. As that was happening, he parted his lips ever so slightly to show me his teeth. There on each side, where the k-9 teeth would have been there was two longer than all the rest that came to a point. Kind of like that of a dog…no more like a needle, long, straight and pointy. As I took in all of these features, I let out a huge gasp.

"Please don't kill me." I choked out, as I started begging for my life. I had read a book about vampires and none of them had made the vampires so pretty or handsome they were monsters and hideous looking. You would know that they were vampires just by one look according to the book. Also in the book, it said that vampires only came out at night because the sunlight would burn them and they would die. I started to wonder if this was some kind of trick but it did not matter, anymore I knew that I had to get away.

"I can't kill you, you are already dead." He said and I immediately started panicking. My mind was telling me to get free and run as fast as you can. At the same time, I was thinking it; I freed myself from his grasp and made a break for it. I ran and ran with him not far behind me.

"Hey stop he shouted at me. Look, I am not going to hurt you. This is not something you can out run." What was he saying; I could not out run my impending doom? Nevertheless, for some reason, those words stopped me dead in my tracks.

"Ok, kill me then." I said shaking with fear.

"I told you I'm not going to kill you. However, it is obvious that you do not know what you are. Come with me I will show you." He reached for my hand. I hesitated but took his hand in return. Wow, this was either a very dumb move or he was telling me the truth either way I knew my life was over even if I would have kept running. I have to admit that I had noticed that some things are a little… no a lot different from what they used to be. The sight, hearing and other things that had been heightened, did have me thinking what was wrong with me. We walked what seemed like forever. We did not speak. Finally, there in the middle of the forest was a house.

"Is that where we are going?" I asked pointing to the house.

"Yes." He replied.

"Is this your house?" I asked trying to make small talk now.

"Yes" He replied again.

We climbed the front steps and went inside. He was still holding my hand as he led me through the veranda and down a hall to a rather large powder room.

He pulled me inside the door with my back to a huge mirror. He looked deep into my eyes and said

"When you are ready to look at yourself, you may turn around. You are slightly different than what you used to look like."

I stared back into his eyes and for the first time saw some concern on his face. I slowly turned around and looked at the person that did not appear to be me in the mirror. My eyes were the light translucent glowing blue color, like his in the forest. My face was pale like his, my hair so healthy and shiny like his. Then as I studied the face in the mirror, I realized it was my reflection. As I took, all of this in red tears ran down my face and I noticed that my heartbeat was gone. I took a deep breath and said

"I'm just like you beautiful and pale I'm a vampire aren't I."

My heart sank as I stumbled over the word vampire. My mind was having a hard time conceiving the truth that, a mythical creature could be real and that I am one. He looked at my face through the mirror.

"Don't cry it is ok." He said in a kind and gentle voice laced with sadness in his eyes.

I turned away from the person in the mirror, fell to my knees, and began sobbing. As I sobbed, he stood there and did not say a word. After my dress was soaked in blood along with some on the floor I pulled it together and made myself stop crying. As I stopped crying Jaxson without saying a word pulled me to my feet, walked me to the kitchen, and sat me in a chair. He placed a finger under my chin and pulled my face up until our eyes meet, then he whispered.

"It will be ok, don't worry. I will teach you what you need to know."

He removed his fingers from my chin and my head slumped back to staring at the floor, my mind in disbelief. I thought about my family, my house and my previous life. As I thought of these things, I blurted out "I have to go." At the same time, I got up and ran for the door.

"Wait, where are you going?" He asked.

"I have to go home my family is probably worried about me." I said still moving towards the door. He was instantly in front of me blocking the door.

"Sam I'm sorry but you can't go home." He said, with sadness written all over his face.

"Why not!" I demanded.

"Remember what you saw in the mirror." He said, I looked away and stared at the floor and replied a simple.

"Yes."

"Well, they are going to see the same thing that person that looks like you but with differences. Most of all you are now a monster." He said.

"They won't care what I look like as long as I'm ok." I rebutted, but nothing could prepare me for what he said next.

"How are you going to feel when you kill them all?" He asked in a warm gentle voice, I could tell he was not trying to anger me but trying to make me see the truth.

"I won't do that." I shouted back at him. He ignored my yelling kept up with the cool, calm, collected attitude, and asked me the question.

"Have you been around humans since the change?"

"No but I know that I will not hurt them I love them." I said with the tears welling up in my eyes.

"What did you have to drink today?" He asked. What a strange question I thought but answered anyway.

"Nothing I replied."

"So that was not you're doing with the dead deer all over the place?" I gasped in horror as the memory of killing the deer flooded my mind. The images of their lifeless bodies danced around in my head and I gasped again.

"Yes that was me, but I'm not thirsty right now." I yelled back at him through my teeth. He pulled my face close to his and looked me straight in the eyes.

"Listen to me closely you will kill them you have not been around any humans and the call of their blood is much more potent than that of the animals that you killed today."

His words sank in to my brain, and I fell to my knees again and stared at the floor. This time he fell to the ground with me and held me close to his body.

"Everything will be ok I promise, I'm sorry that this has happened to you." He said with sincerity. "Someday you will be strong enough to go back and watch from a distance and maybe in some years as you practice controlling yourself you will be able to see them again. I will teach you everything I know but you are going to have to trust me and stay with me."

I sat there nestled into his chest with his arms holding me tight, I came to the resolve that I would stay, and I will learn for my family.

CHAPTER 2

It was morning; the sun was coming up over the trees of the forest. The sky was a beautiful bright orange color. I sat in the chair at the kitchen table staring out into the forest watching bird's leap from tree to tree. A mouse ran across the forest floor and into a hole in a tree trunk. As I sat there, watching, I remembered what my mother, father, brother and sisters looked like. I wondered if they noticed I was gone. I am sure they did notice. They loved me. I had once fell and sprained my ankle walking home and just as it was getting dark here came my brother looking for me. I gasped aloud of the horror that my mind thought of next. What if they were in the forest looking for me? What if the vampire that had tried to kill me finds them? Worse, what if they find me? My mind was starting to go wild with fears of what ifs.

"What's wrong?" A worried voice came from behind me. As my eyes started to fill with tears again, I choked out.

"What if they are looking for me, out there in the forest where I was changed? What if that vampire that turned me is out there killing them?"

"Sh, sh, sh, it is ok, I am sure they are fine." After a long hesitation, he said. "Do you want me to see if they are ok?"

"Yes but can you control yourself enough not to harm them?" I asked.

He replied with a chuckle, and then went on to say. "I have been doing this for a long time I will be fine."

"How do you know where they live?" I asked out of curiosity.

"It is simple all I have to do is follow your trail back to your home." He paused and thought for a second. "I will go just before sundown and I will be back shortly after."

"Ok" I replied. "What are we going to do for the rest of the day?" I ask, but really did not care about the answer. I was just making small talk.

"How do you feel?" he asked.

"I'm ok." I said at first but then decided that I need to be honest. "Actually, I don't really know how I feel…I'm not sure about anything anymore."

"You are looking a little weak. When is the last time you feed?" He asked. I do not know why he asked me a question he already knew the answer too.

"No, I'm not really hungry for food thanks. Nothing really sounds good" I replied not thinking about my answer.

"Oh, Sam, you have a lot to learn. I am not talking about human food I am talking about blood because that is what you drink or feed on now. Or was that some other vampire that massacred all those deer?" He chuckled. "Not to mention you cried most of that out. You should be getting thirsty."

I started to reply no I was fine when the fire in my throat was back with a vengeance. "I guess maybe a little."

"Have you had any human blood since you came to?" Again, with the questions that he already knew the answers too but the way he said it made me appalled and a bit agitated by his question. I snapped the answer in a harsh tone. "No... And I would rather not." He now stood in front of me with each medium sized hand on either side of my face and looked into my eyes.

"To stay strong you must" His whisper sounded like the breeze outside calm and relaxing. "If you don't drink human blood the power to control and resistance will not be there you will never be able to see your family." This information slowly sunk into my head and after a brief silence, I said.

"Ok, I will try."

He grabbed my hand, pulled me from the chair, and led me down a dark hallway to some other part of the house. This appeared to be a bedroom. The drapes were drawn and it was as black as night in the room. If it had not been for my exceptional sight, I would have not been able to see my hand in front of my face. This room was not huge but big enough for a queen size bed and a dresser. There on the bed I saw two people sleeping. I could hear their deep breaths and the pounding of their hearts. My instincts and senses kicked in I could almost taste the blood in the air. I slowly walked closer and closer to the sleeping pair. From behind me, I heard Jaxson chuckle a little bit. "They are not going to hurt you," He said in a whisper so low that I almost could not hear him.

The next thing I knew the blood hit my tongue and down my throat putting out the agonizing fire in my throat. The taste was so amazing it was like eating a steak that was browned only on the outside. Wow, I'm never going back to animal blood again I thought. Now I was on the second human and before I knew it this person was drained as well. When I finished I fell to the floor. I felt dizzy, like when you have a fever and cannot get out of bed.

"Are you ok?" His sweet voice asked from somewhere in the room.

"Yes I'm fine." I replied with a giggle.

He scoped me up off the floor, carried me to another room, and laid me on a soft bed. I still had not opened my eyes after I had fallen to the floor.

"Well you be ok for a few minutes. I have something I need to do." At this point, all I could do is nod and I hoped that he could see me nod. I felt him move so I knew that he must have seen me nod. Then what seemed like two seconds he was back.

"Are you sure you are ok." He asked again.

"Yes I'm fine, the dizziness is starting to wear off I think. Is it like that every time you drink human?" I asked out of curiosity.

"No just the first few times." He said so soft and sweet.

"How often am I supposed to feed?" Was my next question that I needed to know the answer to?

"With you being new, you should feed at least twice per day. When you get older you can cut back to once per day or even every other day." He said playing with a few strands of my hair.

"What about sleep?" I asked because I was feeling tired.

"The older you get you will require less and less sleep until you don't sleep anymore."

"How long does that take?" I asked with a yawn.

"Approximately a few months to a year at most, whenever the chemicals in your brain change to vampire and all human traces are gone. You should sleep now I know you have not slept well in a while. I will wake you later when I get back from checking on your family."

I heard those words and my eye lids closed and I was out like a light.

I woke up screaming. This dream I had scared me. It was about me standing on the remains of my family they were all dead and I guessed that I had killed them. Jaxson was standing over me as the tears began again.

"What is the matter?" he asked.

"I had a horrible dream." I said through the sobs.

"What was it about?" He asked.

"Me, I killed my whole family." I said, throwing me further into the depths of despair.

"Oh Sam, it is ok I will not let you hurt them." He put his arms around me and held me tight, and rubbed my back. He was trying to sooth me. It was helping and I finally stopped crying. "You should go back to sleep you must still be tired." I nodded and was back to sleep as fast as I had waken. The next thing I knew Jaxson was waking me up.

"Wake up sleepy head it is time for breakfast." I sprang out of bed almost knocking him to the floor. I still need to get used to how fast I could move.

"Did I sleep all day and night?" I complained with a yawn.

"Yes you did, told you, you were tired. Come I brought you breakfast."

In the same small room as the last time, there were two people sleeping, and the same as last time I drank them both dry. Unlike last time though the dizziness was not as dizzying, I did not fall on the floor this time even though I wanted too. I managed to sit down in a chair and closed my eyes for a while, as I waited for the dizziness to ware off. While I was sitting there, I could hear things being moved around but did not or could not pay attention to what was going on. What I thought was a few minutes that passed must have been longer because when I opened my eyes the bodies were gone and Jaxson was sitting on the edge of the bed staring at me.

"Did you get a chance to check on my family last night?" I muttered closing my eyes again as a dizzy spell gripped me again.

"Yes, they are all fine, they have been in the forest looking for you but there are no dangers to them, whom ever made you has moved on."

Hearing this gave me a since of relief. "What are we doing today?" I asked not really caring, but I thought the gesture would make him think I was interested in something that he wanted to do.

"You are going to learn something today." He paused then started again. "How about, we start with some vampire history. Vampires go a long way back. They have been in legends and folk lore for centuries. Some of the legends are true and some are not. However, the most important thing you need to learn about is the elders they have been around since the beginning of vampirism. The elders all live together in Heidelberg Germany. There are eight of them. They are the government of the vampire world. They make sure all vampires follow the rules. If you break the rules they will come looking for you, and no vampire would want that." Jaxson explained. As he went on, I became distracted by my own thoughts and was not paying attention to anything he said. Honestly, I really did not care about history or anything that had to do with the past unless it was my past or my families past. As he talked about the history, we changed rooms to the kitchen.

Sitting at the table and staring into the forest. I saw some birds leaping from tree to tree and could hear the tweet, tweet, tweet sounds that they were making. There was a deer laying down taking a nap. It looked so peaceful out there. I was thinking about walking through the forest as I watched the leaves gently blowing in the wind. It was a partly cloudy day and the sun that was hitting my leg felt very warm and it felt good. Jaxson was still talking but I rudely interrupted him.

"Can I go for a walk? I have not been out of the house for a few days, and it looks so nice."

Without waiting for his answer, I jumped to my feet and was out the door in a split second. Standing on the porch, I took a deep breath in. I could smell flowers roses, and lilies in the breeze. The smell of grass, earth and trees was the next thing I could smell. I could feel the sun on my skin again, and felt the light breeze that blew through my hair and across my skin. I took the two-steps down to the earth and was off I wanted to run. Paying no attention to anything, I ran and ran. I finally stopped at a huge ravine in the forest floor. It was the size of a cornfield across and almost as deep as one. I stood there thinking about crossing it when I heard rustling behind me. I spun on the ball of one foot to see what was there. It was just Jaxson. I hadn't noticed that he had followed me. He looked at me with worry in his eyes.

"Where exactly are you going?" As he asked me the question I watched his eyes darting around, it almost seemed like he was looking for something.

"I just wanted to..." I started but decided to ask him a question instead. "Is there something wrong?"

He looked me in the eye and said, "We should not be here. There is something out here in the forest that could kill us both." A wave of panic washed over me for a split second then I though he was bluffing. What out here is more powerful than a vampire I wonder, and decided to ask.

"What are you talking about?"

"I have seen a very large werewolf around here lately." I did not know what I wanted to do laugh or take him seriously. So I settled for asking another question.

"Are they our enemies?" I do not know why but this sounded funny coming out of my mouth.

"No, not really, but they do have the power to kill an unsuspecting vampire. I saw it happen about 100 years ago. A vampire that I knew was trying to keep one as a pet or something like that. One day the werewolf turned on him and ripped him to shreds. That is the story that I heard anyway, I think he was trying to do something else with the werewolf though."

I looked at Jaxson, and the fear and terror of the story was on his face. He was being serious, and that triggered some fear in me. I turned around to look at the ravine one more time just as a cloud was passing overhead. The Forest fell into deep shadow. I scanned the shadows and saw a huge furry creature deep in the brush. As I spotted the animal, it looked directly at me. The eyes seemed to pierce right through me. The eyes were a glowing green color almost like the eyes of a cat. I was frozen in place, the presents of the beast did not scare me it was welcoming like this creature was a long lost friend. I started to walk forward towards the beast when my arm was grabbed and I was being hulled backwards.

"Sam, Sam come we have to go now." he shouted at me.

I could hear him but I could not take my eyes off the eyes that were staring back at me. I was being drug away and finally when I could not see the eyes anymore and whatever gravitational pull that had been there was gone, we were running for home. We entered the comforts of home and threw the door shut. This made the whole house shutter and rattle. Even the windows protested against the force.

"What just happened?" I whispered, trying to figure things out in my own mind what I had just seen.

"That was the werewolf that I was talking about." He said staring out the window.

"No, I mean, why did it feel like the werewolf or whatever it was, was trying to talk to me. I could not resist, there was some kind of gravitational pull I felt, and I just wanted to be near it. Has that ever happened to you?" I said staring at the floor and replaying the encounter in my head. I could see the glowing green eyes again.

"No I have never been attracted to a werewolf." He said with a little bit of a giggle.

"I almost feel like I know that werewolf." I said.

I sat down in a chair trying to make since of it, but no logical explanation was coming to me. While I sat there and pondered, I could see flashes of Jaxson looking out all of the windows. I assumed that he was seeing if the werewolf followed us here. As he calmed down and came to the conclusion that we were not followed. He said "Sam, we have to leave it is no longer safe for us here."

I jumped up, knocking the chair over, and shouted.

"No I'm not leaving my family, especially not with a werewolf on the loose." My shouting shook the whole house and made everything rattle.

"Honey, it would be better for everyone if we leave." He said in a soft sweet tone.

The word honey sank into my mind the quickest. This beautiful smart handsome man was falling in love with me. This was the first time that he had ever called me this and it felt good because I was falling for him too. I let the rest of the relocating thing pass me by for a few minutes. All I could think right now was this is my chance to find that special someone in my life. I do not want to say my family meant nothing at this point but I had a chance for a new life and that one person that loved me, and I could not see my family right now anyway. Therefore, I simply replied in a whisper.

"Okay if you think it would be best."

"It is settled then we will leave tonight. You need to get some rest for our journey."

I started walking towards the hallway to my room feeling high from the word honey still or maybe I was misinterpreting it to be something that it was not. At this point though I was going to allow myself the privilege of thinking, he was in love with me. I had to figure it out soon or it was going to drive me insane. In an effort to figure it out, I started in on some questioning.

"Jaxson, why did you bring me here, that day that you found me in the forest?"

"You must go to sleep we will talk in a little while. Besides we have to have something to talk about on our journey." He chuckled.

I closed the door softly and jumped on the bed, the bed groaned in agony. I was not really sleepy and just stared at the ceiling for a moment before I was back to thinking about him calling me honey. I realized now that it might have been a ploy to get me to stop yelling. I need to leave that subject alone for now though. As a result, I started thinking about the werewolf that I had seen today and started to analyze what it was trying to tell me. I could see those glowing green eyes staring back at me again. I was struggling to put all the pieces to the puzzle together, nothing seemed to fit right. I was annoyed with the subject and decided to leave it be for now. I began reflecting on the past few days, what I knew and what I had learned. I knew that vampires and werewolves existed and that I was a vampire. Then as if a strike of lightning hit me, I wondered what else was real: witches, demons, angels, ghost and fairies. I would have to ask Jaxson about these.

"Sam honey it is time to wake up, we need to get going. I got something for you." He said softly.

I slowly opened my eyes to him staring directly into mine. There was a hint of excitement in his eyes. I slowly sat up and rubbed the sleep out of my eyes. When I removed my hands from my face, I saw next to me on the bed a huge box, the kind that clothing came in. Not just any clothing, but nice fancy dresses from high end dress shops. He pushed the box towards me. I grasped the box in both hands and opened it. The dress was stunning, the type of dress that I had always wanted but could not afford. It was red velvet with white lace over gold inlay. The lace and gold ran down the front in the middle of the dress. I sprang out of bed and took the dress out of the box letting it unfold as I held it up to my small frame.

"Jaxson will you excuse me for a moment, I would love to put this on." I said excitedly. He did not say anything and shut the door behind him. I was out of my old tattered dress in a flash. I threw on this exquisite dress, it fit perfectly. The shoulders had a medium size puff of the red velvet. Where the puff ended, the velvet tightened around my upper arm and came to a point at the top of the sleeve. The sleeve was just a hair shorter than my fingertips. The underside of the sleeve tapered back to free my hands. The inside of the sleeve was lined with the same satiny gold material that ran down the middle of the dress under the lace. The bodice was very tight fitting and held all of my curves well. It was a good thing that I really did not have to breath. Red velvet wrapped around the back and sides of the bodice and skirt to the front of the dress where it joined with the gold silky fabric with a white lace overlay. The neckline on the dress was a box cut, straight down from the shoulders to the top of my bosoms then straight across. The skirt of the dress flared out at the waist and ran down to the floor. I admired myself in the mirror. I was lost in thought, and had not heard Jaxson enter the room. I caught his reflection in the mirror, that startled me, and I did jump a little bit.

"Do you need some help with those buttons?" He whispered in my ear. His breath tickled my ear a bit.

"Yes Please." I whispered back.

He looked through the mirror to see me from the front while he did up the buttons. I was watching his eyes as they went up and down me a few times. Finally, his eyes met mine. I saw something I was not expecting, one tiny tear. I was very surprised to see this but I looked quickly away to avoid tearing up myself. When he got to the top button he hesitated and leaned into my ear and whispered." You are the most exquisite creature that I have ever seen."

Then he spun me in his arms to face him. He leaned in and kissed me. If I had, a heart that was beating it would have been so loud that it would have woken up the forest. If I had blood pumping through my veins, I would have felt the heat warm me from head to toe. It would have been a quick kiss as he started to pull away but, I was not willing to let him go yet I threw my arms around his neck and twined my fingers in his hair, and pulled his face closer to mine and kissed him with all the passion that I could muster. He broke away from me and took both of my hands in his.

"I have been waiting a long time for a kiss like that." He whispered to me.

I felt the prick of a tear forming in my eye.

"I'm sorry I kept you waiting." I replied choking back the tears that were coming. Also, I didn't really know how else to reply. This was the sweetest thing that anyone had ever said to me.

"Come we must go now." He said and dropped one hand leading me out of the room, down the hallway, and out of the front door. I took one last glance at the house, and then it was gone as we disappeared into the forest. I wished that we could stay but the concern for our safety was stronger than anything that would keep us here. Well at least there was no going home for me anyway and Jaxson was all I had. Then again, I could run in the opposite direction of him right now but he would have caught me and forced me to come with him or would he? I wondered then decided that it did not matter anyway because I could not think of a better person to run away with.

CHAPTER 3

We walked for a long time not saying anything to each other just holding hands. I was listening to the crickets and the frogs serenading us with the beautiful music they were making together. Then all of a sudden, the smell of human hit me like a ton of bricks. This set my throat to burning and I lost all control. I let go of Jaxson's hand and ran towards the smell. There in a small clearing was a small camp with a fire burning and two burley men lying on the ground next to the fire covered in blankets. I knelt down by the man closest to me, went straight for his neck, and started drinking him dry. The man on the other side of the fire was awakened by the commotion that his friend was making. The man in my arms was flailing around like a fish out of water. At one point, he even kicked the fire shooting hundreds of sparks in the air. The other man had sprung to his feet and grabbing his rifle. He was taking aim at me but my mind refused to let go of my kill. Also at this point I did not care what he was doing only knew that he would be next. I finished the man I was holding off, and I immediately started looking around for the other man but he was gone. From my crouched position, I stood up and scanned the area for him but he was just gone. Past the flames and smoke from the fire, I spotted Jaxson leaning against a tree looking at his fingers. Almost like, he was admiring how beautiful they were. I brushed myself off and hopped to his side.

"You know the next time you have the urge to kill a human you could let me know." He spoke in a soft sweet mummer. He put his arms around me, pulled me close to his body, and whispered in my ear. "You could have gotten yourself killed." Then he kissed my ear and down my throat and back up again continuing until he found my lips. He spun us around so that my back was against the tree now and kissed me so softly but forcibly at the same time. I let a moan escape my lips on accident. He grabbed both of my hands and left my lips before I was ready, and pulled me back into the forest.

"What am I going to do with you?" He exclaimed then paused for a moment and went on to say. "I can't have you running off and killing people at will we need to work on your control."

I did not say anything my head was still spin-ning from his kiss to really comprehend what he was saying and I guess I did not care right now anyway. Back on the winding forest, trail holding hands, we walked in silence again. I was staring down the trail that we were traveling on when something crossed it up ahead. I only saw a glimpse of it so I had no idea what it was. Then as if in a horrible nightmare, the glowing green eyes that I had seen earlier in the day were now staring at me again. I tried to yank my hand from Jaxson's hand but he pulled me to a stop. He started to ask me what I was doing but quickly realized why. The glowing green eyes peered out from behind the tree and started moving closer to us. Jaxson let go of my hand, grabbed me by the waist, and flung me into a tree. I mean literally picked me up and flung me up into a tree, and in the same second was right behind me yelling at me to climb, climb. The tree trunk had to be every bit of fifty foot around and about two hundred feet tall. We climbed to the top of the tree and stood on a branch.

In a calm collected voice, he said. "Don't look down, please don't look down." He was practically begging me.

I was doing my best not to look, when the tree shook violently, almost knocked us to the ground. I risked a glance down to see what had made the tree tremble under us. The wolf's piercing glowing green eyes were looking straight into mine. I felt the pull of his eyes drawing me in again. Not comprehending anything of what I was doing my body reacted. I had to be with the wolf. I let go of the tree and jumped from my perch. I heard Jaxson in the background yelling, "No don't do it," but it was too late. I landed on my feet with a loud earth-shattering thud. My nose just inches from the wolves' nose. The wolf was bearing his teeth ever so slightly and this frightened me a little bit. However, as I looked back into the wolves eyes I was not scared anymore. There was something calming and soothing about the wolves eyes. The next thing I knew we were walking and Jaxson's screams of terror faded and all I heard again was the crickets and the frog's singing their song. The wolf never dropped his gaze luring me further and further away from Jaxson. As we walked all of my sense's seemed to fade until, I was not hearing, seeing or feeling anything except the wolf. I had no idea where we were going and frankly did not care right now. I started to feel tired and need to rest. The wolf somehow sensed this and almost commanded me to sit down and to close my eyes and sleep, and I did exactly what the wolf told me to do.

I awoke to find myself chained to the floor and behind bars. The bars covered in metal stakes that were welded to my cage and they looked as if they would rip me apart if I even got close to them. Looking around, I realized that I was chained to the center of the room with more metal stakes behind me, I was surrounded. I thought about breaking the chains but knew that it would not do me any good, there was no way out. As I sat there, in my cell of horror, I started thinking about Jaxson. The tears started to fill my eyes. I looked down at my dress and remembered our first kiss and the way he took care of me or was trying to until I ran off with the wolf. Then I came to the realization that I loved him more than he knew or even that I wanted to admit to myself.

My life had not been easy up to this point. I should have been married and had children and had a life similar to my parents. My father was a farmer and my mother took care of the house. My father would spend days in the fields plowing and planting. My mom made sure all of us were feed, the house was tidy, and that the girls were learning how to be a proper wife and mother. The boys were learning how to be a worker like the man of the family should be. Me being the prettiest out of my two sisters my parents set me up with a very handsome and wealthy man in town. We got to know each other well and he eventually did ask for my hand in marriage after a year. My parents agreed to the marriage and we were to be wed in the spring. That was a very harsh winter and my oldest brother disappeared. We do not know if he ran, away, got killed or what happened to him. Grieving for the loss of my brother whom I was very close too, I was still trying to plan a wedding. There were dress fittings, invitations and all of that to plan. As the wedding day was fast, approaching and I knew I needed to get my mind into the wedding. I decided that I would go to town and spend a little time with Tim since I had been too busy the last couple of weeks to even talk to him. I got to town and knocked on his door. He answered the door and invited me in. What a pleasant surprise he boasted. I walked in the door and could hear the sounds of people laughing from the great room of the home. I have some company and they are all dying to meet you, he said. He led the way down the hallway and we entered the room together. There were a few men but a bunch of women as well, dressed in very tight clothing and looking a lot like ladies of the evening. He introduced his gentleman friends first and then introduced me as his bride. He had not introduced me to any of the women. When we were done with the introductions, I whispered in his ear "I have to go, I was just in town and thought I would drop by to say hi." He flashed a drunken smile at me. "Ok then if you must go." He whispered back. He walked me to the door and I left without saying another word. As I walked to the road from the house, I glanced back at the house to see him standing in the big picture window with his arms around one of those girls. I ran most of the way back home, with tears running down my face and my heart broken. I talked to my mom and sisters about what I had seen and they were in shock of my discovery but there was too much at stake for them to let me back out of the marriage. A few days had passed when we had a visit from the sheriff. The news of his death came as a blow to my family and me. I knew that he was going hunting with his friends but I never imagined that he would not come back. To this day, no really knew if he is dead or alive because we never found his body. His friends say that he fell off a cliff but again even after searching his body was never found. The town assumed that he was dead and had a funeral for him. I was all dressed in black and was basically a widow before I was even married. I do not know what the roomer in town was but no man had ever asked to court me or for my hand in marriage again.

Thoughts of that day that I was turned in the forest came rushing back to me as well. I had been there collecting wildflowers for my mother to brighten her day. As things started to pick up on the farm and I had heard her saying that she missed my brother and her friends like she always had said. All of my chores were done and I had a little time left over and I thought it would be a nice gesture. I was also hoping that it would make her smile since I had not seen her smile in a long time. As I sat there flashes of my mom, dad, brothers and sisters faces ran through my memories in happy times and sad and everything in-between. The sound of a door slamming shut interrupted my thoughts.

I could not see anything through the confines of my holding cell, but I could smell something that was not quite human even though I could hear its heart beating. Even though it smelt different, I could still smell the blood pumping through its body. The smell of the blood was very strong so whatever it was must have had an open wound. My throat started to burn and I was thirsty. I struggled with the chains and broke them with ease. However, I made the mistake of moving too fast towards the smell, and several of the metal stakes pierced me, I had forgotten about them in my hunt for blood. This hurt a lot and I stumbled backwards towards the center of the room again and fell to the floor in pain. Then the smell was gone as fast as it had come, the door closed again and I could not hear or smell anything. All the wounds that I had just received were healing; I could feel the skin tug tight and watched as the holes would disappear. This was one advantage to being a vampire. However, I was trapped in this cell though, not going anywhere any time soon. I had no way of knowing how many days passed, but I did know no one had come back since that day and I was growing weaker and weaker. The thirst was driving me insane and there was nothing I could do about it.

All I could do now is lay here on the floor with barely enough energy to lift my head every now and then. What kind of hell is this I thought, wishing that I could just die. This must be what happens to vampires if we do not drink, we just lay here wishing for death to find us. Oh how I wished that I would have paid more attention to Jaxson and had asked more questions about being a vampire. I started drifting in and out of consciousness, and when I could think, I thought about Jaxson. Why has he not found me? I thought, or worse what if the wolf had gone back for him. My eyes pricked but no tears came even though I wanted to cry. The more blood deprived I became the more my thoughts turn to anger. Why has he not come for me? I thought that he was falling in love with me. The way he looked at me those last couple of hours, the dress, holding hands, saving my life from that hunter even though I do not think the hunter would have killed me with that gun. I still had so much to learn about this life. Maybe he did not love me or maybe he just needed me for something else and making me have feelings for him was the only way that he could think of to make me stay with him. He was tricking me and that is why he had not come for me because I had already served my purpose. As I came to these conclusions in my head, I heard a noise. The noise of a small beating heart, using all the strength I could muster, I barely lifting my head to look around I saw a rat down by my feet. How was I going to get the rat to come close enough to my mouth? I looked it in the eyes and thought about it being right in front of me. As I did this, the rat took a few steps closer and closer to my mouth. When the rat was close enough that I could grab it without excreting too much energy I grabbed it and bit down. The few drops of blood that hit my mouth first tasted awful but I could not stop myself I need the blood. This little bit of blood from the rat helped me ever so slightly. I was still thirsty and weak but I could at least sit up now. That was the only rat that I had seen since I had been here and would be the only one that I would see I was sure of it.

More time came and went by and I was sure that I was going to die now. I could not even lift my head. I heard the door creak open. I could smell the fresh air rush in and with it brought the scent of human. I heard the footsteps of this person walk down the stairs and towards my cell. Too weak to move, I just laid there with my throat on fire and no way to put it out. I tried to will myself to get up but my body would not respond. The footsteps grew closer and closer. A light lit up my holding cell it was so bright it hurt my eyes. Even though the pain I forced myself to look, I wanted to see who was there. I tried to talk but no words would come out my voice was gone. A man peered into my cell; I could see his eyes sparkling in the flame that he carried. He did not say anything, and then he was gone. I heard him go back up the stairs and out the door slamming it shut behind him. I wanted to cry again, why did this man not help me? Sure, I would have killed him but he could have let me out.

Later that day or night I am not sure which as it was dark in here with no sunlight or any other light for that matter. I heard a wolf howl outside it sounded close. As I lay there listening the howl seemed to get closer and closer. The door opened with a crash, as if it was ripped off its hinges and thrown. I could hear the sound of heavy breathing, a huge thudding heart, the soft sound of paws on the floor. I was so weak I could barely open my eyes now. I forced them open to revile the glowing green eyes of the wolf. The door to the cell was ripped from the hinges and thrown to the floor with a loud ear piercing crash. The sound of metal sliding across a concrete floor seared my ears rattling my brain and made me grind my teeth together. Then the sound of wood and metal creaked and squealing as it was being crushed this also hurt my ears but was not as intense. I wanted to put my hands over my ears but I just could not make them move. The wolf walked slowly towards me. In my mind I was think finally the pain and misery was over the wolf would kill me. The wolf stopped his advance and lay down on the floor a few feet from me. Why is this wolf torturing me and not ripping me to shreds? I tried to find my voice again but nothing would come out. I wanted to know why the wolf did this to me. The wolf crept back out of the cell. I tried with all I had to move but my body just would not respond. Freedom was right there I could see it. I tried repeatedly with all of my will to move but nothing was happening. I closed my eyes for a moment and opened them again when I heard my name being called.

"Sam, I know you can hear me, I'm sorry I'm going to get some help." A voice said from the darkness.

Then there was nothing again. With the only thing working being my mind, I thought about the voice there was something I heard in the voice that was familiar to me. I just could not put my finger on it. I knew that I had heard this voice before. However, I was too tired to care anymore and I closed my eyes again.

As I slept, I was dreaming about that day in the forest. The vampire women that had meant to kill me. There was something there in this dream this time though something that I had not seen when I was changed. The wolf with the glowing green eyes was the one that had pulled her off me. As the dream progressed, I could see things that my memory had blocked me from seeing before. As I was getting to the part of the dream that was going to show me what happen to the women a voice, a familiar voice in my ear.

"Sam Honey, I'm here I going to take you home."

I recognized this voice instantly it was Jaxson. He slid his arms under me and picked me up, and ran with me all the way home. If I could only show him how happy, I was to see him but all I could do is open one eye and look at his face. His face had a hint of worry in it almost as if he was too late to save me. I wished I could have spoken to reassure him that it was going to be ok. However, all I could do was close my eyes and besides I did not even know that I was going to be ok. However now that I was with him I felt like I was going to be okay.

At home finally, he laid me on the bed.

"You must drink." He said in a soft whisper. Then he placed his arm over my mouth. I could not even part my lips. It was as if my lips had been sewn shut. He pulled his arm away and whispered, "I will be right back."

He was gone and back in a second. I saw something silver and shiny in one hand. He slowly approached the bed. This was it, what I had been waiting for he was going to kill me. I must have been too far gone to save. Finally, the pain and suffering would be over. I closed my eyes. I did not want to see it coming.

I felt him kneel on the bed and heard the sound of skin being cut open. Why could I not feel any pain? Still waiting for the pain I felt something wet on my lips. This covered my lip and seemed to dissolve the stitches that had been there before. Through a tiny crack, the wet stuff had leaked through. The taste of blood made me break the rest of my lips open as well as my eyes.

Jaxson looked deep into my eyes whispered "drink my love."

Just then, he pressed his arm closer to my lips and the flow of blood soared down my throat. My arms responded and I clutched at his arm refusing to let stitches go. I was feeling my strength coming back.

He whispered to me. "That is enough or you will kill me."

I still did not want to let go, but I was still little weak and he forced me to let go.

Holding something on his arm, he asked, "Can you get up?"

I tried sitting up but nothing was happening. I shook my head, as I could not find my voice yet. He picked me up again and carried me to the room where he kept people for me to drink. He propped me up beside the bed, took one of the human's arms, and cut it open for me. How these humans that he brought me did not wake up I never knew. I finished this one and was strong enough to pick myself up off the floor and go to the next one. After I drank the second person dry, I laid down on the floor feeling dizzy and delusional. He picked me up and carried me back to our bed. As I lay there, I could feel the strength coming back to my body and finally found my voice.

"Jaxson" I whispered.

"I'm right here." he replied in a very soft mummer.

"I'm sorry I never meant for this to happen." I said choking back tears.

"Sh… It is not your fault it is mine. You should rest, I will be right here when you wake up." He said and placed his hand over mine and squeezed it lightly.

"No I have had enough rest to last me a life time." I said through a yawn. "There are things that I want to know more about. Like, How come I did not die?" I asked.

"There are two ways that vampires die. One is to be staked in the heart and the other is too be ripped to shreds and your body burned. If you don't drink you will grow very weak like you did but you won't die." He put his arms around me. "Now you must sleep I can see that you are tired."

"But I don't..." I started to say but he put one finger to my lips to silence them. He leaned in closer, inches from my face. He pulled me closer and he kissed me as if he had never kissed me before. I felt tingly all over from this kiss. He follow my jaw line to my throat and back up again. As he did that, he pulled my leg on top of his and wound his fingers in my hair. Our lips locked around each other's. I took my hand and placed it in his hair not willing or wanting to let him go. His lips left mine again, kissed me to my ear, stopped there, and whispered.

"I love you, and I'm glad that you are home. I promise that I will never let you go again. You don't know how hard it was for me not knowing if you were alive or dead." His breath tickled my ear. If I could get goose bumps, I would have had them. I sighed as his lips moved away from my ear. I wanted him right here right now, but he pulled away.

"You must sleep we can continue this when you wake up if you want."

How was I supposed to sleep now? I thought to myself.

"I would rather finish this now if you don't mind I blurted out." Not thinking about what I was saying.

"No it will be better when you are not half high from the blood and sleepy." I sighed again and crushed myself closer to him. With my eyelids growing heavy with sleep and closing at a rapid pace I whispered, "I love you too."

I was feeling like I had spent most of my new life in some kind of comatose state. What was up with all of this sleeping and when will it stop I started to question. I knew that Jaxson had told me but it was not going to be fast enough for me. As I drifted to sleep, nothing could prepare me for the dream I was going to have.

Dreaming again about the day that I was transformed and what had happened. The dream always started from the beginning. The women's eyes full of red hunger. Her face so pale and white, so fragile looking. Her out stretched hand asking for mine in return, but this time however I was not fixed on the women's eyes in my dream I was free to look where I wanted. I looked to the left behind her on the edge of the forest was the wolf with the glowing green eyes watching and maybe waiting for his chance. On the other side was another wolf the one that has the gravitational pull on me, staring in our direction. I saw the wolves how did she not know they were there I wondered. I took the woman's hand and watched as she raised my hand to her mouth. As my hand drew closer and closer to her mouth, I glanced around the women to see what the wolves were doing. They had started making the advance towards us. The dream was so real that I could feel the women bite into my arm again. This caught my attention and I looked back at the women now. We were falling backwards towards the ground. We hit the ground and then towering over me I seen the wolf, the wolf that I have some kind of connection with. They pounced on the woman and pulled her away. Off in the distance I could hear the sounds of growling wolves and breaking branches or trees not sure which. Then out of no were there he was. Jaxson with his angel face peering down at me. His eyes locked on mine. I could not break his gaze he stretched out his arm and put it to my lips just like when I was too weak to move. As this happened I could taste his blood on my tongue. Then everything went black, I could not see, hear or feel any-thing.

I was awakened by the sound of growling. Jaxson I whispered knowing that if he were there he would hear me. There was no reply so I felt for him but he was not there. I sprang out of bed and ran for the door. I stopped in my tracks when I got to the huge room at the end of the hall. Jaxson was sitting in a chair facing me and on the other side of the room was anoth-er man. I was assuming it was a man by his hair. That is all I could see of the man but I could hear his heartbeat. Jaxson realized that I was standing there and my thirst was threating to take over, he stood up from the chair.

"Sam you need to go back to the room I will be there in a minute." There was something in his tone, a hint of panic, worry I am not really sure he had never used this tone before. The thirst started to block out the sound of his voice and was pulling me closer to the beating heart. This time he turned and looked at me as he caught my gaze his eyes were green flames burning through me I could do nothing this time but obey him. Before I had time to think, my feet were carrying me back to the room. I opened and shut the door behind me. My mind was now cleared from the fog or released from his control. What the hell was that I thought to myself? I really need to talk to him right now about my dream. I started for the door again this time I was determined to talk to him. As my hand touched the doorknob, I heard Jaxson excused himself from his guest. Then the door was opening. I backed away from the door. I let him get through the door and shut it.

"Jaxson I know what happened that day that I was changed" I stated. "You are the one that did not just let me die. Why didn't you just let me die instead of cursing me to this life?" I said with anger in my voice. I was now very mad and upset that he had not told me. I felt betrayed.

He reached out for me to come closer to him but I refused. Sadness was written all over his face one tiny tear forming in the corner of his eye.

"I am sorry Sam I cannot tell you anything other than I had too. I will tell you someday but not right now it is complicated." This made me even madder than I had been a second ago. I think I could have torn the house down with one quick movement. How could I have been so stupid to fall for this guy? Sensing my mood Jaxson backed towards the door.

"Listen to me." He said slowly trying to lock eyes with me to control my mood again. I refused to look at him and turned my back towards him. The emotions washed through me of hate, pain and deceit. Why was this happening to me again? I clenched my teeth and hands into fists of anger. I wanted to tear him into shreds right now.

With my teeth clenched and speaking through them and my voice full of anger. I yelled "GET OUT NOW." So mad I growled the words.

Then I started counting back words from 10 trying to calm myself. I turned around to find that Jaxson had left the room. I could hear low murmuring from the other room. I had calmed myself a little and tried to relax but I was determined to get an answer. I opened the door and walked into the hallway and down to the room. Again, Jaxson stood and turned to look at me.

"Sam you should not-" I cut him off.

"I will do what I want you are not telling me anything." I growled.

"Sam you are not alright you need to cool off." He growled back at me. This made me tense even more. I was ready for a fight now. I felt indestructible at this moment and I partly was. I was so mad my eyes had made everything have a red hue to it.

"You should go my friend, this is not good." He said slowly to his friend not taking his eyes off me.

His friend stood up and said. "I will come back later." The voice caught me off guard. I knew that voice. I automatically glance up to see this persons face. I could not believe what I was seeing. I can see ghost now I thought. The face of my brother that had disappeared was staring back at me. He looked the same as the day he had disappeared. All of the anger disappeared as fast as it had begun. I fell to my knees looking at him and back to Jaxson. My mind not being able to comprehend what I was seeing. Jaxson gazed into my eyes and could see the questions that my mouth could not speak.

"Yes he is alive." He said softly and slowly walked to me and knelt down in front of me. My brother came to stand behind him.

"It is ok Sammy we have something in common now and when you get a little stronger and don't feel like you want to kill me we can do stuff together."

The tears came streaming down my face. "I have missed you so much you know. I wished every day that you would come home."

"I know Sammy I have been watching."

As his word sank into my head, I put two things together and I blurted out "You are the wolf that I feel connected to and now I know why because you are a part of me. It all makes sense now."

"You are right Sammy, I am the wolf." As I thought about this for a minute, the anger came back to me. I jumped to my feet. "Why did you lead me to that place and starve me." I spat at him with anger and contempt.

"Easy Sammy there is a lot to the story and I'm sorry for that but I had too. I had to protect you." He said back to me with sorrow and sadness in his voice.

"Protect me from what?" I growled at him. "Do you know how much pain and agony I went through? You have to tell me why!" Jaxson and my brother exchanged a glance. In that glance, I could see that they were not going to tell me why.

"Sam (Jaxson said) it is best that we leave this one for another day. I know that you feel betrayed but really this one is for your own good."

The anger still in my voice I tried to concentrate on something else.

"Bill *(I said harshly and sarcastically)* what have you been doing these last few years?"

"I have been watching over you and the rest of the family but you the most. You seemed to always be wandering into places that you should not have been. The day that you were in the field picking the flowers, why were you there anyway?" He asked sincerely.

"I was picking flowers for mom to brighten her day she was having a bad day and I had heard her mumbling about missing you. I had finished my chores early and decided that the gesture would make her smile again." I said and the sadness over took me. I am sure she was missing me now too. Who was taking care of her and trying to make her smile now? I wondered to myself.

"Oh…I wish you would not have been there that day. We knew there was a vampire in the forest and we were tracking her, but she found you first."

"So why didn't you kill her before she had the chance to kill me?" I asked not understanding how or why it had gotten that far before he tried to save me.

"Well it is complicated you see, when you vampires *(he gestured to Jaxson and I)* are in hunt mode you will kill anything that gets in your way, so we had to wait for the right opportunity. Unfortunately that was after she bit you and by the time we got to her she had almost drained you dead. My friend Jaxson, had smelled the blood and knew about her being in the forest. Therefore, instead of letting you die like that I begged him to change you. It would have been so hard to see you die that way. I thought maybe, just maybe we could be brother and sister again."

I stared at his face in disbelief I saw the tears roll down his face. Tears filled my eyes as well and started rolling down my face. I instantly wanted to hug him but I did not know if I could trust myself that close to him. Jaxson sensing what I wanted to do put one hand on my shoulder. "Jaxson, please help me." I begged him.

"Clench you teeth together and try not to think of the heart beat and the warmth of his body and defiantly don't look at the veins in his neck. I must tell you this is very dangerous I don't know what would happen if you bit him."

I listened to his warning but did not care at that moment. I went to my brother and gave him a quick but huge hug. As the warmth of his skin touched mine, I saw him shiver a little. I must have been cold I thought but I did not feel cold. I logged that to memory and would ask about it later but for now, I had to catch up with him.

Jaxson placed both arms around me and whispered in my ear "are you sure you are ok"

I was more than ok I thought but simply replied "Yes."

"I would feel much better with this after you have feed some more." He said. I thought about these words for a minute as I did the burn in my throat was there but nothing that I could not control I thought.

"Come you need to feed, your brother will be here when we get back." He released me, took my hand, and pulled me to the door. This was strange.

"Where are we going?" I asked.

"We are going out tonight I know of some campers that smell appetizing. With one backwards, glace I looked at my brother. I still could not believe it. Jaxson lead me away from the house.

"Ok it is your turn to find them and show us the way to the camp. It is easy all you need to do is smell the air." I closed my eyes, took in a lung full of air, and could smell the earth, flowers and water. I did it again knowing that is not what I was looking for. This time the smell of human, this set my throat to burning again. My feet reacted first and I was running towards the smell. I was running so fast that to the human eye I would have looked like a blur.

CHAPTER 4

Slowing as I reached the human camp. The smell of the human blood mixed with the smell of the fire that was crackling in the middle of the camp. The smell of the fire burned my nose a bit it was like smelling last year's burning leaves in the Fall. I walked carefully around the camp watching for any signs of activity but all I heard was snoring and loud breathing. I fell to my knees next to a man that was sleeping outside the tent by the fire. He was the closest to me and I watched as Jaxson made his way to the other man. I bit down on the man's arm he didn't even twitch. I listened to his heartbeat slow and stop and I was done. The dizziness that used to cripple me to the point of euphoria was getting better. This time I was a little dizzy but I could still function. I stood and watched as Jaxson finishing up. The whole thrill of the hunt wore off and I found myself in a hurry all of a sudden to get back to the house, well not really the house but more specifically my brother. I was looking forward to talking with him and finding answers to question that I had about him leaving us and I just wanted to catch up and see what he has been doing all of this time. With my head stuck on my brother, I did not say a word to Jaxson and started running for the house. I was half way to the house when I looked back to see if Jaxson was coming but I did not see him anywhere. I stopped in my tracks I called out, "Jaxson where are you?" I did not hear a response and turned around to look for him. I walked back towards the camp at a fast pace looking everywhere for him. "Jaxson" I shouted again, still nothing. I was starting to worry that something happened to him. My pace was getting quicker and I was listening for anything that would make a noise. I passed under this huge oak tree and something hit me from behind and flung me to the ground. I landed face down in the dirt. I tried to move to get up but something was on top of me, I was getting ready to put a little more effort into moving but there was a voice in my ear.

"We are going to have to work on you paying attention to your soundings." Then he laughed a very evil laugh and helped me up, then went on to say. "Sorry love I just wanted to see what would happen if you were surprised." He smiled at me and extended on hand for me to take.

"That was not very nice you know. I was really worried that something might have happened to you." I said with sadness in my voice.

"Oh so you were worried about me for once." He said with a smile and a wicked grin. Then he twined his arms around me and pulled me close to him. Before I could answer him, he kissed me and I kissed him back as well even though I was a little mad at him right now. "Come I know you want to get back to see your brother and I'm not going to keep you any longer." He released me and took my hand, we ran for home.

The closer we got to home I could smell something funny in the air, something that did not belong here. It was a strange smell it smelled like burnt toast and roses I stopped and pulled on Jaxson's arm to stop with me.

"Do you smell that? What is that smell?" I asked.

A strange look crossed Jaxson's face and he began to pull me in the opposite direction of the house. I put up a fight struggling against his grasp I want to see my brother. "Let me go Jaxson, I want to see my brother." I growled at him.

He pulled me close to him and whispered in my ear. "It is not safe there is something very wrong. Your brother is not there he left shortly after we did." He pulled me back into the cover of the forest. "We have to stay here until they leave. We must be very quiet." He whispered.

He pulled me under some brush and held me close. We were both on edge, I wanted to ask what was going on but I knew that I should not say anything right now. We sat there waiting, not sure what I was waiting to see but I was on edge.

I heard a noise of a breaking branch behind us and half jumped out of my skin but did not make a sound. He must have noticed my tension because he leaned down and whispered in my ear so low that I could barely make out what he was saying.

"It is ok it is your brother. Worst case scenario you run with your brother far away from here." I was about to speak when the door opened to the house. Jaxson whispered one last time

"Do not move until I tell you to if it comes to that."

I was focused on the house now. I saw a tall figure walk out first. He was draped in a black cloak with the hood over his head. Just then, Jaxson took his hand and covered my eyes. I wanted to struggle and be able to look but I knew that our lives depended on me not to make any sudden movements or noise for that matter. We sat there like this for a long time. All I could do was listening for movement. I could hear the footsteps leaving the porch of the house on to the grass and walking away from us but one set of footsteps were getting closer to us. His hand almost felt like it would crush my head. Although this was very uncomfortable, I knew that I could not move.

Then at last, what had seemed like days Jaxson moved his hand and whispered in my ear. "They are gone but we must be still until I'm completely sure."

Just then, I heard footsteps behind us again and just about lost it. Just before I was getting ready to scream, I heard my brother's voice. "They are gone."

"Are you sure they are all gone?" Jaxson asked

"Yes there were ten of them and I counted ten leave." My brother replied.

Jaxson rose to his feet and pulled me up with him. He did not say anything as we approached the house with caution. Jaxson looking everywhere and my brother was right behind us, we entered the house and he turned to me and took both of my hands in his.

"We must leave now. You need to gather your things. Go now and be quick." He said with sadness and sorrow in his voice.

I ran to our room and grabbed and few things and was back to Jaxson's side in a flash. Jaxson exchanged a glance with my brother and my brother looked at me.

"I'm sorry I can't go with you right now, I have a pack to worry about and I need to keep an eye on the family and this place so that you may come back someday." As he spoke, the tears filled my eyes. It figures I just found out that my brother is alive and now I have to leave. My brother came to me, scooped me up in a bear hug, and whispered in my ear. "Everything will be ok, but you must go this is the only way and don't give Jaxson a hard time it is not his fault. I love you sis and I always will." I was now sobbing getting blood all over his shirt. Jaxson pulled me away from him and held me close to his body.

"As soon as it is clear my love we will come back. Your brother will still be here. I promise." I heard the door open and close softly. I knew my brother had gone. I buried my face in Jaxson's chest and tried to hold back the tears but they were coming no matter what I did. Then off in the distance I heard one lonely wolf cry.

"Come we must go." He pulled away from me, took my hand, and pulled me towards the door. I took one last glance at the room. All of the furniture had been covered with white sheets and I knew that this would be the last time I would see this lovely house for a long time. We jumped off the porch and ran towards the forest. I hesitated for a minute at the edge of the forest and took one more glance at the house. Jaxson was holding my hand and we started our long journey walking through the brush, which tore at my dress and skin. While my dress was being shredded and torn to pieces by the sticks, briars and thorns but felt like creasing kisses on my skin. I was lost in my feelings and thoughts when Jaxson's voice broke the silence between us.

"I need to talk to you. You are going to have to exert a lot of control over your thirst, we are going to be around humans and we have to be very careful not to be detected. So you are going to have to try and contain your hunger as much as you can, I will make sure that you get to drink every night and this should make it a little easier. I believe that you can do it after seeing you with your brother."

"My brother is different he is a wolf." I said back, sounding very unsure of myself.

"Yes but he does have a beating heart, warmth and blood pumping through his veins." He said back to me trying to prove a point to me. Then he pulled my hand and said. "Come I have a surprise for you."

We walked a little bit further and the forest gave way to a farm. It was my family's farm I instantly recognized it. Filled with excitement to see everyone I wanted to run but Jaxson grabbed me with both arms around the waist.

"Whoa, you must be very careful." He whispered in my ear.

Under the cover of darkness, we crept closer to the house and could see there were no lights burning inside the house. Everyone must be tucked in and sleeping I thought to myself. I took Jaxson's advice and slowly started walking towards the house. As I got closer and closer, the smell of human was burning my throat. My drive to see my family was winning the raging war inside of me over blood. Out of the corner of my eye, I saw the glowing green eyes of the wolf that must have been my brother there to make sure nothing happened to our sleeping family. I slowly approached the front, door and gradually turned the knob and cracked the door open. The strong scent of human hit me like a ton of bricks. It must have hit Jaxson like that too, because he tightened his grip on me. I let the scent wash over me and tried to gain control over the inner monster that wanted to slaughter the sleeping family inside. I took the first unsure step into the house sucked in a large breath of air and let my throat burn out of control. I pictured my family laughing and playing like we always did. The inner monster went silent for a moment. Jaxson with his hands still on me refusing to let me go took the step into the house as well and I was grateful for it. I took another step, now fully engulfed in the human scent. I wanted the blood but I just kept telling myself no this is your family and you cannot harm them. I can do this, I will do this, I am stronger than the inner beast that was trying to come out and ruin everything. I told myself repeatedly. When I had control of myself, I turned in Jaxson's arms and looked him in the eyes.

"Can I see them just for a second, but please don't let me go." I whispered to him, my eyes were begging and my lips were pouting.

He looked back into my eyes with the words no written all over his face but said

"Yes, you may and I will not let you go I will keep you from hurting them. We must be very careful though because I can see the hunger in your eyes."

He walked with his arms tight around me to my parent's rooms. I slowly opened the door being extremely careful not to make a sound. Jaxson tighten his grip on me even more waiting for me to react but I was ok. The feeling of love was over powering the beast inside of me for the moment. I went to my mom's side of the bed first and lightly touched her face. Then slowly bent down, kissed her check, and whispered. "I love you and I'm sorry." She fidgeted a little bit but did not wake up. My dad was much harder to say good-bye too. We had a bond that seemed like it was unbreakable by anything. I bent down, kissed his check, and whispered, "I love you forever." One single tear rolled down my check and hit his check. I wanted to wipe it away but did not want to wake him. We left the room and I knew that this was the last time I would ever see them again. I had the feeling of sorrow and sadness in the pit of my stomach. I wanted to cry my eyes out but I could not leave the bloodstains on the floor. I choked down the tears and continued on to my sisters, then my younger brother. We were walking toward the front door now when I twisted in Jaxson's arms and stared into his eyes.

"Can I do one more thing before we go?" I inquired not knowing what he would say.

"Whatever you desire honey." He said knowing that I was in pain and he hated it.

"Can you let me go I think I'm fine?" He released me and I walked over to a drawer in the kitchen where we kept paper, quill, and ink. I took a sheet of paper, the quill and ink, sat down at the table, and wrote.

Dear Mom and Dad,

I just wanted to let you both know that I am sorry for disappearing, but it is very complicated situation and I have no choice. Maybe someday, I will be able to come back and see you but it is too dangerous for you if I am around right now. Just know that I love you and we will be watching over you. So do not cry or worry about me I am a strong person. We love you very much.
Love
Sam.

P.S. Bill is ok too, that is what I mean by us. Do not look for us it is too dangerous, and please stay out of the forest.

I placed the quill across the paper on the table where they would find it soon enough. I rose from the chair looked at Jaxson, the tears filling my eyes again. He embraced me and we started walking towards the door. We heard a howl off in the distance. This must have been a warning howl, because Jaxson grabbed my hand and said.

"We must go now and fast."

Jaxson grabbed my hand and pulled me through the door, I took one more glance at the house and we were off, running as fast as we could away from my family. As we ran holding hands, the tears were streaming down my face. We ran for a long time, jumping over streams and rivers. I could smell the scent of human again and we slowed our pace. The stronger the wonderful smell got the more we slowed and eventually stopped by the river that cut through the forest on the edge of a town. Jaxson turned and looked at my face.

"Wow you are a mess. Let us wash your face off and get the blood out of your hair. You look like you have been in a fight or killed someone." He said with a giggle trying to lighten my mood and make me smile.

The blood on my face and in my hair was from crying as we ran. I was going to miss my family even more now that I knew my brother was alive. I began to hate what had happened to me. I also hated the tears that my family would cry for me. I knelt down by the river and splashed the water on my face trying to scrub the blood away and the thoughts of my family. The sun shining off the river showed me a reflection of my face, and Jaxson was right I looked like hell. I thought about the note that I left for my family and maybe I should not have done that but it was too late now. Jaxson was helping me wash blood out of my hair. He broke the silence and brought me out of my depths of grief for the moment.

"Are you ready for this?" He asked with concern in his voice, he could see that I was already in pain.

"Yes I am ready I think. Is there anything that I should not do?" I asked to keep the conversation going and my mind distracted from the sadness.

He chuckled. "You should not kill anyone and try not to look at anyone. Your eyes are pale blue and this would frighten people. We are just going to pass through town in and out."

"When do my eyes turn back to their original color?" I asked really wanting to know that answer to this question.

"That happens about the same time you stop sleeping. Come let's go." He grabbed my hand and held it tight. The closer we got the more the scent of blood was getting to me. I started to hesitate, I wanted to run in the opposite direction away from town or I could just start slaughtering the whole town the inner beast whispered to me. No, no I reasoned with it I have to do this. I focused on the ground and putting one foot in front of the other, we made it to the other side of the town quickly.

"You can look now Sam, we are out of town that was very good. I'm proud of you." He patted my hand and kept pulling me along by his side.

I was not welling to unclench my teeth just yet because I could still smell the blood that swirling around me. In addition, I knew if I did let myself open my mouth I was going back and killing the first person that I came across. Therefore, I looked at Jaxson and just smiled. He must have noticed that I was really struggling to stay by his side. He put one arm around my waist, pulled my hand across my body, and held me tight to him. He barely gave me enough room to keep my legs moving. I got relief from my blood lust as we walked back into the forest and the scent of the forest washed away the scent of the human blood. I broke the silence first this time.

"I need to drink, if we are going to be in any-more towns, I don't think I can control myself next time." He did not reply and we just kept walking.

As we walked further into the forest, the scent of human crossed our path. At once, I was on it, heading in that direction of the wonderful scent. As the scent got stronger and stronger, I slowed so that I did not make any sound what so ever. I found a hunter sitting at the base of a big oak tree. My mind was working overtime telling my feet and hands what to do. I have never drank someone that was still awake and alert to their surroundings. This was all new to me and exciting. I walked out into the clearing and the hunter spotted me.

"Hey you, are you lost?" He called out to me.

"Yes, I'm lost I was hoping that you could help me find my way back to town." I said in a sweet innocent voice.

"Sure I can help you find your way back when I'm done hunting. Why don't you come sit down next to me?" he said.

I walked over to where the man was sitting, sat down and leaned against the tree. The thirst was driving me insane. However, I lacked the know how to approach drinking him dry I was going to have to wait for the right moment I thought.

"So what is a pretty lady like you doing out here in these forest?" He asked in a whisper.

Oh, crap what to say. I was not planning to have a conversation with this man. This broke my thought concentration of how to kill him and I needed to come up with something quick for an answer.

"Umm… I was looking for a wild flower that I heard only grows in certain spots of the forest." Dumb, dumb, dumb I thought he is never going to believe that.

"Oh I have seen those flowers they are very pretty, I take some home every once in a while for my faience." He replied.

My mind instantly noticed the fact that he had someone special in his life. I cannot do this I thought, I cannot ruin her life, and I knew the consequence that she would have to face for the rest of her life. However, the inner beast was trying to win the fight with my conscious. Raging inside my head and the thirst in my throat burning out of control, I had to make a decision quickly before the beast won. I saw Jaxson just then standing by a tree where the man could not see him. The love I had for him helped me decided that I could not ruin his faience's life and I made a break for it, running not holding a normal human pace. I ran until he was a distant memory. When I was far enough away and knew that, I would not turn around now. I stopped running. I gathered my thoughts as Jaxson approached me.

"What happened?" He asked with the look of confusion on his face.

"I couldn't do I, I could not take his life he had a faience I could not ruin her life like that." The tears started again as I remembered what that had felt like. I was sure Jaxson had no idea what I had been through and why I was crying but he did not ask and just wrapped his arms around me and pulled me close to him.

"It is ok sweetheart, we will find someone else." He placed a finger under my chin and lifted my face up to look into my eyes.

"This just proves that you are not a mindless killing machine." He put both hands on my face and kissed me. The tingling sensation was there again and it made me forget why I was sad. I was defiantly in love with this wonderful man. I pulled him closer to me and wrapped my arms around his neck. In that moment I forgot about everything, why we were running away from home, who those other vampires where, and where we were going. In that instant I knew that, I was insanely in love with this man. As I reveled in this realization, he whispered in my ear.

"We must keep moving. We both should drink. I am getting a little thirsty myself. I was too lost in my thoughts of him to acknowledge what he had said. My mind was swirling with images of him and I in bed again and him holding me while I slept, keeping me safe. Thinking about sleep was making me tired though. Even though I loved it when he held me like that, I still was ready for the sleeping part of this life to be over. I was starting to require less and less sleep so this was a good thing but it was not gone yet. Then I had a revelation that maybe when I did not sleep anymore that Jaxson would fill that time with other things. The longer I did not move the more I starting to feel exhausted.

"Jaxson can we stop and rest for a while I'm getting sleepy." I said with a yawn.

"Do you want me to carry you?" He asked looking somewhat annoyed.

"No, I think I just need a few minutes." Not waiting for his answer, I sat down beside a big tree and was out cold.

As I slept, I dreamt about Jaxson and me running away from a black cloud that was following us. No not following us but chasing us. We were running as fast as we could but it was no use though they were gaining on us. As the black cloud got closer and closer, it started morphing into human like figures. I could now make out that there were three of them. All three had a pair of red glowing eyes. There was no face it was just black with the red glowing eyes. However, this too changed, as they came closer and closer. I could start making out faces of porcelain just like mine. One had the features of a handsome boy, his eyes had changed from the glowing crimson to the pale almost translucent blue eyes that Jaxson, and I shared when we were hungry. The other two had feminine facial features with the same eyes, but they were not as pretty or handsome as the boy they just looked average nothing special about them. I started to make out other features as the black cloud surrounding them dissipated completely and gave way to the black Cloaks with the hoods pulled up to cover their hair. The only indication of their hair color was their bangs that stopped just above their eyes. So From what I could see of the girl's hair they both had black flowing hair. As I studied their features, I had not notice how close they had gotten to me. Standing just inches from me now, and staring into my eyes. They did not say anything and just flashed a toothy smile at me. The one woman stood in front of me while the other two slipped behind me forming a triangle around me. The women still did not say anything she glanced at the other female then to the male. As this happened they grabbed my wrist with one, hand and put the other on my shoulder. They pushed me down to my knees. Staring at the ground because I did not want to see what was next, the woman put her hand under my chin and pulled my face up until my eyes meet hers again. When my eyes meet hers, she put the other hand on the side of my face. Then as if she was using some kind of magic images of my past started flashing through my head, first baby images of my mom, dad, brother and sister. Then later and later, until we got to the transformation scene at this point the images slowed down to a crawl. In these images she saw exactly what had happened. She removed her hand.

"Well child." She croaked out. Her voice sounded like an old women's voice that had been abused for ages from drinking and smoking. It was really raspy and sound almost like it hurt to talk. This caught me by surprise and was unexpected for the way she looked. "It seems that we have the wrong vampire and that you did not cause the harm to my sister, but however you are going to be very valuable to me." She smiled at me and let out an evil laugh.

I knew what she saw, my brother killing her sister, and I was now the bait to lure him to his death. The other two vampires lifted me to a standing position and loosened their grips ever so slightly, here is my chance I thought to myself and I pulled away from them and ran knocking the woman in front of me to the ground and out of my way. The old woman yelled to the other two

"GET HER!"

I was running as fast as I could but they were faster. The boy knocked me to the ground and hovered over me with a steak right at my chest. He looked at me and plunged the steak into my chest. As this happened in my dream I must have screamed aloud and that jolted my eyes open. Jaxson was there with his arms around me, I felt safe for the moment and the tears came again.

"It's ok Sam it was just a dream." He said trying to reassure me that we were safe.

"I know but it was really bad and scary." I said not really wanting to go into detail or to relive the dream.

"Why don't you tell me about it?" He asked trying to help. I hesitated about telling him but decided that it might actually help me to talk about it. So I told him what I saw, as he took it all in not say anything just the look of fear washed over his face. He tried to hide it from me but was doing a really poor job at it and I sensed that he knew something about it.

So I asked. "What do you think it means?"

"I'm not sure. It could mean many things. I am sure that it was just a dream and nothing more. We should get moving I'm starving and I know that you are." He said changing the subject.

"Yes I'm starving too." I answered back leaving everything else alone for now.

He helped me to my feet and we started walking again, but something was different though he was acting a little strange. Usually he took my hand and we walked together.

"Is everything ok?" I ask after a few minutes

"Um…yeah everything is fine." He replied in an unsure tone.

As we walked, I watched his facial expressions out of the corner of my eye. They would go from thinking to an angry look, and then morphed into something completely different. We walk in silence not saying anything. I too though about that dream and tried to decipher what it meant. I was coming up with nothing that made since. I was deep in thought when the smell of human jolted me out of my thoughts. The smell hit Jaxson as well and, he reached for my hand and we were now running together just like we had always done.

CHAPTER 5

This was the biggest town that I had ever been too since I became a vampire. It was full of people walking, riding horses and buck wagons here and there getting supplies before the general store closed for the day. Some I suspected where making an appearance in town to catch up on the recent gossip.

At the beginning of the town, there is a black-smith shop. I could smell the burning wood and the melted metal in the pot. The combination of the wood and metal smelt bitter and sweat at the same time. I could also hear the ting, ting, ting as he was hammering on a horseshoe. This was extremely loud to my vampire ears. The ringing was as if I had put my head inside a bell and had someone ring it. The sound and smell distract me from my thirst though until someone walked in very close proximity to us. Jaxson sensed my reaction to the human grabbed and spun me around to face him and kissed me. This did the trick, and completely distracted me from the human that I was going to lunge for. I was tingly all over and had no interest in the human for the moment. As the danger passed, he released me and took my hand again. As we moseyed through the town, I was taking in all of the sights trying to ignore the thirst that burned out of control in my throat.

The general store was a wood structure that looked newly built. All of the siding still had that beautiful golden honey brown color to it. The part that I liked the most was the huge picture windows on both sides of a wooden door that held two small panes of glass. Inside I could hear two men bartering about what they could trade for some goods. I peered into the window to see the two men but saw my reflection instead. I was a mess my beautiful dress had been tattered and had dirt stains all over it. Now I felt like everyone was staring at me and saying wow look at that messy girl. Jaxson on the other hand did not look as bad as I did it seemed like he never got dirty and his clothing was always neat and tidy. How did he do that I thought.

The barbershop was next to the general store. There was a long line of men waiting for their turn in the barber chair for a haircut and a shave. It looked like it was going to be a long night for the barber. I was watching the barber pulling the hair up then cut it with a pair of shears. For some reason it was amazing to watch him do the motion repeatedly. Something shined off the window brightly and was almost blinding. When I looked away, I saw what had caused the blinding light. Something shimmered from the window of a shop across the street. I looked closer to see a dress in the shop's window. The setting sun was bouncing off the sequence of the dress. Sending rainbow colored sparkles everywhere. I wanted to get a better look at the dress in the window, so I pulled Jaxson's hand in that direction to cross the street. The dress was the most exquisite thing that I had ever seen. It was slim fitting and clung to the curves of the manikin. The ruby red satin covered in diamond like gems. The dress otherwise was simple with just a touch of white lace around the short sleeves. I was picturing myself in the dress. Twirling around and looking into the mirrors.

"Do you want that dress?" Jaxson's voice startled me a bit.

"Umm… I would love to have that dress." I replied. I was going to go on and say *that I did not have the money for it,* but Jaxson grabbed my arm and pulled me to the door. The owner was getting ready to close but let us come in anyway.

"What can I get for you fine people this evening?" She said looking at me in disgust. If only she knew that, I could kill her maybe she would have kept the look to herself. I thought about returning the look but then decided it was not worth it and settled for smiling.

"We would like that dress in the window" Jaxson said. The woman turned and almost hopped to the window excited about the sale that she was going to make.

"This dress is beautiful she shrieked but it is really expensive." She said and eyed Jaxson speculatively, almost to say are you sure you have the money for this? But, before she could ask the question, Jaxson replied to the unspoken question.

"Money is not an object." Jaxson said. However, the voice that he used sounded different. I had never heard him use it before. I started to analyze the tone while the woman took the dress off the manikin but forgot about it as she showed me to a fitting room in the back of the store. I quickly undress and put the new dress on it fit perfectly, as if it were made just for me. I went out of the fitting room and to the front of the store where Jaxson and the woman were talking. Jaxson had his back to me so I cleared my throat to get his attention. As he turned around his jaw hit, the floor and I think I may have even seen him drool. I watched him look me up and down about four times. There was silence for a few minutes while they both examined me.

"I did not think it was possible to make you prettier then you already are." Jaxson was barely able to say.

The woman running the shop said, "So then you want the dress.

Jaxson did not even turn to look at the woman and said, "Yes we do and she will be wearing it out of the store."

As the woman went to get my old rag Jaxson kissed me on the forehead and seemed like he wanted to do something else but the woman was back just then with the old dress. She took her place behind the counter and started to write the bill for the dress. Taking his eyes off me for a moment, he got her attention, gazed into her eyes and with that tone again, told her that.

"The dress was on the house."

The woman blankly stared back into Jason's eyes and repeated his words. "The dress is on the house and you folks have a nice night." She seemed to be under some kind of spell. We existed the shop back to the street. I glanced back through the window were the dress had stood on the manikin to see what she was doing. She was still standing their blankly staring out the window as if her mind was gone. I logged it to memory and would ask about it later. I was too distracted right now by all the attention that I was getting to think about it. Women that walked by looked at me and turned their noises up or gave me dirty looks but their men stared at me. Some drooling one even tripped over his own feet. There In the men's faces was the real test they all wanted me and considered Jaxson a very lucky man. One women that walked by slapped her husband's arm to get his attention back to her, I laughed. I was having fun. The attention was ending as the sun was sinking even lower in the sky and people were deserting the town and making their way home for the night. I was coming down from my high of having this beautiful dress and the smell of human was setting my throat to burning again.

The muffled screaming of a woman caught my attention. The screams were not loud enough for human ears. I grabbed Jaxson's hand and started towards the screams. Jaxson did not put up any fight at all and just let me pull him along. Behind one of the buildings on the outer edge of the town were two men and a woman. One man had his hand over the woman's mouth and the other man was starting to rip the women's clothing off. Jaxson let me go and stood in the shadows so that he was not visible to the humans. I walked towards the men. However they did not seem to notice me, I cleared my throat and said. "Hey leave her alone."

Catching both of the men off guard, they jumped a little bit before looking at me. Stunned by either the fact that they were caught or the fact that I was so beautiful or maybe they could not believe that I would interrupt. Whatever the reason they let the woman go. The woman ran as fast as she could away from the scene. I stopped walking when I was a few feet from them.

"Hey there sexy, what are you doing in a place like this." One of the men said holding up his hands towards his surroundings. He was grinning at me. His grin looked mischievous and devilish. His eyes glowed with the excitement of what he thought he was going to do to me.

I did not reply and stood still. The man that had spoken approached me head on while the other man started to the side and was trying to slip behind me without me noticing. The man in front of me and forcibly grabbed my face and started in for a kiss but stopped short.

"Look at this one she is fearless." He said to his partner. Then he resumed his advance to kiss me, as he got closer and closer to my lips. I slid one hand slowly up his arm and to his hair. I grabbed a hand full of his hair, bent his head to the side, and bit down. Ah, at last the blood started to pour down my throat and put the burning to rest.

I heard the other man behind me and his muffled scream as Jaxson took him out. We drained these men of every drop of blood then tore chunks out of them to make it look like they had been attacked by some kind of wild animal. It was all for show to through to throw the humans off. My mind was no longer stuck on feeding, I thought back to the dress shop. I just had to know how hc had made her give us the dress. So I asked slowly and unsurely, unsurely because I was not sure how to ask the question. "Jaxson how did you do that?" The look of confusion washed over his face. I tried to clarify the question. "With the lady at the dress shop?"

He laughed, he must have figured out what I was asking, then proceeded to answer my question. "That is a gift that all vampires have, you will be able to do it someday."

Without skipping a beat, I asked excitedly. "Can you teach me how to do that?"

I anxiously waited for his answer that seemed like it was taking hours of deliberation but was really only seconds. "I'm sorry Sam I can't teach you yet, you are not ready and you are still too young." This is not what I thought he was going to say and I knew that there was no sense in begging, so I changed the subject.

"Where are we going exactly?" I asked with a touch of announce in my voice.

"I have some friends that would love to have us." He said not giving away any more information as to whom these people where.

"Do you think that we should go there, and bring our troubles to them?" I asked trying to get him to talk to me and tell me more about these people that we would be staying with.

"Oh, Sam, You think too much!" He snapped at me. I was going to ask some more questions but I decided that I had better not. I shut my mouth and kept walking.

I still wanted to figure out how he did that at the dress shop so I kept playing it over and over again in my head. Studying his posture and the way he looked at the woman and decided I would focus on that as we walked. I practiced with my face to try and get the look down. I need to have the look of loving, adoring and sincerity in my eyes. I quite paying attention to my surroundings and my mind was stuck on trying to figure out the mind thing. Just when I thought I was getting it Jaxson voice broke me away from my concentration.

"It is not too far now we will be there in a few minutes. Is there anything you need before we get there?" I had a long list of things that I wanted. Nevertheless, I knew that they were not going to happen, so I simply replied.

"No, I don't think so."

We approached a plantation house it was huge and magnificent. The lawn sprawled out from the home in all directions and was lush and green. Four huge oak trees two in the front and two in the side yards complemented the house and the grass. The house was well maintained and bolstered white wooden siding with green shutters. The front of the house had a wraparound porch and pillars that went from the third story balcony down to the top of the porch. The spindle railings and pillars framed the entryway perfectly. On top of the railing, half way in-between each pillar there was flower planters filled with pretty purple flowers. The flowers draped over the sides and halfway down the porch and swayed in the light breeze. We followed the U shaped two tracks up to the front of the house and paused slightly at the steps leading upwards to the front door. Sitting on the porch in-between two huge windows was two chairs and a table that look to be very enjoyable for sitting outside and reading or maybe even a quick nap. I turned to take in the magnificent view from the top step of the porch. The scrolling lawn ran out to green rolling hills on one side. On the other side, the lawn ended at the dense forest. On the hilly side, you could see the white fences rolling with the hills, which kept the horses in. This was undeniably a breath taking view.

Jaxson did not get a chance to knock before the front door swung open. Inside the house stood a man, he was tall with short black hair and a mustache.

"Jaxson" he said excitedly. "So happy to see you my old friend." The man said with a thick southern drawl. The only way you got this accent is from living in the deep south your whole life.

"It is great to see you too Ezra. This is my companion Samantha." Jaxson gestured towards me; I smiled as he met my eyes.

"Um…please call me Sam." I said in a soft whisper not sure that I should have said anything or not.

"Why don't you come in?" Ezra said then stepped to the side of the door and gestured with his hand for us to come in. As we walked through the door,

Ezra called out "Lilly our guests are here." She was standing next to him in a flash. He shut the door and formally introduced us to Lilly. She was beautiful; she had blond hair that wrapped neatly into a bun on the back of her head. She was tall lean and very attractive. I was starting wondering if this was what all female vampires looked like.

"Jaxson she looks horrible, how old is she?" She asked Jaxson but her eyes were on me. She looked me up and down with disgust in her eyes.

That was extremely rude of her and I was almost certain that I was not going to like her at all. I was in raged over the fact that she said that I looked horrible. How could you say something like that miss primp and proper, I am better than you are attitude. This was going to be a long visit. I wanted to yell at her and make her feel bad for saying anything about me. I was just about ready to say something when Jaxson's voice broke through my thoughts.

"It has been a long journey and she is only a month old." He said making it clear that he was not going to tolerate her saying that about me. He looked at her with the utmost contempt in his narrowed eyes.

At once Lilly back down and tried to explain what she had meant. "I did not mean any disrespect I was just trying to say that she looks as though she could use a bath, some clean clothing and possibly a nap." Her eyes meet mine and were apologetic, for what we thought she meant the first time. I could agree with her now that I was dirty and did need a bath. Looking down at my dress, I discover that it was filthy. This sadden me a bit I really like this dress.

"That would be great, thank you." Jaxson re-plied, nodded and quickly smirked.

"Come Sam I will show you around and where you and Jaxson will be staying."

She took my hand and pulled me towards the grand staircase. This house was just as impressive in-side as it was outside. The foyer that we had been standing in had marble floors and walls that jetted up to the ceiling of the second story. The foyer shaped neatly into an oval with help from the pair of U shaped stairs. The walls covered in beautiful wallpaper; it had a white background with a silver floral lace pattern. A chair rail split the wall and the boasted a different kind of wall-paper, of vertical stripes of white and silver. We climbed the stairs, when I got to the top I looked over the railing down at Jaxson. I wanted to say something to him but settled for just meeting his eyes. I turned and walked through the doorway that leads to a hallway. Lilly was standing there waiting for me on the right side of the doorway. The motif from below carried through these walls as well. The only difference was the wood floors with a wonderful running rug. The rug stood out from the floor and walls by its color's red and white mostly with hints of blue, green and yellow. We went all the way down the hallway to the last door on the right. I peered around the corner to see a huge bathtub filled with bubbles overflowing the sides. The bathtub sat in the middle of the large space. I was only concentrating on getting in the bath and did not pay any attention to the rest of the room.

"We knew that you were coming, Ezra could feel Jaxson and we knew that you were close so I made this bath knowing that you would most likely need to relax. I will leave you to get undress." Lilly walked over to the door and grabbed the handle without saying another word. She almost silently shut the door and then she was gone, it was just this inviting bath and me.

I got undress and got into the bath. I could feel the dirt and dust melting into the water off my stone like body. I started to relax, sinking further and further into the water, dipping my head under the water to get my hair wet. I closed my eyes just to pop them open again when I heard the doorknob jiggled a little bit then I heard the small squeak of the hinges as the door slowly opened. I popped my head above the water as Jaxson came through the door.

"Are you ok in here?" He asked, but I was not sure what he meant by it. He looked at me and then to the wall trying not to stare at me.

"Yeah I'm fine." I finally replied after a moment of awkward silence. It had dawned on me that he was making sure that I was fine with Lilly because he already knew that I was not in any danger from anything else right now.

I looked down at the bubbles in the bath and was thankful for them. I looked up at Jaxson and noticed that he was also staring at the bubbles. I wondered what he was thinking but really, I already knew what he was thinking he is still a man vampire or not. I started to daydream of him taking me right here and now. I was imagining him slowly sinking into the bath with me when he broke the silence that had fallen between us again.

"Um… Lilly is going to come back in here if you don't mind, she would like to wash and brush your hair and bond with you she does not have any friends to do girl stuff with." He glanced at me just then to see my reaction to his words, but I did not have a reaction for him to see.

"Ok that is fine." I said with a hint of reluctance in my tone. I am sure he did not hear it though.

He turned his attention back to the wall and said. "Ezra and I are going for a walk to talk about things, I will be back soon."

I was going to say something about sticking close to here but Lilly came bouncing through the door and I thought that I had better not say anything. He glanced at me one more time and was out the door.

"Are you ready for your hair to be washed?" Lilly asked then hesitated and said, "I could come back if you need a minute." I think that she felt like she may have intruded on Jaxson's and I's conversation. Jaxson did not say anything else and quietly slipped out the door.

I quickly answered her. "No, no, stay; it would be an honor for you to wash my hair." I said in the most exciting tone I could manage. What I really wanted right now was to be with Jaxson or left alone. She grabbed something from behind me and lathered it into my hair I could hear the bubbles popping and crackling in my ear.

"Thank you for letting me do this." She said in a very womanly soft voice. It was almost as if she was talking to a baby and was keeping her voice low as to not startle the baby and make it cry. My mind still distracted by thoughts of Jaxson made me slow to reply.

"No problem I think I'm enjoying it as much as you." I said dryly but trying to be convincing at the same time.

"You know he loves you." She said

"I know and I think I love him to I admitted. What is your story?" I asked to get the attention off me and on to her.

"Well Ezra and I meet about twenty years ago. He saw me walking along the street one day, approached me, and said you are the most beautiful women that I have ever seen." There was a long pause as she seen that day in her mind again. "He asked me if he could court me and mesmerized by his looks and voice, I said yes. I knew something was different about him but I had no idea what. We dated for a couple of months then he asked me to marry him. Of course, I said yes. The night before we were to wed, he came to me and explained he was a vampire and that he would understand if I did not want to marry him anymore. I was upset for a minute but then I decided that it did not matter what he was and that I was in love with him too. The next day we were wed and that night when most people have a honeymoon he was changing me. Then I awoke to this new life. I have not thought about anything else other than I get to spend an eternity with my man. I still feel the same way about him as I did that first day I meet him. What about you what is your story?" She asked in return.

Oh no my mind screamed at me. Should I make up a story or should I tell her the truth. Crap, crap, crap what do I say? Without wasting any, more time I blurted out, "My story is not as sweet as yours." Still not knowing if I should tell the truth I made up a story in my head hoping that she would not ask for more detail than what I could makeup and still sound reasonable.

I started out with "I was dying from a gun shoot wound and Jaxson found me and changed me."

"Oh that sounds horrible. How did you get shot?" She said, I could hear the horror in her voice and I was sure that if I looked at her face I would have seen it there as well.

Without hesitation, I answered. "I was in the wrong place at the wrong time. A hunter mistook me for a deer. When he noticed that he had shot a human he ran, I am guessing he was afraid of the consequences. He left me there to die, then like a knight in shining armor Jaxson appeared and that is all that I remember."

"Oh honey that sounds very horrible, I'm so sorry that the transformation was not good for you. We should probably rinse the soap out of your hair now." She sounded so sincere in her statement. I think that it had really made her sad for me. I felt a little triumphant at the thought that she believed my story.

She poured the water over my head and I could feel all of the dirt and debris fall out of my hair. I then washed my body and it was time to get out. Lilly was standing outside of the bathroom waiting on me. I opened the door and walked out into the hall with just a huge bath towel rapped around me. She gestured with her hand to follow her.

On the very far side of the hallway was a door as she opened the door it gave way to a huge room. There was a bed nestled between two windows. This bed was a huge four-poster bed made out of a dark wood. A very intricate flowers and leave design was carved into the dark wood. The bed was about hip high on me and covered in a lacy looking bed covering. The same lacy material was also used as cartons on the windows. On the other wall across from the bed was a dresser also made out of the same wood and carvings on it. On top of the dresser was a vase full of different color wild flowers, these gave the room a sweet smell. Beautiful paintings of flowers hung on the walls. As I took in the sights of the room, I did not notice that Lilly had slipped out of the room and come back with a long black dress that was made of satin. I had almost forgotten that I was still wrapped in a towel. I glided over and took the dress from her.

"I will leave you to change." She said in a sweet soft voice. As she left that room, I dropped the towel from around me. I slipped on the dress and was about to zip it up when a voice startled me. I whirled around to see Jaxson standing there. I ran to him, and threw my arms around him.

"Did you miss me or was that too much girl time for you to handle?" He said sarcastically knowing that I did not want to do in the first place so yes he must have caught my tone earlier.

"Yes and no." I replied mockingly.

"What about that zipper?" He said with a grin on his face. I did not say anything and just turned to let him zip my dress. He ran is fingers ever so slightly from my shoulder down to my lower back where the zipper started. If I could get goose bumps, I would have had them all over. He hesitated to zip my dress this made the urge for him even stronger I wanted him right now. I was going to turn and try to seduce him further but he was pulling the zipper up and said we should go visit for a little bit. My heart sank to my stomach in disappointment. I had never done anything with a man and have never come this close before now. I had only been kissed up to this point and I think that is why my cravings for him were getting stronger and stronger with each passing second. I turned to face him once again before we left the room. I think he saw the disappointment in my face. He leaned in and kissed me quickly then grabbed my hands in his and looked me in the eye.

"I love you. Come lets go visit." He dropped my left hand and pulled me towards the door. Jaxson lead me though the house to the back porch. Lilly and Ezra were sitting in a couple of wooden rocking chairs looking over their fields of corn growing in the summer sun.

"I see the dress fits you Sam." Lilly said as we entered the porch. I caught Ezra glance over and then quickly look away. I knew that he only had eyes for Lilly and all he was doing was acknowledging our entrance.

"Very well" Jaxson added with an excessive amount of ecstasy in his voice.

If I could have blushed, I would have several times over.

We sat down in two more rocking chairs on the porch. The sun was touching my legs and warming them through the black dress. This felt really good and I rested my head against the back of the chair, closed my eyes, and was just basking in the sun. I was listening to their casual conversation about everyday news. There was no talk other vampires or anything else that was of interest to me. Somewhere in their conversations, I drifted to sleep. I was dreaming about the black mist again. My mind already knew how the story went and this allowed me to be able to see past the mist and pay more attention to the details of the surroundings.

I felt someone touch me, and my eyes popped open instantly. I turned my head and looked at Jaxson. He mouthed the words that Lilly had been talking to me. Not knowing what she said I was not sure how to answer so Jaxson answered for me.

"Yes she would love to do that." Paused then added in. "Go dress shopping with you." That last part was for my benefit.

I started to shake my head no but it was already too late. I instantly started looking for a way out of shopping when a slight burn came to my throat. I took it to the extreme and pretended that my throat was on fire burning out of control. I spotted one of the slaves that they had on the farm and pretended that I was going to go for him. Then I showed a slight bit of control, grabbed Jaxson's hand, and pulled a little bit. I could not wait to be alone with him any longer. He slowly rose from his seat and turned to face Lilly and Ezra.

"Where is the best place to find something to drink?"

"Follow the trail to the north and there are a few villages." Ezra said eyeing him speculatively but did not say anything. He pointed to a trail on the left side of the house.

"Please be careful with that dress." Lilly called after us.

Running until we were out of sight and hearing range. I put myself in front of him. I placed my arms around his neck and pulled him in for a kiss. As our lips touched each other, the tingly feeling was back. His lips left mine and kissed me from my mouth to my throat to my ear.

"This is really what you want, you are thirsty, but not for blood." He whispered in my ear.

We fell to the earth with him on top of me. The last thing I remember hearing was a few stitches in the dress pop.

He rolled to the side off me still holding my hand. I tried to move, I wanted to rest my head on his chest but my body just would not respond to anything that I was telling it to do for the moment. I stared up at the sky that had gone black and the stars were gleaming brightly.

"We should go quench our other thirst now." He said in a whisper trying not to disturb the moment.

"We should I'm truly thirsty now." I said still trying to comprehend what had just happened. It was the most amazing thing that I had ever done in my life.

Jaxson sprang to his feet, offered me a hand, and pulled me to my feet. I took a couple of steps and realized that the dress was not as tight as before. I looked down and seen that the seams on the sides of the dress had been split halfway up the sides.

"We are going to have to get Lilly a new dress to replace this one." I said somberly, trying to make a joke about it.

"Yes we will. Come we need to feed and then get back to the house, maybe we can try that again but in a bed" My mind going through the detail of what had just happened I answered late.

"Yes that would be great." I would be up for skipping drinking if that meant that we could have sex again. I was going to say let us just skip it when the Scent of human crossed our path and that erased any thoughts in my mind. The thirst for the blood and the burning in my throat was the only things I could think about now. Perfect a couple of cowboys lying by a fire in the middle of the forest. I hurried and drank mine dry. Wanting to get back to Lilly's and Ezra quickly in anticipation of what was to come.

Getting closer and closer to the house a strange smell filled the air. The smell was familiar but I could not remember whom it went with at that moment. I grabbed Jaxson's arm and pulled him to a stop. He placed his hand over my hand.

"It is ok it is just your brother." He said and patted the back of my hand.

How did my brother find us I wondered to myself, but at the same time I did not care. I was excited to see him. We walked a little further and the glowing green eyes of my brother were in front of us. I let go of Jaxson and ran towards the glowing green eyes. Just before I got to him, he shifted to human and held his arms wide open for me. I leapt into his arms knocking us to the ground.

"I thought I would never see you again." I said through sobs of joy. Then Jaxson grabbed me around the waist and pulled me to my feet. Then he offered a hand to my brother and pulled him to his feet.

"What brings you hear?" Jaxson said as he gave him a hug.

"I just missed my little sister." He smiled and scoped me up into a bear hug.

"We are on our way back to my friend's house where we have been staying would you like to come?" Jaxson asked but he sounded a bit nervous.

"Am I welcome there?" My brother said and re-leased me at the same time.

"Yes, I would not have invited you if you were not." Jaxson replied to my brother then added. "Ezra and Lilly don't have a problem with wolves and if you're a friend of mine you are a friend of theirs as well."

As I got over the joy of seeing my brother, I had a nagging suspicion that something was wrong. I was not sure what but I was going to try to find out.

"Brother, I know that you came here because you have news from back home." I was looking at his face as I said this but there was nothing on his face that I could read and he did not say anything so I let it go for the moment and was back to being happy to see him.

Jaxson grabbed my arm and pulled me behind Bill and him. "There is something wrong." Jaxson said in a very low whisper that I had a really hard time hearing. He pointed in the direction of the house. My brother, shift back into the wolf form. He grabbed my arm in his jaws and pulled me along with him. Why was he pulling me away from Jaxson? I started to struggle against him but he tightened his toothy grip on my arm.

"No we must not be separate this is dangerous." I said but it seemed to fall on deaf ears.

I finally broke free of him and ran towards Jaxson. I was back at the spot where we parted ways and nothing in my whole life could prepare me for what happened next. I saw Jaxson approaching the house and the black figures standing on the porch in the light of the moon. Jaxson stepped onto the porch and knelt down. He spread his arms wide a black figure on each side of him took his arms holding him by the wrists. Just then, my brother put his arms around me and started pulling me away from the scene. I saw something shimmer in the moonlight and then the screams of my lover pierced my ears. I knew he was gone as I took one more glance back at the porch and only saw the black figures standing there. I let out a small cry and one of the hooded heads turned in our direction. The danger was now on my brother and I. We ran through the forest. I did not look behind to see if they were chasing me but I knew that they were. I was running beside this wolf now and we were running as fast as we could.

"You must go they will kill you if they find you with me. It is really you that they want you killed the elder's wife. I love you just know that no matter what happens now we keep running." He started to veer away from me. Then he was gone and I was alone. I kept running as I ran things started to become more familiar to me. I knew what this meant it was my turn to suffer as Jaxson did. I glanced over my shoulder but did not see anything there. I wanted to tell my feet to stop running and to just wait here for my fate but my mind said no that I had to try and out run them for my family more than anything else. I glanced over my shoulder again and there in the shadows was the sight that I did not want to see but at the same time, it was welcoming I knew that my existence would be over soon. My mind knew how everything was going to happen now and this helped my feet from moving. I did not turn to face them like I had in the dreams but as I heard them slow behind me and stop I took a deep breath, even though I did not need it then turned to face them. It was just like my dream two women and one man. I did not make any moves towards them I just fell to my knees and assumed the position with my arms out stretched. I was determined to get this over with fast. They all had a weird look on their faces as I did this and were not sure what to make of it. The man and one of the women walked over and grabbed hold of my arms. The women that was in the middle walked towards me now. In the little bit of moonlight that snuck past the leaves and tree branches glanced off something shinny in her hand. I closed my eyes, looked up to the sky, and started re-membering things of the past. I was expecting pain of the shiny knife straight to my heart but I felt something touch my check. It felt like a hand, this took me by sur-prise and I opened my eyes. Everything around me had a red tent to it this must have been from the tears that I knew were streaming down my face. My tears were not from fear but from relief. My eyes found her eyes and I peered into the black holes as she spoke.

"You know why I am here child?" She said in a raspy hard voice. I nodded but did not say or make any sound.

"I know that you are not to blame for this but all the same you must pay the price." She said then I could see thoughts in my head that I had not recalled or thought about in a long time flashed past. I came to the realization that she was searching my memories look-ing for that day that I was turned. The memories of the field and that women vampire popped in my head she had the ability to slow the images down. Then she re-moved her hand from my face. She closed her eyes and

I let my eyes slide closed and my head slump back towards the ground. I knew what was coming next it was almost over. I opened my eyes, could see the puddle of tears forming on a leaf, and wished that she would just do it and get it over with. Kill this monster inside me and set me free the way that it should have been that day in the field. Instead, she spoke again.

"Child it is not your fault and therefore I cannot kill you for something that you did not do."

I could not believe what I was hearing. They were going to let me go. The man and the women holding my arms released me and steeped away from me. I did nothing even though everything in my body wanted to jump up and kill them.

"I'm sorry about your lover he was the killer and now we must go." The women said. Then they were gone as fast as they had come.

I was all alone left with a broken heart and crying. I lay down in the dirt and leaves and cried for the people that I had lost even though it was a different life I still had no choice in this life. I do not know how long it was that I was there but I kind of remembered the sun coming up and going down twice before I even twitched. I still could not will myself to get up and I had cried my eyes dry. Finally, on the fourth day my body made me get up and start searching for something to drink. I was so uncoordinated and weak that I was running into trees and tripping over whatever was on the ground. Finally, I fell to the ground and was too weak to make myself get back up. I closed my eyes and hoped that they would come back and kill me. I was daydreaming or dreaming not really sure, at this point, Jaxson had his arms wrapped tightly around me. This feeling made me feel better and I refused to open my eyes or to feel anything at this point and I did not care what happened to my body. I do not know how many days I laid there like this but I did open my eyes because I heard a noise that registered in my mind. A sweat soft sing sung voice that I would recognize anywhere.

"Sam are you ok?"

My eyes did not see anything at the time but felt arms under me lifting me from the earth. As my body twisted and my face turned to look at my brother, he was a live and the vampires had not found him my head rang with joy that I still had someone to hold on to. I closed my eyes again; I could feel the cool wind on my face and blowing through my hair. The next thing I remember is being laid on something soft with a familiar smell in the air. I remembered this smell from the house that Jaxson and I used to occupy. I opened my eyes and I was right. This brought back too many painful memories of the one that I had lost, my true love. Now I had eternity to live without him. As I lay there thinking of Jaxson and being overwhelmed by the feelings that I still had for him and always will, I started contemplating about what this whole life had meant and what it meant now. I was nothing but a monster now that killed people to survive. I knew I would not die just laying here though and I knew that Jaxson would not want me to be in this position. I willed my leg to move and then the other one to the edge of the bed. My feet dangled off the side of the bed, I made my abdominal muscles contract and pull me into a setting position on the edge of the bed. I placed both hands on the bed and pushed with all I had my but rose off the bed just a hair before my arms gave out. I was starting to become frustrated with not being able to move very well and pushed even harder this time. I was now in a standing position my legs felt very wobbly and could fail at any minute. As the first spark of sunlight pierced through the glass, I caught a reflection of myself in a mirror. I look horrible, my skin so pale I looked like a walking corpse. I had to get something to drink the thirst in my throat was burning out of control and was the only thing now that I could think about. My feet started to move on their own shuffling me to the door. Stumbling occasionally and catching myself on whatever furniture was nearby, I slowly made my way to the door. I opened the door, and to my surprise, I saw my brother curled up on the floor sleeping by the door. I could hear his heart thudding and the slow deep breaths he was taking in. The rhythm of his pulse was drawing me in my mind in turmoil over killing my brother over the thick rich blood pulsing in his veins. I fell to my knees by his head and touched his hair. In a split second, he had me pinned to the ground.

"I have something for you if you don't kill me first." He said then helped me to my feet. He led me to the back part of the house and the sound of four hearts beating took me by surprise. He opened the door to reveal people talking amongst each other. He pushed me into the room and closed the door behind me. I could see them but I was sure that they could not see me as the room was as dark as night and there was no windows for sunlight to shine through. The blood lust took over and I slaughtered all four of the people in the room with in minutes. I was full to the brim and did not think I could have held any more if I wanted to. I sat in the room for a few minutes feeling the high of the blood rushing through me. I slowly rose to my feet from the seated position on the floor pushing the last body off me. I turned and faced the door and slowly walked to the door feeling a little tipsy. I walked out of the room and back to my room. I went straight to the closet and opened the doors. The smell of my lover hit me. I choked down the tears that were coming and grabbed a few items to remember him by. I turned and faced the doors again and closed them with the smell of my lover locked in there. I walked out of the room and down the all too familiar hall towards the front door. I caught a glimpse of my brother lounging on the sofa and motioned him to come with me. We walked out of the door I turned placing my hand on the doorknob and staring back into the room burning the images of the inside of the house to my memory. I shut the front door and that chapter of my life inside. I placed both of my hands on the door, closed my eyes, and took in a deep breath. I could feel heat emanating from somewhere. I opened my eyes to see my hands in flames, and catching the door on fire. I don't know what came over me but I ran around the house once and set the rest of it on fire. When I was finished I closed my eyes again I shook my hands a bit to put out the flames. I opened my eyes and the flames were gone. I took my brothers hand we started walking away from the blazing inferno. This was a new power that I had no idea existed among our kind, but then again what did I know about my kind. I still have a lot to learn about this life. What other things could I be capable of doing?

My brother and I walked a ways into the forest. We got to a certain place when he turned and looked at me. He took both of my hands and had the look of sorrow in his eyes. He looked away and I could see that he was getting ready to tell me something that I didn't want to hear. A small tear rolled down the side of his check, he looked at the ground and started.

"Sam I'm sorry but I can't take you with me. The others don't want vampires around and I am sure that I can't protect you right now against them. I wish that I could run away with you but I have an obligation here. Also, what if the cloaked figures catch up with you and I, they would certainly kill us both. I think for now we should go our separate ways. I love you and you will always be in my heart. Where will you go since you burnt the only place that you could call home?"

The tears welled up in my eyes and I could not find the words to say. I was broken and had lost everything. I choked back the tears and pulled my hands away from him. I turned so that he could not see the pain and anguish on my face and simply said.

"I love you too, until then." Then ran.

CHAPTER 6

I guess when I left that house I left any kind of self-control that I had. The first little town that I came to, made of about one hundred people, I killed them all. The whole entire town even the babies and children. My dress was soaked in blood by the time I was done but that was ok because there were dresses at the general store that I took. Then I was on to the next town. I arrived in the next town and word of my killing spree had already made it there. The towns' people were saying it was the plague or some kind of sickness. Little did they know that the sickness was listening to them chatter about what they were going to do to prevent it from coming to their town. I laughed to myself as they said they were going to quarantine the whole town no one leaves and no one comes in, one man said. As I listened to them, I planned whom I would attack that night. As night fell and I was heading to my first victims house. I was not thinking of anything as I went in through the window and wipeout the whole house. My mind was completely blank no thoughts at all except to kill, drink, and be happy. The blood monster had taken over and there was no one or anything that could stop me.

The people of the town the next day were in frenzy. The plague was coming to get them. I watched some people pack their belongings and leave the town. Standing there, I watched people as they bustled around while I planned my next attack. The man that had suggested that *no one leaves and no comes in* looked in my direction with a curious look. Then he pointed his plump finger at me and said. "It was her she brought the plague with her."

I thought to myself, well I did not bring it with me I am the plague. A mob of people stood around me now discussing what they should do with me. "Lock her up in a jail and throw away the key" one woman said. Another man said "We should burier her six feet in a hole.

Wow, how did I make these people so angry? I looked at the man right in the eyes and whispered the words to him to make it right and stop accusing me of things that are not true. I tried to use the mind trick that Jaxson had used but the man did nothing. I kept trying but still nothing. I could not control his mind. I wished that I could have learned that skill but maybe I was just the odd vampire that could not have that one skill that came so easy to others. That was neither here or there right now. I needed to escape from here before they brought out the pitchforks or something. The man turned and started saying something to the people, their attention was off me, and I slipped between two building and into the forest nearby. I found a huge tree and climbed it to the top. Lounging on a branch I closed my eyes not to sleep but just to relax I had quite sleeping after Jaxson had been killed. My mind was racing around who would be the first victim on the list for tonight and who was next after that. Now all I had to do was wait for nightfall.

As night fell, I jumped down from where I had been perched all day and headed into town. I started with the man and his family that had accused me of bringing the plague. I slaughter four families that night and I would finish off the rest of the town the next night. My killing spree went on to the next town and the next town. Finally, after about two hundred small towns and a few years later, I was board of the killing sprees. The monster inside me grew quiet.

I wondered the earth from sea to sea, becoming a nomad and only killed to keep me strong. In my wandering I would take in the sights of the world and watched as they built huge buildings each one a little bigger than the last, but I found that this was very lonesome. I wished that I could share this with someone special but I had never found any one more special than my Jaxson. I had block my whole short life with Jaxson from my thoughts and kept all of the memories locked away in my mind. One day I found a place that reminded me of home, and him the memories unlocked them self's under their own will, they all came flooding back to me overwhelming me to tears. The images of him and me together flashed through my mind I started running trying to get away from them and locking them back up one by one. After the episode, I found myself running for home even though I was still trying to get away from the memories. One minute I would run in the direction of home but then I would turn around and run away. I didn't know what I wanted to do.

CHAPTER 7

Two hundred years had passed since I had been home. The town had changed a lot the streets were paved with the black asphalt. There are houses where farm fields had been and where I played as a child. There was one old house in town that I remembered or at least it looked the same anyway. Where the old general store used to be now stood a huge grocery store with an attached strip mall. In the downtown area, some of the buildings looked old but I knew that they had not always been there. These buildings formed another strip mall but had apartments above the stores. All of this sparked my curiosity of what happened to Jaxson's old house site. I could not believe my eyes as I turned the corner and a sea of endless house stood for miles. I had no landmarks to go by to find the old house site but I could feel it in my bones. The ground felt different here almost sacred to me anyway. I know that I should not have been surprised to see a house standing in its place but I was still stunned. This land was now part of a subdivision with paved streets, sidewalks and light poles. I stood on the sidewalk just staring at the house for a few moments when I noticed people staring at me as they drove by. I don't know why but I wanted the house I needed the house, I had to have it. I decided that I would come back in the cover of darkness and talk to the people that lived there. The darkness would conceal my intentions for them to leave me the house or I would kill them at that moment.

The next thing that popped into my head was I need to see if my brother then wondered if he was still here somewhere. We had decided to go our separate ways back then, because it was not a good idea for us a vampire and werewolf to run together and that I might hurt him someday. The only problem is that I had no idea where to look for him. I decided that I would start in the place where I was reborn, besides I had to see if that was still there or if that too had changed. To my delight, it was still kind of the same meadow but some-one had turned into a park. There was a huge play scape surrounded by some kind of squishy matting. There was a nice gravel path leading around the huge park. Parts of the path disappeared into the woods and then reappeared a few hundred feet later. In the middle of all that, there were some kind of fields to play sports on. But at the far end just past the pathway was taller grass with the most beautiful wildflowers growing in it. The park was absolutely stunning and all I could think was thank you someone for seeing the beauty in it and not turned into a subdivision.

A little girl and her mom playing in the wildflowers on the far side of the park caught my eye. As I watched them play in my meadow waves emotions washed over me. First sadness because I knew that I would never have the chance to play with a son or daughter of my own. Second was loneliness. I mean I had thought it would be nice to share my life with another person or vampire but I was thinking more of the kind of love that a woman and man shared. I couldn't help but think about how my vampire life would have turned out if Jaxson had not been taken away from me. There was his name again and the drawers in my mind started to rattle and threaten to open up again. This brought on the anger, I was angry now about the fact that I should have died long ago.

To, calm myself I diverted my attention elsewhere away from the mom and daughter. My keen eye sight saw a figure standing just inside the tree. Whoever it was noticed that they had my attention and disappeared into the forest. It moved to fast to be human that was for sure. It could be another vampire and I was in its territory. I had run across one or two other vampires and even stayed with one for a day until I found out that he only wanted me to leave his territory alone. For now I would just leave, I had more important things I wanted to do than chase him down. Besides, I wanted to visit one other place before I tried to track down my brother. My parents' house, if it was still there. Then I needed to find that cave that I was lock in when I was younger to see if my brother may be there or maybe pick up his scent to see if he was still hear on earth somewhere.

I walked down the street that used to be a two track to my parent's house. This had changed a lot too. The road that used to be all dirt now was paved with the black asphalt and there were house everywhere. Is there anything that the new world did not touch I wondered as I walked. I came to the spot where the house used to stand. In its place was a modern two-story house with green shutters and white siding. The land that my father used to farm was now a subdivision full of houses. Ok I was expecting that the house would be different from what I had already observed, but I thought that the land would still be the same beautiful rolling hills that I had grew up on. How someone could have taken and sold the beautiful land to develop houses was beyond me. I was sadden by this I was hoping that one thing, just one thing, would have been the same.

I walked up to the door and knocked but no one answered I just wanted to know if descendants of my family still lived there. I knew that it would not be my mother, father sisters or brother but it could have been great, great, great somebody. As I walked away, I noticed the name on the mailbox. It was my last name there printed in some sparkly letters gleaming in the afternoon sun. This little discovery perked me up a little bit. Seeing's how no one was home I decided that I would maybe come back just to meet them. Then again what would I say, hi I'm a long lost cousin from two hundred years ago and wanted to know more about the family. This even sounded awkward in my head. They would have called the cops for sure and had me arrested and thrown in jail. Being stuck in jail would have not done me any good. I would have had to kill everyone in the jail to escape. Then I would be a wanted person and forced into hiding. So maybe some things are better left alone. I walked away feeling a little sad and disheartened by the whole thing.

I came across a sign that said Bear National Forest with an arrow pointing to my left. I followed the road to a huge wrought iron gate. The gate opened in the middle and was held up on either side by brick pillars. Above the gate stood an arch also formed in the same black wrought iron. In the middle of the arch in five foot, high lettering was the words Bear Forest. As I passed through the open gates, I noticed a silhouette of a bear in copper, the front half of the bear silhouette on the right hand gate and the back half on the left hand gate. After passing the gates and walking down the gravel road into nothingness it took me back to how it used to be. No houses on top of each connected by the black roads. It was just the birds chirping and the smell of the pine trees mixed with honeysuckle, lilac and wildflowers in the air and no noises of the subdivision. I could smell the humans but I was not going to let that ruin the moment for me. As I walked down the dirt road leading to a parking area I decided that it was a good idea that I take the path less traveled. Stepping into the forest was like stepping back in time, my mind started flashing through old memories. Mostly of Jaxson no matter how much it hurt, maybe it was time to face them head on. I was wandering around the trees and through the thick underbrush not really heading in a certain direction and sorting through my feelings when a familiar smell hit me, the smell of wolf. My body reacted and carried me forward towards the smell at a faster pace and for now, all those memories were packed back up and stowed away I would have to deal with them another day. When the smell became intense and I knew I was close, I slowed my pace and started listening for the thudding heart. I found my wolf sitting under a huge oak tree with his back towards me. This wolf was black as Cole. This wolf was not my brother even though I wanted so badly for it to be him. I approached the wolf and it turned its head to look at me and started to bare his teeth and snarl at me.

"I'm not here to hurt you I just thought you may have been someone that I know." I said aloud to the wolf. I knew that he had heard me but that didn't stop his snarl and the blank stare in his eyes. I started backing away, turned, and started walking in the opposite direction when a someone cleared their throat behind me. I turned back around to see a man standing there looking back at me with four other wolfs. I stood frozen in place, not sure, what I should do but I did manage to find my voice.

"I mean no harm." I said to them.

"What do you want vampire?" He asked in a serious harsh tone.

"I was just looking for someone that I used to know, I will just go if you will let me. Sorry to bother you." I said and started walking backwards again keeping an eye on all of them for movement. No one even twitched their tails. Then all of a sudden, one of the wolves' started waging its tale. Then from behind me, I heard a voice.

"Where are you going Sam?" I recognized this voice immediately and spun around so quick that I made myself a little dizzy. My brother stood there looking the same from when we were younger adults. I ran toward him with my arms open wide. As I hit him, we both fell to the ground.

"I missed you very much." The tears started falling. I couldn't control them no matter how hard I tried.

"I missed you too." He said as tears of joy poured from his eyes as well.

"You have to tell me everything that I missed." I said with a frown, wishing that I would not have stayed away so long.

"Yes I will but you have to meet someone first." He said and tried to free himself from my grip. "Can I get up now?"

"Of course you can." I felt a little embraced that he had to ask me to let him go. I leapt to my feet and offered my hand to help him up he took my hand and we were both standing now. He brushed himself off a bit and called out "James"

As I turned around to see who James was I saw the big black wolf again coming towards us. "Sam this is James he is the one that runs things when I'm not around. James this is my sister Sam can you let everyone know that she is back and is the only vampire allowed in this forest." He nodded his big wolf head then turned on his hunches and took off.

"Come we have a lot of catching up to do." My brother said as he grabbed my hand and pulled me away from the crowd that had gathered. We found a fallen tree that was nicely supported by the earth and sat down. It made a perfect seat. We sat there staring at each other in disbelief for a few minutes. I knew that I was having a reality check and almost felt like I was talking to a stranger that was really not a stranger. To break the silence that had fallen between us my brother asked me.

"The first thing I want to know is where have you been for the past two hundred years?"

What should I tell him I really hadn't done any-thing except roam the earth. I really had nothing to tell him. So I simply replied "I have been here and there."

"You know that I looked for you several times but every time I thought I was close you had already moved on." He said with tears welling up in his eyes. Somehow, though he managed to choke them back down.

"Really you looked for me?" I was a bit sur-prised that he had looked for me but really he was still my brother and it shouldn't have been a surprise especially after what we had gone through together.

"Yeah, I was trying to find you when dad got sick so that you could come and say goodbye. Then again, when mom was sick, I really tried to find you. I still looked for you even after that." He said with sorrow on his face. I could feel the tears welling up in my eyes now and I wished that I would have not been so caught up in myself and what I didn't have and should have come home much sooner.

"Does that mean that you actually went and seen them?" I wondered if he had tried to make amends with dad and to help mom with the farm when dad was gone.

"No, I stayed in the shadows and watched from a distance. I would go and sit outside the window sometimes at dinner to get the latest gossip but I never let them know that I was there." He said and I could see the regret in his eyes. He wished he could have done more.

"What else did I miss?" I asked sensing that was all he was going to say about that. I tried to make the conversation a little more upbeat by asking this question with more excitement than it really need.

"Nothing else really except for our sisters and brother getting married, and then everyone dying. That's about it in a nut shell."

"What happened to mom and dad's farm?" I ask out of curiosity of how it became a subdivision.

"When they passed away our brother kept it and had a few kids and he taught them how to farm. When he passed the oldest boy took the house, got married, and had more kids that also farmed. Then when oldest sister out of them moved in for a while, she decided that she didn't like it so the house sat vacant for a long time. Then one-day big trucks pulled in and turned it into the subdivision that it is now. The house was the first thing tore down and replaced with a newer more modern house." He said and relived the moment over again in his mind. I could almost see the images that he was thinking. The house leveled and the ground tore up then almost like magic the house were built and occupied.

"When did they turn the place where Jaxson's house sat into a subdivision?" As I said Jaxson's name aloud an old ache in my dead heart shot a pain through me. I hid the pain from my brother though. I didn't want him to see that I was still in pain over Jaxson.

"That happened about three years ago. The county enforced the taxes on the property and when no one came to pay them they took the land and turned it into a subdivision." He said glancing at me from time to time trying to read my reaction. I must have hid it well though because he didn't say anything.

"What about you?" Well I found a special someone, fell in love and married her. She passed away a few years ago." He said and I could see that it still pained him a bit to talk about it.

"Oh my, I'm so sorry." I knew exactly how he felt to lose that one person that you loved with all of your heart no matter what. Silence fell upon our conversation as we both reflected back to the person and people that we lost all too soon. The silence was broken by a howl in the distance. My brother's head snapped in the direction of the howl, and then another howl broke that silence.

"I have to go something is wrong." He said already in motion shifting into wolf. Not sure if I should follow, him or not I ran behind him a ways. We came to a clearing in the forest I stopped just inside the tree line and stood in the deep shadows from the trees. I could see other wolf's in the clearing. I could not understand what was going on there was a series of short barks and howls. As I stood there watching I came to notice that the black wolf was staring in my direction. Why is this wolf staring at me I wondered? Then just like that, it was over each wolf went its own direction and they were gone. My brother turned back to human form and sauntered over to me.

"What was that all about?" I asked trying to figure out what they had been talking about in wolf.

"One of the wolves thought that they smelled vampire in the area, but it was nothing it was just your scent from earlier in the day.

"So what is the deal with that, you don't allow vampires in or around this area?"

"Yes we all banded together and protect the forest and keep all vampires from bothering the humans while they camp here." He stopped and took in a deep breath, then began again. "While you were gone we had a huge infestation of vampires coming in after they made this a national forest and killing the campers. It was getting so bad that people started calling it dead-wood forest. They also were starting to talk about shutting down the park and turning it in to one of those subdivisions. I just couldn't let them do that I love this place too much for that to happen. Besides this is where I was turned and for sentimental reasons I wanted to keep it the beautiful forest it is today. We moved in and took over the boundary of the park to keep the vampires out it took a few years but the campers started returning and the park was saved. We drove out the vampires and told them that they got a free pass this time but next time we would kill them. We have only had one death in the park since then but we were not sure that it was vampire related."

"So I never did get to ask you how you were made a werewolf."

He looked at the ground and I could see that he was seeing a different time in his mind. "Well it was a mutual agreement between me and my maker. He had been watching me for a long time and talked to me one day when I was walking through the woods, pissed off at dad as usual. He told me what he was and that he was looking for his replacement for this area as he was going to move on. He asked me if I wanted to take over, I said no at first. Then after a month or two, he just did it anyway without my permission then disappeared. At least I knew what I was but I didn't know everything about what I was or who I was. Then I met Jaxson by accident and he contacted some people he knew and helped me though the rough times. The rest of the story you already know.

My mind flashed back to when I was made and watching the wolves rip that vampire apart. This made a shutter go down my spine. The images of that day kept repeating in my head the only thing that stopped it was the sound of my brother's voice.

It was like he could tell what I was thinking judging by his reply. "It is ok they are not going to hurt you, as long as you stay away from the campers and or help keep other vampires out."

"I guess I can keep from feeding here but I do need to feed somewhere." I said then paused and said, "how about you I bet you taste good and started in towards him like I was going to bite him." Jokingly of course, I would never harm my brother.

A low menacing growl came from behind me just them. I turned quickly to see the whitish gray wolf pulled back into a spring stance and was ready to strike. My brother was rolling with laughter behind me. "It is ok, she is not going to hurt me, she is joking." The wolf relaxed and I realized it was the same wolf that stared at me in the clearing earlier.

"Sam this is Aidan, Aidan this is Sam my sister." My brother said gesturing to the whitish gray wolf, then back to me.

The wolf changed shape to give way to a beautiful young man. His eyes were a cool sky blue the kind that would cut through you like a knife or the kind that were so kind that you got lost in them. His hair was shiny and beautiful light brown color and sticking out everywhere. I was studying his features and did not realize I was staring until my brother cleared his throat behind me.

"Well I'm going to go sleep for a while do you want to stay here with Aidan and he will show you the ropes or do you want to come watch me sleep?" He said jokingly with a bit of sarcasm. I thought about my option of watching my brother sleep and how boring that would be or staying with this cute guy and I decided to go with Aidan.

"Aidan take good care of my little sister!" Then he was gone. Aidan and I looked at each other awkwardly for a few minutes. Neither one of us sure of what to say or do.

"Um… this is kind of crazy." He said. His voice was a deep tenor and very smooth sounding. The most beautiful sound that I had ever heard, snap out of it Sam I thought to myself he is a wolf and you are a vampire this would never work. We started walking down a trail in silence for a bit. I had no idea what to say but knew I needed to say something. Come on Sam find something to talk about but what. Music is always a good topic I thought. I was just getting ready to talk when he blurted out we have company and he transformed to the wolf before I could ask my question about what kind of music he liked. We stood there and waited a few minutes. Then out of the shadows emerged what seemed to look like people at first but then I could smell the dried blood on them and could not hear beating hearts. I knew what they were and it was my job now to talk them out of going into the park. I took the lead

"Hey what are you doing here? This park is a no vampire zone and unless you turn around and leave it will be ugly." I said and stood very straight and tall trying to make sure they didn't want to pass.

"Why should we what are you going to do?" The leader of the threesome came forward and challenged me. He started towards me in a manor to fight. I heard the sounds of paws in the forest and knew that I would be safe from there attack. When the wolves showed up behind me and made there self's known, I said.

"This forest is protected by a wolf clan and they will kill you if you don't leave."

"We are not leaving so get out of our way." He stepped towards me and so did the other two people with him. I was not expecting that, I thought for sure they would have ran away. I looked over my shoulder to see only me and one other wolf I thought there would have been more to back me up. It sure sounded like there was more. I turned back to face them again and put up my hands in fists and said.

"I'm afraid I can't do that." Laughter erupted from them and they all put up their fists. I started to prepare myself for the battle that was coming. I had never been in a fight with another vampire before so I was unsure of what to expect. I started to wonder if they knew I was a vampire too. Then all of a sudden, like he could read my mind the man in the front said.

"Ok we are going to leave this time but next time we will not." Then he winked at me and vanished just as fast as he had appeared. I was so glad that they left because I was sure that I would have lost even with the wolves on my side. When I turned, I noticed that more wolves had appeared behind me. Then they started too dissipated back to their posts as the danger passed and Aidan and I were the only ones left standing there.

"Aidan I'm going to need you to teach me how to fight. If they would have pursued I would have been in trouble." I said in a whisper not really wanting to admit that I was weak loud enough for everyone to hear. I heard a low whine come from behind me and jumped a little because I had thought he had shifted back to human form.

"Are we still in danger is that way you have not changed back?" I asked but heard nothing in response except the crickets chirping and frogs bellowing. I whirled around to find no one there, wolf, vampire or human. Where could he have gone I wondered? Great I'm here by myself with some blood crazed vampires out here somewhere. I heard a stick break to my left and deeper into the forest. Should I run the opposite direction or should I go towards the sound I questioned in my head. It could be Aidan but then again it could be the other vampires. I stood almost to the point of being frozen in fear of who or what it could be. Another stick cracked a little bit farther away from me and I decided that maybe I should go check it out. It was my job now to help protect the forest and running in the opposite direction was not doing my job. But, what if it is the vampires, what am I going to do then? Well the wolves will hear the scuffle and come running I think I can hold it down until then or I would be dead. I started running towards the noise of the braking sticks. As I came to the location, of where I thought that I heard the breaking sticks I slowed and was very careful not to make a sound. I was not breathing; my footfalls were so soft that I could barely hear them myself with my super sensitive hearing. As I silently approached, the area there was nothing there. To my right I heard another branch break. I very quietly went in that direction making sure not to make a noise. As I approached, there was no one there again. Then out of the corner of my eye, I saw a shadow. Even with my more than perfect eyesight, I could not make out what it was. It blended in with the trees and underbrush. I crouched and started toward the shadow that didn't seem to notice I was there. The closer I got I could make out some features four legs, a beating heart, ears that stood up off its head. Then I realized that I had been hunting a deer. I recorded all the sounds that it had made to my memory and started to turn and walk away from it but as I did, the deer took off like a shot. I didn't know if I scared it or something else. I decided to get off the ground to have a better view so, I climbed the nearest big tree and sat there in silence listening to the deer running away, the hooves of the deer's pitter pater on the forest floor were being mimicked by something else. As I sat perched in the tree the foot falls were getting closer and closer to where I was I prepared myself to jump just in case. This time I could make out the human figure of Aidan running through the forest. He slowed as he passed the tree. In a very soft whisper, he said.

"Sam are you here?" He waited a minute and then said "I knew you are here I can smell you."

I still did not make a sound and waited for him to turn his back towards me and jumped landing just inches behind him. He jumped and spun almost knocking me to the ground. He grabbed a hold of me to help me catch my balance. We were standing chest to chest. This felt too good to me and I instantly pulled away from him. I had not had that feeling in two hundred years. He looked at me a little strange. I had to say something this was so awkward.

"Ummm…. Thanks for keeping me upright. I think I have had enough for one night though. I need to go feed anyway. I'll see you later." Before he could answer, I was already running. As I was running to get away from Aidan, my mind was trying to wrap around what had just happened. The longer I thought about it I decided that maybe I shouldn't go back to the park. A wolf and a vampire there had to be some laws against that. If not a vampire law there surly had to be a werewolf law. My mind was now in such turmoil about staying away or going back, at this point I wished that I knew more about vampire laws and rules, if only I could find another vampire that would teach me them. The only problem I had with that was the fact that I just did not trust other vampire, what if they were working for the elders and reported me. What if they kill me? The floodgates to all the question were wide open in my mind. My throat stared burning and I realized that I was thirsty. I had no idea where I was but the sweet smell of the blood took over and shut down all the questions. I was walking now not to startle the potential blood donor, willing or unwilling. I walked around the small town and finally found a drunk guy behind a building smoking a cigarette.

"Hey sexy lady, are you looking to have some fun?" He stumbled as he pushed himself off the wall and staggered towards me. I walked towards him too. He threw his arms around me and put most of his weight on me to hold himself up. We stood there for a minute as he gained his balance and I was leaning in for the kill and the wonderful taste of blood when I heard a noise behind me. Someone had cleared their throat, to make their presents known.

"Hey little lady you are in my territory now." I had heard this voice earlier in the park. Oh crap I thought to myself. I dropped the man and stood there for a minute contemplating on running and what direction would be best. As I glanced around dark figures started appearing out of the dark shadows. I was in deep shit this time. How am I going to get out of this one I thought. I turned towards the leader and said.

"I will just go in peace and never come back." Trying to have a convincing attitude and sound to my voice. I was hoping that he would just say ok and let me go but I knew that it was too good to be true.

"I don't think I can let you do that my dear." He said in a calm relaxed voice.

"Why not?" I asked with anger in my voice.

"Because vampires are not supposed to run with wolves, you have broken the law and we are going to turn you into the elders." My one encounter that I had with the elder's henchmen a long time ago came back to me in flashes with the death of my lover and maker in the front of the line. The chase through the forest from the Cloaks that should have killed me but for some reason they spared me. I could not be taken to the elders now that I had my brother back. As my mind re-alized this, I began to become fearful and decided that I need to try to make a run for it. I searched for a way out, looking up a building to the roof, and decided to make a leap for it. At the same time that I leapt for the rooftop, I noticed flames had engulfed my hands. I hadn't used them or seen them since I had burnt the house down. I wanted to stop and admire them once again but knew it was better keep running across the building tops. The rooftops ended and I had to jump down to the street. Some of the vampires chased me across the rooftops while others ran through the alleys. I just had to make it back to the park where I would be safe under the protection of the wolves. Even though I didn't know how they would feel about me bring danger to them, but I did know one thing for certain my brother would stop at nothing to protect me.

I ran as fast as I could and it was just fast enough for them not to catch me. I could smell the park and the wolves and knew that I was almost there. As loud, as I could I called for my brother and Aidan. To my delight, I was meet at the edge of the park by them. They let out a quick howl to warn the others and to come. I skidded to a stop right behind them and waited for the vampires to approach. The leader was there first to stop just feet away from the wolves and the park line.

"We mean no harm we just want the girl!" The leader said in a demanding but sweet voice. He stared at me the whole time almost as if he could not see the wolves or maybe he saw them but he just refused to take his eyes off me. The wolves adjusted their posture and laid their ears back against their heads. As soon as every wolf was there, my brother made a risky move and transformed to human form.

"What do you want with her?" My brother said in an equally demanding voice.

"She has broken the law by hanging out with you." The leader said and pointed his finger at the all the wolves there. He still didn't take his eyes off me though. I wanted to creep back into the forest and just let my brother deal with it but if something happened to him, I would be hurt.

"Exactly whose law would that be?" My brother snapped back at him not wasting any time.

"The elders." The leader replied and put his hands on his hips. I saw my brother fidget slightly and I didn't have to see his face to know what he was thinking at that moment.

After a short moment, my brother demanded that they leave. I don't know how he did it but his voice was calm and collected. His whole demeanor changed slightly and it seemed like he was trying to say that he had no idea of who or what The Elders were or are and he didn't care either. I knew he knew though.

Without hesitation, the leader said, "We are not leaving without her."

My brother changed back to wolf form instantly and let out a menacing growl. It was very disturbing for even me to hear. The vampires took a few steps forward and so did the wolves. The wolves that were behind me in the forest also made their self's known. When the vampires realized that they were outnumbered, they started to back away a few steps. The leader gave the order to leave and they started to run away one by one until the leader was the only one left standing there. He turned and glanced over all of the wolves. His eyes stopped at me and glared at me again.

"We will be back to get her, we will follow her anywhere she might go. I'll see you soon darling."

Then he was gone. As the danger disappeared, my brother shifted back to human form. I ran to him threw my arms around him and started to cry.

"Come now little sis I will not let them hurt you." He wrapped his arms around me in a bear hug. I pushed him a way a bit although I didn't want to let him go I had to I was still thirsty and the pulsing under his skin was starting to draw me in. I pulled away quickly and to get far enough away from him so that I would not take him at that moment. He gave me a strange look then it hit him like a ton of brick.

"You're still thirsty."

So that I did not lose, control and I clenched my teeth tightly together as I nodded. Everyone can go back to their posts he said in a monotone – nothing is going on voice. As they, left one by one the burning in my throat started to dissipate ever so slightly. I was confident now that it would be ok to unclench my teeth and at least talk.

"Sorry I did not get a chance to quench my thirst. I have to find a way out of here before something happens."

"I know, I will get you out of here come let's try the north side of the park." He said and shifted to wolf.

"Just stay away from the people I don't think I could control myself right now." I said back to him.

We ran to the north side of the park and I was able to escape out into the world again and search for food. "I whispered thank you to my brother then bolted keeping my direction north, northeast.

CHAPTER 8

I pushed everything from my mind and was free for the ten minutes that it took me to run across two state lines and to where I was sure I was alone. I slowed my pace as I entered town so that I didn't startle anyone. I took in a huge gulp of air. The fresh summer breeze of lilies, honeysuckle and petunia filled the air along with the smell of wet soil and worms that was coming from a freshly plowed farmer's field. The closer to a town that I got I could hear loud music and people yelling to talk over the noise. Entering town there was a banner above the road flapping in the slight breeze that read Blueberry Festival. The loud obnoxious music was coming from a tent that had a country band on a small make shift stage. There were people everywhere some drunk, some sober and some that were just being plan weirdoes. The raging fire in my throat was burning out of control and it took all I had to keep my mouth shut and locked down tight so that I did not kill everyone here. In today's times that would be a very bad idea. The monster inside me jumped at the chance to ask questions though. What if I did kill everyone would they blame it on some kind of poison or plague of the past? No, no, I'm not a killer, I'm not a killer. I repeated several time in my head forcing the monster back down. But, I was a killer just not a ruthless killer I only take what I need to survive and nothing more. One person and one person alone will get me through a few days. I had made a pact with myself after my massacre stage not to do that anymore. I had let the monster inside thrive and win all the battles over my human thoughts. It was a struggle to silence the monster after I let it rage out of control. I felt helpless sometimes against the monster inside but eventually my humanity took over and put it to rest.

I was walking around the dark edges of the tent eyeing out the potential blood donor. But really I was just watching people act really stupid because they were drunk. Like this one girl that was showing off her tits to everyone that would look at them. There was this guy in the back corner of the darkest part of the tent who was sleeping and his friends were paying girls to take pictures with him. Wow what is wrong with people I thought as I kept walking staying just inside the dark shadows. I found a place to stand that was just inside the shadows and where I had a good view of the tent and what was going on inside of it. To act casual I leaned up against a tree. I heard something behind me but didn't turn to look because I could smell his sweat and the funkiness of a man that had forgot to put deodorant on. Not to mention his beating heart gave him away.

He rounded the tree and asked. "Are you lost little lady?"

Without even looking at the man, I said. "No I'm not lost." I was hoping that he would just go away but he lingered there. I'm guessing he was mustering up enough courage to ask me his next question.

"Would you like to dance with me?" He said, his voice shaking he sounded even scared to ask and he should have been scared. I didn't reply to him hoping that he would get the hint but no he just asked another question.

"Are you waiting on someone?" He said and looked around to see if anyone was coming.

"No, I'm just watching the party from the outside." I said sarcastically trying to drop the hint that he should go but he still stood there. So finally, I gave in and asked, "What is your name?"

"Umm…well my people call me sly but my real name is Scott." He said this time he sounded kind of excited that I was even talking to him.

"Ok Scott why don't you go back to the tent and find you a nice lady in there to dance with. I'm not the right height for you." I was blunt and to the point now. I needed him gone before I did something stupid. I knew that if he got any closer to me I would take him right here right now and then I would have to kill any-one that sees and that would have turned into a blood bath.

"Sorry to bother you mam have a nice night." He finally said and walked off to the tent.

MAM he called me MAM, I went off in side my head do I really look that old this vampire thing is not keeping my looks very well. I think he was hoping that I would change my mind though because he looked back at me one last time before entering the tent. I could have killed him but I don't think he would have wondered far enough with me away from the party so that I could feed without worrying about someone spotting us. I could have used force and made him go but he seemed like a nice enough person to at least have one more day on this earth. I kept waiting and watching for the right opportunity. A strong gust of wind blew from the south with it came the smell of other vampires. I recognized the smell of the vampires as the ones that were hunting me. I had to go again without getting so much as a drop of blood from anyone here. I placed my scent on everything that I could touch and snagged a coat from a car trying to hide some of my scent as I ran away from here going to the East my idea was to hit the next town to hopefully find a quick meal and then back to the forest under the protection of the wolves.

The next town that I came to was a quiet little town where they practically roll up the sidewalks when it gets dark. So I just kept running through the town. I knew there had to be one more town before I needed to turn and run back southwest to get to the park. There were a few people out and about in this town. I actually had a choice of who would be a blood donor. There was a couple taking a midnight stroll. An old man sitting on his porch looking like he should have been dead already, and a young women just returning home from somewhere. The couple was out because I would have to kill both of them so that would be a waste of human life. Not to mention I didn't think I had time for that. The woman was already at the back door of her house and almost inside. I had enough time to get to her but I didn't know if there were people inside or not just in case she screamed. My choices boiled down to the old man. I snuck up behind him, whispered sorry in his ear, and sank my teeth into his leathery hard wrinkly skin. The first drops of blood hit my mouth and I drained him completely in the matter of seconds. I started to stand up and was ready to run home when I heard the familiar voice of the head vampire.

"Jarod give me a report."

"She is here I can smell her. She has been a few places he said."

Oh, crap I had to get out of here and fast.

"Well track her down dip shit what are you waiting for." I heard the leader say.

I heard him take in a lung full of air. Then nothing was said I had to go now. I jumped off the porch and ran to the back of the home. I hoped a couple of fences and started to make a break for the park when an

Idea hit me. No literally, hit me I ran through some clothing that had been hung out to dry on a close line. They smelled of flowers and soap. Maybe just maybe if I took some clothing off the line and exchanged them I would be able to escape. I quickly undress and re-dressed in this clothing. I didn't want to leave my old clothing just lying there to be found so I picked them up and held them as far away from my body as I could then threw them down a sewer hole. That should keep them looking long enough for me to get out of here. I ran for the cover of the park and my wolves.

As I entered the park I slowed my pace to a walk now that I felt safe. Something seemed wrong though there were no wolves to greet me at the border. Then I was knocked to the ground and licked every-where.

"Thanks brother I need the dog spit bath." I said sarcastically.

He barked out a laugh and changed to human form.

"I was so worried about you."

"I didn't notice!" I replied still wiping the spit off my face. When I completed wiping my face I said

"New rule don't do that again the dog breath is horrible smelling." We both laughed.

"What happened to your clothes?" He asked eyeing me speculatively; he already knew something had happened. I was not ready to tell him just yet though so I said.

"I decided I liked these ones better." In my haste, I had not stopped to look at what I was putting on. The shirt was plaid long sleeve and the pants were not much better, different colored polka dots on a black background.

"So what did you do, dribble blood on them or something?" He said trying to be funny.

"Yeah, that is because I'm such a messy drinker." I said sarcastically but quickly changed my attitude to be serious. "No I had a run in with our friends." I said with shame.

He instantly snapped into parent mode and looked me over and when he could not find anything that said I was hurt he asked. "Are you hurt anywhere?"

"No, no, I'm fine I tricked them by changing into these clothing."

"What are we going to do we can't protect you out there when you go to feed. I have to talk to the others." He said with haste then instantly changed to wolf and let out a ear piercing howl. The howl was so loud that it made my brain feel like it swelled and left my ears ringing.

"About what?

I shouted half deaf from the howl. He didn't even turn to look at me. All of the wolves gathered except one. Where is he I wondered? My brother was talking in wolf I didn't understand any of it. A series of short barks, and wines, and other little sounds that I had no idea wolves could make. Except every once in a while all the wolves eyes would quickly glance at me then away, so I figured they were talking about me. When I thought no one was looking I slipped behind the tree and up to the top of the next one without making a noise. Just to get away from the stares. Where was Aidan? I caught a small movement off to the left. Then I heard the hooves of a deer sinking into the mud and breaking through the grass and the roots. Then off to right another movement. This was the same thing just a deer walking through the forest. Then there was more and more deer making their way through the forest. As each of them passed, a thought occurred to me. I could use the deer as my main source of food until it was safe for me to leave the park. The other option would be to run and keep running until they caught up with me someday. The only thing keeping me here was the sense of family that I had been without for two hundred years. My mind was back on the deer moving through the park. What if I could use the animals in the forest for food instead? But what If I can't stand the taste of the deer blood? I thought back to the day that I was born and all the deer that I had killed that day, I remember their blood tasting ok. I wondered what other options I might have for animal blood in the park. As I was deep in thought about this, I heard my brother call my name. I jumped from my perch way above the ground and landing with a soft thud. He was just getting ready to call me again when I walked up behind him

"yes brother."

He turned and reached for my hand.

"The other wolves and I had a chat about you hunting in the park. We all agree if you don't take too many humans and the human has to be alone you can feed here in the park. This way we can label them as a missing hiker, but you must stay in control of yourself."

I nodded and stepped around my brother to address all of the wolves.

"Thank you for letting me feed in a no feeding zone. I do have an idea that would not involve humans though. I can live off the blood of animals so if it would make you all more comfortable and still be able to keep the peace I can hunt animals."

They all just stared at me with blank expressions. I started to wonder if they had heard what I had said or understood. I guess I was expecting them to do something whether it was a bark or some other kind of acknowledgment that they understood what I had said.

I whispered back to my brother. "Can I get a little help?"

As he passed by me, I caught a glimpse of his face and it was lit up with a smile he nodded. He looked at all of them and as he did they all would shake their heads yes or no. the majority was yes but there was a couple of no's but I suspected they said no to begin with. Ok then it is settled no human's just animals.

"Thanks you for all coming. You may return to your posts now." My brother said. Then he turned and looked at me with an elated smile on his face.

"So what made you decided that animals would be the answer?"

"I don't know just a hunch I guess." I paused not sure, if I should ask but I really wanted to know where Aidan was. I looked to the ground trying to hide what I was feeling from my brother and asked. "Where is Aidan?"

"I'm not sure I think he may be sleeping, he ran patrol all night waiting for your safe return. When I found him he was so exhausted that he almost collapsed." I looked up at him out of the corner of my eye and could see that he was wondering why I asked. I didn't let that stop me though from asking the next question.

"If I wanted to find him where should I look?" I said then quickly thought that my brother might be on to me and added. "I just want to let him know that I'm ok, of course."

"Is there something going on between you two?" He asked eyeing me speculatively. I knew that I had to answer quickly and that I cannot hesitate or what I was going to say would be discredited. So, I quickly replied.

"No, we are just friends."

My brother eyed me speculatively some more but this time I was able to look straight back into his eyes without a trace of anything on my face other than we are just friends. I knew that I liked him but that is all we really were just friends.

"Ok then, come I will show you the way." He turned and started walking. I quickly joined him and started another conversation that needed to happen but I really didn't want to talk about it though.

"There is something that I have to tell you." I started and paused and waited for him to say something but he just nodded his head in a manor saying go on. I took in a gulp of air and started again. "One of the vampires out their looking for me was able to track my scent. In all of your years that you were friends with Jaxson did he say anything to you about a vampire like that?"

The name opened a wound so deep that it hurt my cold dead heart. I shoved those feeling back down before the tears came and waited for him to answer.

"No he never mentioned anything about what his kind could do." He replied a bit puzzled but I could tell that he was still thinking. What about you with the fire touch?" He then asked.

"I have only done that twice in my whole life, once to burn the house down then once the other night when I first ran into those vampires."

He had a point though, and I could not ignore it. If I had something special what was to stop other vampires from having something special as well? I thought about that question as we walked in silence. Then another thought occurred to me. What other special powers were out there?

I was so deep in thought that I had not paid any attention to where we were going. The next thing I knew we were in front of a wooden door carved in the hillside. I knew this place. It was the place where I had been held captive. I hesitated a little bit.

"You are not going to lock me in there are you?" I asked sounding a bit terrified to myself. This place brought back bad memories for me. My brother looked at me and cracked a small nervous smile. I could tell at first he was going to say something else but he must have seen the panic on my face and decided not to.

"No, it is ok, this is where Aidan is." He said quietly.

Just then, a howl broke and rang though the forest.

"I have to go I will see you soon."

Then he was gone in a blink of an eye and I was on my own. I slowly opened the door and walked inside the smell gave me chills. I could hear Aidan's breath in a steady whishing motion in and out in and out. As I found him curled up into a ball on the floor in my cell, I hated the idea of even stepping foot in it. All of the metal stakes had been removed and put in a pile in the corner. I laid down beside Aidan and he wrinkled his nose ever so slightly. I knew that he could smell me. He laid his big noise on me and sniffed again. Then as if to put his mind at ease, he took an even bigger sniff.

I finally patted his head and said.

"It's ok go back to sleep. I'm going to lay with you a little while if you don't mind."

He took his paw and put it across me. I closed my eyes and vivid thoughts of that time I had spent here came racing back to me. I saw the cell as it was when the last time I was here panic raced through me until I got to the part were Jaxson saving me. The longer that I lay here, the more I started seeing other things. It was almost like dreaming but I didn't sleep anymore. The dream was about the vampires that were hunting me and they had finally captured me. In the dream, it turned out that the head vampire just wanted me to be his wife. Until I agreed to be his wife, he was not going to let me go or feed. Then that shifted to a battle between the cloaks and the leader. My brother was there to save me. Then Aidan whispered in my ear.

"Are you ok?" Of course, this startled me and I jumped about fifteen feet in the air. So when I replied my voice sounded a bit shaky.

"Yeah I'm fine why?"

"You where growling through your teeth at someone or something."

I looked at him as he was wiping the sleep from his eyes. Then I instantly felt bad for waking him up and said. "Oh, I'm sorry did I wake you?"

"No, I was waking up anyway." He said but I knew that he was just trying to be nice so he didn't hurt my feelings.

He kissed me just then on the check. Almost to say apology accepted.

"I'm sure glad that you came back, I was really worried about you."

"I'm sorry that I made you worry."

He put an arm around me and pulled his self-closer to me, then without warning, he kissed me. I thought about pulling away but this kiss felt so good. I started to kiss him back. I had not realized that I was so starved for affection. All though at the same time, memories of Jaxson flooded my head. I tried to shake them off but they just kept coming each one more intense than the last. This felt right but at the same time, it was so wrong. I could not let myself continue to kiss him any longer if I was going to think about someone else. I pulled away, rolled over on my back, and sprang to my feet.

"Where are you going? I'm sorry if I hurt you."
His voice rang out in a panic.

I had to say something to put his mind at ease.
"No it is not you it is me."

I ran out the door and to the far end of the park I
wanted to keep going but I knew that I couldn't, I knew
that the hunting vampires were just waiting for me to
cross the line in any direction. I climbed to the top of
the tree, sat there, and cried, the tears soaking my clothing. I was crying because of Jaxson still, I needed to get
a grip on myself. Pull it together come on, he has been
dead for two hundred years. What was wrong with me?
I needed to talk to someone about this instead of keeping it all inside and not sharing it with anyone. As I
came to this resolve my brother appeared out of no
were. Sam he called, I did not answer still trying to
stuff the emotions that I was feeling down back were
they came from. Sam I know that you are here and I
know where you are please come down. With the way
his voice sounded, I knew that Aidan must have told
him something.

"Come on Sam we can talk about this." He said
begging.

I jumped down making no sound as I landed on my feet. I slumped down with my back against the tree. I looked down at my shirt and realized that it was completely soaked in blood.

"Brother, please stay over there, I'm a mess." I finally managed to say.

"Did Aidan hurt you?"

"No, it is me all me. I think I'm finally ready to talk about this?" I paused and summoned all my strength to say one name. "Jaxson"

"I know I miss him too he was a very good friend of mine." He paused for a moment. I knew that he was remembering something about Jaxson. Then he started talking again. "It is ok to miss someone you love sis. Even though you are a vampire that does not mean you have to be thoughtless or soulless. You still have human emotions inside of you."

"I know but being here, reminds me of him. I would give up everything to have him touch me once more." I paused to remember his kind and loving touch. "I shared a kiss with Aidan and all I could think about is the way that Jaxson used to kiss me. Maybe I just need to go away from here and try to start a new life somewhere else. I mean look I have only been here for a week and I have already caused you too may problems."

My brother flew around the tree and scoped me up in a bear hug. "No I don't want you to leave; I will not lose you again!" He demanded, then shook that off and began in a quieter sweeter and softer voice. "Look I know that you loved Jaxson and with him being your first lover and all but sis you have to let him go. You can't hold on to a ghost. I know one thing that he confided in me was that he loved you too and that if anything were to happen to him he would want you to move on with your life. I know the way things happened really sucked but sis you can't bring him back. Let me tell you a little story. I too once fell in love but with a girl. She was my stars, moon and the sun, my everything that was good on this earth. She understood that there were things that I could not tell her and she accepted that and did not ask any questions when I had to go out late at night to keep this park safe. One night when I was out, she slipped and fell down the basement stairs. When she fell she broke her neck, that severed her spinal cord, and she died. I sat in that dark basement for days just holding her. I don't know if I was hoping that she would wake up even though I knew she was gone. Aidan was the one that found me sitting there holding a dead bloated corpse. I had not realized how much time had passed when he found me but he said that it had been a week. I had not moved from that spot. I had not eaten, drank and had urinated and defecated all over myself. He pulled me away, he got me cleaned up and something to eat and drink. The anger came I tried to kill myself a few times but unless you have a silver bullet that does not work out so well. All my suicide attempt did was give me more pain and agony. Anyway, I still think of her to this day. Yes, I have been with a few other girls and I have thought about her when I was with them. I guess what I'm telling you is that you have to move on. It is hard and yes, you will get there.

I turned just then to look at his face and there sparkling in the moon light was one single tear on his check. As I sat there in my brothers arms I decided that I would try again and keep trying I would not give up just like my brother has not given up. I turned and hugged him around the neck.

"Thank you I need that." I said trying to comfort him. I knew that it must have been hard for him to tell me his story. I wished then that I had not stayed away so long. I could have comforted him as he was comforting me now.

"Anytime you need to talk I'm here for you, I love you." He said back to me wiping the tear from his face.

"I love you too." As I said that, one more tear fell from my eye and rolled down my check.

After sitting there for a while both of us in our own little worlds, my brother left me to go get some sleep. But not before making sure, I would be ok and would not do anything rash. I sat there leaning against the tree for a long time thinking about what my brother had said. I let the memories pass through my mind of the time that Jaxson and I had been together and ran through all the emotions that went with it, I did cry a little here and there but I also smiled. The next thing I knew the sun was coming up and casting a beautiful orange red glow through the forest. The forest looked like it was on fire and the fog was so thick it looked like smoke in the air. As I sat their Aidan's voice broke through into my thoughts.

"Sam where are you? I'm so sorry, I didn't mean to hurt you." He said with sadness oozing from his voice.

Oh, crap I have to get out of here before he sees me. I was not ready to confront him just yet and I still need to go through things in my head.

"Come on Sam where are you?" I heard him say and he was getting closer to me.

I leapt to my feet but in the same instant, I saw him he had spotted me. I ran to the other side of the tree where he could not see me but he was right there staring at me.

"Oh my, are you bleeding or something?" His voice had an edge of panic to it.

"No I'm fine." I said and patted my body showing him that I had not been harmed in anyway. Then He reached out for my hand and I hesitated but gave him mine in return.

"It is ok, I'm fine." I said again trying to reassure him that nothing was wrong with me. "I'm sorry about last night umm..I, well." He cut me off though probably sensing that whatever it was that was bothering me he didn't need to know about right now. So he said.

"It is ok no need for explanation. It was my fault I should not have been so forward."

"No, Aidan don't blame yourself. It is all me. I'm not sure how to explain this to you but here it goes." I just knew that I needed to tell him wither he wanted to know or not. This time I wasn't having a hard time finding the right words I just let it flow. "For all of the years that I have been here on this earth I have only been with one person and when you kissed me it threw me unexpectedly into memories that I have been trying so hard to suppress and not think about. You see when he died he took a part of me with him. You are a very nice guy but I don't think that you are right for me at this time, I have to work through some personal issues as you can tell."

"I'll wait as long as I have to." He said this made butterflies swirl around in my head at that moment and I almost lost my resolve that I had just given him.

"Can I at least have a hug?" He asked. I opened my arms, threw them around his neck, and buried my face into his chest. Then all at once the scent of his blood started to overwhelm me and I pulled back quickly.

"I have to go, I need to feed." I said through clenched teeth. I don't know what he seen on my face but it was enough to make him back away and blur once like he was going to shift and call in reinforcements. I gave him one parting glance and was off running. As soon as I was far enough away that I could not hear his beating heart any more I slowed my pace. I closed my eyes and listened for movement. I heard the pitter pater of hooves nearby and went in that direction. I caught up with a small heard of deer in a small clearing in the forest. I excreted very little energy to catch one and bit into it, the blood that hit the inside of my mouth was not the sweet taste of human but more of a bitter taste like a lemon. I didn't really like the taste but I made myself drink until the deer was drained anyway. I wished that I had other options but I knew that I didn't. I could try risking everything to go out for human blood my inner demon said. I was almost convinced to go but my human side caught up and said no this will do for now. The argument between the two started but the human side prevailed this time.

Now I was board and needed something to do since it was my night off from guarding the park. As the days and nights passed I was starting to feel like a prisoner here with nothing much to do at all. I felt restless and really needed to find something before I went crazy.

As the darkness turned into another long lonely night, I found myself wandering through the forest up and down the hill. Staying as far away from the humans as possible, I did not want to be tempted by their blood. However, I found myself in that situation with a human anyway. I walked as fast as I could in the opposite direction, holding my breath and clenching my teeth, my mind was thinking of ways to kill this one lone girl wandering around. I could kill her and stuff her body somewhere where it will never be found. I could make it look like a drowning accident; they would not find her for days the killer in me said. The more I thought about this the more my feet started carrying me in her direction. Come on you are stronger than this the human in me was trying to say. However, the demon in me was winning the fight this time. I got closer and closer to her getting ready to take her down. Then unexpectedly I saw him. The one that my heart, and mind had been trapped with, my maker, my teacher and my lover.

"No don't do it he yelled to me. No my love." I melted to my knees and forgot all about the women walking down the road.

I could not help but cry out "Jaxson my love." I got one more look at him through a haze of red that also blurred my vision then he disappeared as fast as he appeared. My first thought was that I had to find my brother. I jumped to my feet and ran calling him. I caught him on the edge of the forest in wolf form of course.

"I saw him." I shouted. He blurred back to human instantly.

"who?"

"Jaxson, I saw Jaxson." I said excitedly, then the pain came again but I pushed it down trying to hide it.

"What do you mean you saw him?" He eyed me speculatively, I'm sure that he was think that I had finally cracked and gone insane. But, I didn't care what he thought right now.

"I saw him he was a ghost but I did see him." The excitement of seeing him for the first time in two hundred years wore down to sadness of missing him. The sadness took hold of me and broke me down to tears. My mind and heart were in overload. What was I going to do I can't continue to live my life like this. Then I had an epiphany that might work. I wanted the other vampires to capture me and hopefully with any luck they would destroy me. Then I could be with him again. I weighed my options of staying and being a prisoner to this park that was growing smaller and smaller every day or turn myself over and hopefully be put out of my misery of missing Jaxson. What would this do to my brother though I thought as I stood there staring at him. It seems as though coming back here may have been the worst decision that I had ever made. I feel stuck in to worlds and neither one of them did I belong too. I did get to see my brother but I was starting to think that I was wearing out my welcome with the rest of the wolves. Then there was the thing with Aidan that seemed to be getting weirder every time I saw him. I just had such mixed emotions when I was around him. I liked him but, I could not let go of Jaxson at the same time. I knew that I would only end up hurting him in the end anyway. As I was thinking this all over in my head, my brother was standing over me watching me.

"I love you sis but I really do need to get back to patrol, are you going to be ok?" I don't think he knew what else to say at the moment but he did have his job to do.

"Yeah, yeah I'm fine. Umm I'll talk to you later?"

"Ok love you sis."

I waited for him to get far enough away and ran for the border. I was out of here no matter what waited for me on the other side. I ran for the boarder and about the same time that I crossed it, I heard two howls one that I knew and the other for the first time. As I cleared the boarder, I kept running not slowing down, I yelled, "I'm sorry brother".

CHAPTER 9

When I felt like I was far enough away from the park, I slowed to a walk. As I walked, my head was clear for the first time in a very long time. I just watched as the birds flew from tree to tree and the wind rustled the leaves. There was a stream nearby humming a lullaby as the water washed over the rocks. It was such beautiful music. I heard the first signs of life in the form of voices. Then I heard more and more voices and decided that I need to go that way since I was hungry for human blood that I hadn't had in a long time. Oh, this was going to be so good. I picked up my pace a bit, as the aroma of sweet tasteful blood crossed my nose. The wind swirled around me just then like a tornado with it brought the scent of my hunting party. Crap, they are close but I really wanted to feed at least one last time if it was going to come to that. I decided to go for it anyway I might be able to just slip by them I thought. The smell of the blood got closer and closer and I blocked everything else out. Just as I found someone to feed upon there they were.

"Well, well look who came out to play." The leader said, taunting me to fight him.

"I know what you want can I just please have one last drink before you do what you wish with me. Consider it my last request and I will come peacefully without a fight."

"Ok as you wish."

I sank my teeth into the woman and sucked her dry not leaving a drop of blood left in her. Then as had promised I dropped to my knees and surrendered. The two strongest looking men came to help me to my feet and intertwined their arms in mine.

"Don't try anything funny." They said in unison, I could tell that they seemed a little scared of me. Little did they know that I couldn't control my fire power. Right now, I was not scared or upset about anything and so far that was the only times that it had worked. At this moment in time, I just didn't care if they were going to kill me. Besides that defiantly would not be a punishment at this point. We walked to an old abandoned warehouse. This is where it all ends for me I thought. We went through to steel double doors down a wide hallway to another set of steel double doors.

"Well babe how do you like my lair?" The leader said stretching his arms wide gesturing to all of room.

I looked up from watching my feet to see a room full of stuff; it was upscale for this old abandoned warehouse. I looked around there were red velvet couches mostly along the walls. In the front of the room, there is a stage with a thrown sitting on it. The thrown was made of gold and covered in the red velvet. About twenty chandlers hung in beautiful lines across the ceiling. They were all different, some had long glass panes and others had glass diamond like beads. The lead man came and stood in front of me.

"This is your new home now and I'm the leader you are to do as I say." His tone was demanding and he seemed not to be kidding at all.

Me however I wanted to bust out laughing. What this guy was going to order me around I don't think so. But, what leverage did I have right now absolutely nothing. One thing did come to mind I could try to use this as a way to learn more about being a vampire.

"Frank, could you please get this girl some decent clothing, oh and honey you need to take a shower frankly, you stink." A devious smile covered his face.

"Sure thing sir." I replied in the most sarcastic voice I could manage.

"Sir, sir, that is really cute, but from now on call me Ted." He demanded in a playful but serious tone.

"Ok Ted it is." I said back sarcastically.

"Frank, would you please show her to the shower."

I stepped into the bathroom it was pretty plain and felt like a prison cell more than a bathroom. A white porcelain sink hung off the wall with a small square mirror above it. The shower was made of small tan tiles with a matching tan vinyl shower curtain the kind that sticks to you no matter what you do. I was thinking about trying to escape but there were no windows and it would have taken too long to go through the cement wall. I leaned back against the door for a few minutes then wondered over to the shower and turned it on. I turned on just the hot water even though I was a vampire I could still feel the heat from the shower and it somehow soothed me a little bit. I lathered up my hair with the soap, watched all of the dirt rinse out, and swirl down the drain. Then I lathered up my body in the same fashion. When I was done, I stood in the water letting it roll over my face and body. I didn't want to get out, it was so peaceful and relaxing. I finally convinced myself to turn the shower off when the water got cold. I grabbed my towel off the back of the toilet and wrapped it around me. I went to the door and asked for my clothing. Frank who was still standing outside the door handed them too me. I dried myself off and then held out the clothing that was given to me. This looked more like something that should be worn to bed. It was all red with black lace everywhere. I put it on and took a step back from the mirror to get a look at it. The skirt was very short if I bent over everyone would see my lady parts. The skirt and the bra top were connected with lace that my skin shown through. The bra had barely enough material to cover my nipples and I was sure if I bent over my breasts would fall out. The bra was also strapless but had quite of bit of support. All in all there was just enough material to cover up my business and that was it. I may have been better off just tearing a few pieces off my old clothing and just wearing that over my lady parts. As I stood in the mirror for a little while longer too embarrassed to come out I started to hear the thump, thump of music playing from down the hall. Then there were three quick raps on the door.

"Are you ever going to come out of there?" Frank asked through the door.

This shook me out of my blank stares into the mirror. I stumbled over my words.

"Y-y-yes, just give me a few minutes more." I said slow at first but picking up the pace at the end.

I quickly brushed my hair and sauntered over to the door. I put one hand on the doorknob, took a deep breath in, and pulled the door out of my way. There waiting for me was Frank he took one look at me and his eyes bugged out and his jaw hit the floor as he took in my five foot five inch frame. He was probably seeing me naked since my outfit didn't leave much to the imagination. He realized that he was staring and made his self-look away.

"Well then umm... yeah we should get you to the party." He slowly said stumbling over his words.

We walked down the hallway back to the big room with the couches and thrown. As we entered the room of about a hundred vampires, everyone stopped what they were doing to stare at my grand entrance. I looked around, noticed that all the other women there were wearing the same thing as me of course in different colors and styles but they were all short, and showed lots of skin. As my eyes fluttered around the room, they caught on one person, the leader of the group. He stared back at me. He slowly extended one hand towards me for me to take. I hesitated a little bit then slowly started walking towards him. I extended my hand too; I did not want to take his hand but did anyway.

He pulled me in close, threw both arms around me, and whispered in my ear. "You are truly amazing. Come meet my friends."

We slowly walked around and met everyone their by the time we got to the last person I could smell blood in the air.

"The food has arrived." I heard someone in the crowd say.

Ted shot a glance at me and smiled. He finally let go of the hand that he had been dragging me around by all night. The door to the party swung open and in came quite a mob of humans. After they were all inside, I could hear the sounds of bolts being locked from the outside of the room. I stood in one spot, watched him flutter around the room, and gathered five people. He glanced over his shoulder at me and nodded. What is he nodding about I wondered to myself. Then as he nodded, again I got the clue that these were our humans and I was supposed to join him. I slowly walked over to him and the humans trying to be careful not to move too fast. By the time, that I got to his side the burning in my throat was so intense that I was having a hard time controlling it. I wanted to slaughtering them all and my monster inside was outweighing the human; I forced the monster to be quiet as we sat on the couches. We sat there and I listened as Ted made conversation with these people. I however knew that if I opened my mouth for any reason they would all be dead in a matter of seconds, so I sat waiting quietly for Ted to signal that it was ok for me to drink. At this point, I didn't know if he was try to torture me but he was doing a great job of that. What seemed like an eternity but was really only a few minutes he finally got tired of the boring human conversations.

"Hey why don't we all go to a quitter location so we can get to know each other better?" He nodded towards the door and I knew that he wanted me to follow him.

They were all a little hesitant but obeyed anyway. I had seen Jaxson use this trick before but never could master it. We all rose to our feet and walked over to the door, Ted lightly tapped on the door it was only auditable to vampire ears. I heard the locks being unlocked and the door opened. We sauntered down the hallway to another room. I glanced behind me and saw Frank following us. I stepped through the doorway to a huge room that had a king size four-poster bed in one part of the room. The room was so big it made the bed look like a twin-size bed. On the other side across the room from the bed were two corner couches set around a projector screen TV and a coffee table in between the couches. On the coffee table was a bouquet of red roses in a crystal vase with beautiful etching of vines and roses. I'm sure the roses would have add a pleasant fragrance to the room if I could get past the smell of the humans. Ted came around behind me and placed one arm around me.

"You need to feed. I can see that you are hungry. Just pick one and I will keep the others calm." He said in a whisper low enough that the humans couldn't hear.

I did need to feed there was no doubt about that. I picked the tall well taller than me blond women to feed upon first. Ted did keep all of the others quiet and entertained while I feed in the shadows of the far corner of the room.

"Sam please come join me for another." He motioned with his hand for me to join him.

I ran this time not having to worry about who saw me. I picked another and another, by the end of the third human I was blood drunk and didn't have a care in the world at this point. I threw my arms around Ted and started to kiss him. For once, this did not bring back the pain of my lost lover. I kissed him, and then started to undress him. I took, his shirt off to reveal a body that looked like he could have been a body builder in his past life. You could see all of the muscles under his white velvet skin and they flexed with every movement he made. Then off came the leather pants that you would have seen a rock stars wear. Then in one swift movement, my supposed dress was torn off and I too was naked. He pressed his body to mine and held me there with one arm, if I wanted to get away I could but I didn't want to. He swept me off my feet and carried me over to the bed. With our lips still locked together in the heat of passion. After we were done he lay down beside me and pulled me close to him.

"Sam why don't you tell me about who you are and who made you oh yeah and how old are you?" He asked twirling a piece of my long hair around his finger.

I thought about how to answer the questions for a split second and decided that I would tell him parts of the story but would omit other parts. I told the story about how I came to be but I left out the part about the wolves and the elder vampire that tried to kill me. I also made it sound like a freak accident that killed my maker. As I finished my story, he started to tell me his story. He was older than I was by one hundred years. He told me about his maker and that he was a tall handsome man and lived in the middle of the forest. As he kept talking and describing him, I started deriving a conclusion and it was looking like we could have the same maker. I just blurted out the name

"Jaxson?"

He thought for a minute, Yes I think that was his name.

"What happened how come you were not around when he made me?"

This caught him off guard, the look on his face told the story. He stared blankly at the ceiling for a few minutes the silence was getting awkward. I was just about to say something anything but he started talking again.

"I have not seen him in hundreds of years ever since you were made. He just disappeared one day and then a few months later his house was burned to the ground."

I thought about telling him what happened but decided that maybe at a later date I would.

"Do you know what happened to him?" He asked, I should have known that he would ask me but it still took me off guard and snapped my response at him.

"I already told you what I know."

"It is just a shame he was an awesome teacher."

"Yeah I know I loved him." The pain tore through me and I managed to hide it from him.

Three quick raps on the door changed the mood quickly. He sprang out of the bed and called "just a minute."

"Stay very still doesn't move." He whispered in my ear not even another vampire would have heard him. He threw the blanket and pillows over me to disguise me being there. He quickly ran to the door and flung it open.

"What is going on here Ted?" A man said with a husky voice.

"You really should clean up this mess it is very disgusting to leave dead bodies everywhere. I heard him throw a body to the floor and sit on the couch.

"You know why I'm here Ted?" The man said in a matter of fact voice.

"Yeah I know and we don't have her yet."

"What is the problem don't you have enough man power to break through the wolves and get her?" The man sounded angry and seemed like he was going to rip his head off at any moment.

"No there are more of them than you have seen."

"I will send one of my guards then." I heard the clothing on the man's pants rustle he was slowly walking somewhere.

"Ted I want that girl she has a gift that I want and it would be a great addition to my arsenal."

"Yes sir." Ted said enthusiastically.

"The new guard will be here in a week." The door slammed shut with a loud thud.

I was as still as still could be when Ted came over and removed everything off me.

"It is safe now."

I jumped up and back from him instantly. Not sure, what kind of game he was playing with me.

"Thanks for not turning me over, but I believe that I need to go now."

I made a break for the door but he was already in front of it blocking my way. I glanced around for another option but there was not any other ways out.

"Sam stop listen, if I wanted to turn you over I would have. We can figure this thing out together." He took his hands, placed them on both sides of my face, and made me look into his eyes.

"Sam I have to protect you at all costs we have the same maker. I can't let them take you now. For me it is kind of like finding a sister that you never knew you had. Sam please?" He begged me to listen.

"Ted I really need to go back to my brother and sort things out he is in as much danger as I am." In the heat of the moment, I had just said too much. Ted just stared into my eyes waiting for an explanation. I started to give him one.

"Ted I was not one hundred percent honest with you about my story. Well more or less I left out the part about my brother being the leader of the wolf pack in the park."

"What are you serious?" He spat at me.

"Yeah."

"That explains a lot of why they are protective of you. I could not figure out why they would want to protect a vampire when they tried so hard to keep them out of the park. This really complicates things." He said dropping his hands from my face. My mind was bouncing back and forth about telling him why and how I was made but I decided to save that for another time.

"Yeah I know, I must go and talk to my brother." I said trying to sound demanding this time.

"Will you come back to me?" He asked but I was not sure how I wanted to answer.

"I will when I can, when I know that my brother and his pack are safe. I would love to spend more time with you and get to know you better." I said adding that last part in for good measure. I paused thoughtfully for a second then said. "Look you can come visit me but you must stay away from the park."

He pulled me in close to him, gave me a big hug, and kissed my forehead.

"I'm glad that I did not turn you in when I had the chance." He smiled at me then turned away. He pulled the door open for me and as I took one more glace back at his face one single tear started to roll down his check. Why exactly was he crying I wondered to myself. He has only known me exactly one whole day. I ran down the hallway, out the door, and into the forest. I was shocked that he had let me go.

CHAPTER 10

I ran at top speed all the way back through the forest to the park. I slowed as I approached the park. I stepped one foot inside the park and there was a wolf standing there snarling at me.

"It is ok I'm Bill's sister Sam." I said trying to calm the wolf.

The wolf did not stand down what the hell was going on. I back up a few steps until I was on the outer edge of the park.

"Aidan!" I yelled at the top of my voice I am sure he would hear me for miles. Then a few seconds later, I heard a howl. It was Aidan, as I stood there; waiting for him to show up the other wolf was still inches away snarling and snapping at me. When Aidan finally arrived the wolf relaxed as Aidan shifted to human. He stared at me like there was something wrong with me, and then I realized what I was wearing the red lacy thing that had holes in it. Then he snapped out of it.

"You have to come quick, it is your brother."
Then I'm assuming that he did not want to say anything else because he shifted back to wolf and we ran together. We arrived at the little shack that was my prison in my younger days. I flung open the door and all I could smell was blood, it was a good thing that I was not thirsty. I ran to his side and knelt down.

"What happened?" I demanded

"It was a vampire that ran into the park and he was all alone in human form." Aidan answered me.

"Has this ever happened before?" I was hoping that someone here would have seen this before and that he would just snap out of it and be fine.

"No to our knowledge no wolf has ever been bitten."

"Is he going to die?" I said though sobs now barely able to form the word die.

"Again we don't know Sam."

Just then, my brother moaned and blinked his eyes open then closed then opened again. He jumped a little when he saw me knelling beside him. He parted his lips ever so slightly as if he was going to say something but nothing came out.

"Aidan I need to go back I think that I may be able to find the answers of what is going to happen. Is there anyone that you would trust to follow me so that you know the way? That way if something changes you can come get me right away."

"Well, no, everyone here is not going to respond well to a vampire right now." He said

"Ok is there anyone that can watch the park or that you can put in charge for a little while so you can go with me?"

"Yeah I think that would work. I will be right back he left and was gone for a few seconds. When he came back, he nodded his big wolf head at me. I knew that then that he was going with me. I leaned in, kissed my brothers forehead, and whispered in his ear.

"I'm so sorry this is all my fault, I will fix this." One tear ran down my face and hit his and he blinked his eyes open and closed; as if to say I do hear you.

"I love you and I will be back soon." Tears flowed from my eyes. It took all I had to leave his side but I must find the answers on how to fix him.

Aidan and I ran through the forest and back to the warehouse. When we were close, we stopped and I whispered to Aidan.

"This is close enough Aidan. If anything changes, you come and get me right away. I put both hands on the sides of Aidan's snout and kissed his forehead. "I owe you a lot and will make it up to you when this is all over."

I turned without another glance and started running I did not look back because I did not want him to see me crying. I threw the first door open and started running down the hallway back to Ted's room. As I approached Ted's room, someone grabbed me from behind putting one hand over my mouth. Then he started dragging me backwards down the hallway to another room. I tried to struggle but it was not doing me any good. The heat started to burn in my hands. I was almost to the point of ignition when I was released and spun at the same time. I was getting ready to scream and fight, when I realized that it was Frank.

"Sh don't say anything. He is back he came back for Ted. He found out that you had been here the last time he is furious that he did not turn you over. Just then, a scream came from the hall.

"You must go." He whispered in my ear.

"I have to talk to Ted my brother's life depends on it." I whispered back. We heard the door down the hall open and slam back against the wall.

"Come I must hide you so he can't find you." Frank did not say another word he just gestured for me to follow him. He twisted and pulled a couple things then a hole in the wall popped open. I pushed the door opened and pushed it shut without saying a word or making a sound. The room was made of concrete walls with no way out. My mind started racing as usual how did I know that Frank would not turn me in? I just had to trust that he wouldn't do that at this point. I had no other choice but to stand in the corner and wait until he let me out or turned me in. I could try and tunnel out through the concrete but that would be too noisy. Then I could hear the main door open and slam back against the wall.

"Frank, you will be in charge from now on." The man's voice boomed through the room.

Nothing more was said. The door to my temporary holding cell opened and I walked out. A since of relief washed over me, and surprise that he was true to his word.

"I think that you need to leave now. I held back telling him this time but there will not be a next time. I'm not sure why Ted kept you safe the first time and nor do I care." My mouth fell open at the words he spat at me.

"Thank you Frank and good luck with everything." I said back not really know what else to say.

I quickly left the room and was out of the warehouse in a split second. I ran for the park. Not sure what to do now, I still needed answers. I stopped dead in my tracks as I heard footsteps behind me at this point not knowing who it was, it could have been anyone. Coming into view, I could make out what looked like Ted. My mind argued with me no it could not be he is dead, but it was Ted.

"Sam I'm so sorry." he said when he got close enough for me to hear. I didn't think I just started running towards him. I threw my arms around him.

"I thought you were dead."

"Yeah me too."

"I need your help, my brother has been bitten by a vampire. Come I'll show you the way" I grabbed his hand and pulled him along with me.

We neared the edge of the park and I yelled for Aidan. As we waited for Aidan to come other wolves showed up too. As the big black mass approached us, I could see Ted backing up, for every step Aidan took towards me Ted took one back.

"Aidan this is Ted, I know that he is a vampire and that everyone will not be comfortable with this but I need to take him to see my brother."

Aidan eyed Ted and I a couple of times before he shook his head yes. He turned and I got the idea that we were supposed to follow him. As we entered, the park I could hear wolfs on both sides of us and behind us. We had an escort of wolves.

We approached the place where my brother was and Aidan finally transformed back to human. He did not turn to look at us he just lead the way in. My brother was still lying motionless on a make shift bed.

"Ted what do you think, how can I save him?" I questioned

Listening to all the sounds in the room, I waited for Ted to respond, but something caught my attention. The way my brother's heart beat sounded. It was really slow and would miss a beat here and there. He was dying I could feel it.

Now with a little more panic in my voice. "Ted what do I do, please tell me how do I save him?" I begged panic oozing from me.

"He just needs some blood, I'll show you." He grabbed my arm bit into my skin and my blood began to run.

"Now just put a few drops on your brother's mouth."

I did what he told me to do but nothing prepared me for my brother grabbing a hold of my arm and clamping down on it. I could feel the blood being sucked out of my body and was starting to grow weaker by the second.

"Sam pull your arm free." Ted said in the most calm, collected and monotone voice. Then when my arm was free, he said, "Now we wait."

Seconds turned into minutes and minutes turned into days. As I watched him shift from human to wolf then back again uncontrollably, on the third day, he finally stopped shifting and was in human form again. His eyes popped open and he looked straight at me. There in his eyes was something different, but what I wondered, however it did not matter right now.

"It is ok, you are ok." I whispered. I wanted to run to him and hug him but I was very unsure of if I should or not.

"Ted, he is a wake." Ted walked to my side.

"We need to get him something to drink, I'm sure he is thirsty."

My brother still had not found his voice, he just stared at everyone and it was very eerie. We all watched his eyes turn from vampire blue to wolf green and back to human brown a few different times. Then he took two steps in my direction. Flash backs from my first days came in a rush back to me.

I know you maybe disoriented but you will be ok now." I put my arms out in a gesture for a hug but he still just stared at me. Then he took another step forward and started to shift to wolf.

"No, no wait don't shift I started saying." Then right on, cue the door flew open and in came Ted with a few humans. My brother's eyes shifted to vampire and all of his attention was on Ted and the humans.

"Go ahead brother they are for you." I said gesturing towards them.

I shot a glance at Ted and he backed away from the humans a few steps. The people were frightened and started screaming and running in all directions. I made eye contact with my brother for a split second and realized that he did not know what to do.

"Go with you instances." I shouted above the noise and confusion.

I watched as my brother shifted to wolf form and bolted after one person. As soon as the person was caught he shifted back to human form well technically vampire. I watched him take down two or three people that way. As he finished the last person off he just collapsed on the floor. Not caring anymore, I ran to his side.

"Brother are you ok?"

"Sam, Sam, Sam you are always worried about the wrong things. I never felt better.

"I'm so sorry for what happened I did not want to do this to you but I had no other choice."

"It is ok, don't worry."

"I have someone for you to meet." I gestured to Ted to come over. "Bill this is Ted, Ted this is my brother Bill. Ted is also a vampire and he is going to teach us everything we need to know about being a vampire. Ted and I come from the same maker. My brother glanced up at Ted and looked at me.

"Yeah I know him we meet several years ago before you were made into a vampire." At that moment, I wanted to blast him one for not telling me that sooner.

"So you knew the whole time that he was chasing me around that he was a part of Jaxson?" I spat the words at my brother. "You know you could have introduced us then we would not be in the shit that we are in now." I said.

"Sam, I'm sorry we had only met once and I didn't remember his face all that well. I do however recognize the name." My bother said back to me, begging forgiveness with his eyes. Of course it worked and I instantly forgave him.

CHAPTER 11

A couple of weeks went by with no outside interference from any vampires trying to get into the park everything felt weird. My brother still shifted to his wolf form to run his lines and protect the people of the park. For the most part, he stayed clear of all the humans in the park just because he did not trust himself to be close. Ted and I did not talk much anymore, he was busy doing his thing and I was busy doing my thing. My thing well mostly sitting around in the tree tops watching the animals wonder around the forest floor and helping my brother adjust. Wow, I guess I turned into an old boring vampire. Now that my brother was ok and he had Ted. I was free to do whatever I wanted. I decided that I wanted to go traveling again maybe to South America, Germany, England, or even Canada. As I pondered my options of where I wanted to go I heard a warring howl. It was my brothers howl I jumped down from my perch and ran across the forest towards him. Upon my approach, I saw three cloaked figures standing just outside of the parks line. The images from when I was a younger vampire came back to haunt me. The same three that were sent for me the first time. Being a chicken, I stood behind a tree. Ted arrived and ran to my brother's side.

"State your business here." Ted said in a strong stern voice. The woman in the middle the leader of the small hunting group said.

"We are here for one reason, to collect a vampire named Sam."

"What is it that you want with her?"

"She is in violation of the vampire code and must be punished for her crimes."

"What code is that may I ask?"

"She created this half vampire half wolf and that is strictly forbidden to mingle with werewolves. And you would be wise to leave this area."

"We don't know where she is. She left from here three days ago."

"We will stay here and wait for her to return, and you all shall be warned that if you try to interfere with her capture you will die."

With that, they stepped back into the shadows of the forest but I knew that they did not leave. I ran as fast as I could to the far edge of the park. My brother and Ted caught up to me as I had started pacing back and forth wearing a hole in the ground.

"What am I going to do? I have seen this before they won't stop until they get what they came here for."

I caught the eyes of my brother first and there was one tear running down his wolf face matted in his fur. He knew that they would not let me live this time. Then I glanced to Ted and he had a dumb founded expression on his face.

"What do you mean you have seen this before?" Ted said after a minute. I glanced back at my brother and he nodded. My brother was right it was time to tell him what happened to our maker.

"Well Ted you see I still have not told you the whole truth of what happened to Jaxson. He did not just disappear into thin air like I lead you to believe, they killed him. The sadness came through my voice and he knew that it was the truth.

"What do you mean? For what?" He shouted at me, his voice full of anger. I shut down, fell to my knees, and started to sob.

My brother's arms were around me holding me together. He whispered in my ear "We must tell him everything maybe he can help."

I choked back the tears that wanted to come out and started telling Ted the accounts that lead to our makers demise. As I finished the story, he looked at my brother and me, not saying anything. Anger and hate for us filled his face as he looked upon the both of us.

"How could you let him die for something your wolf pack did?" He yelled at my brother after a long silence.

"I'm sorry it was not supposed to happen that way. Jaxson never told me that they were coming for the killer of the elder's wife he just told me they had to leave the area. If I had to do it all over again I would have confessed to them and they would have killed me instead of Jaxson." My brother spat the words back at Ted. I could see in his face that he was wounded by his confession. He paused for his mind to catch up with him then said. "You have to understand that I would have died for my sister just so that she could have been with Jaxson for the rest of her life." I knew that he was telling the truth and tears ran down my face again. Ted was too infuriated to see that my brother meant what he had said.

"I'm sorry I can't help you anymore, I'm leaving and going back to what I used to call home and try to get reinstated as leader with my friends." Then just like that he was gone. My brother and I sat there for a long while not saying anything. We heard footsteps approaching but they were not human by the sounds of it.

"Hey are you guys ok?" A very familiar but hesitant voice said from the darkened forest.

"Yeah we are fine Aidan can you come and sit with Sam for a few minutes I have to talk to the rest of the pack." Aidan did as he was told. He took my brothers place behind me and gently put his arms around me.

"Sam what is going on?" He asked in a soft whisper.

"I don't really want to talk about it right now Aidan.

"I saw Ted leaving the park, where was he going?"

"Home." I said angrily.

"I thought he was banned from there or something like that."

"Well he was but he does not want to be here anymore, he is tired of the wolf thing." I paused then said. "Aidan you really don't want to know what is going on ok so please stop asking me questions." I snapped at him.

"Sam I do want to know what is going on, especially if it involves you."

"Aidan please I'm not really in the mood for flattery right now."

"Please, please, please tell me." He begged.

"Ok fine you want to know, here it is. Bill, my brother, killed an elder's wife because she was killing me and Jaxson made me a vampire so that Bill did not have to see me die that way. Jaxson fell in love with me and ultimately paid the price for Bill killing the elder's wife. Now they are after me again because I made Bill into a vampire and that is something that is unheard of and against vampire law for a half wolf and half vampire. There now you have the whole story, feel better." I pushed his arms off me and stood up. I did not look back at him but could feel the torment that was going through his body.

"Sam, are (he took a big gulp of air) they going to (another big gulp of air) kill you too?"

"I don't know most likely yes." I said trying to keep all emotion out of my words.

"Sam I love you, I'm not going to let them hurt you."

"Oh Aidan, there is nothing you can do to make them stop hunting me."

"We could run away together." He suggested.

"Aidan there is no place we can run, Jaxson and I tried to out run them or out maneuver them. I must face the music, so this is good-bye Aidan. I want you to know that I love you too and I want you to keep that love with you always and forever. But, please take my advice if a girl comes along love her the way you would have loved me if I would have not been so messed up. One more thing tell my brother that I love him and that everything will be fine, he will always have a piece of me in him." When I finished speaking, I glanced back at his face for a quick second and realized how much he loved me and knew he was going to miss me. But, I had made my mind up, this ended right her, right now. I made myself run. I ran faster than I had ever ran before on a straight line towards my waiting death. As I breached the park line, I heard howling from all over the park they knew that I was gone. I kept running until I reached a safe distance away from the park were they would not hear my cries of agony. I stopped and stood very still for a few minutes scanning the forest for any sign of them but there was nothing.

"I'm here, come and get me, I surrender to you." I shouted aloud. I stood there for what seemed like an eternity and nothing happened. I heard some leaves rustling to my left so I turned in that direction to face them. I did not see anyone or anything. Then I heard rustling to my right but still did not see anything. This kept happening so I was now spinning in a circle. On the fifth revolution, I finally saw someone standing there. I looked twice because I thought that my mind was playing tricks on me. There before me stood Ted.

"What are you doing here?" I said a little angri-ly because I really wanted it to be the Cloaks and have this done an over with right now.

"I have come to take you in so that I may return to my former position." He said with a deviant smile. He paused then said, "You owe me that."

"Ok well I guess maybe I do owe you that." I said this time more relaxed. I was actually happy that it was him and not the Cloaks that found me. I guess after all I was not really ready to die just yet.

I watched as he glanced to my right then to my left. Then in that split second, there were now hands on me holding me in place. The fire that wanted to burn them crept through my veins but I knew that I needed to hold it back at all costs.

As they lead me to the warehouse I could not help but think that Ted was now involved with the Cloaks somehow and I wondered what they offered him in return for me.

"Ted, can I ask you a question?" I said softly.

"No you can't ask me anything."

I decided to ask anyway. "Where are the Cloaks?"

He did not answer my question so I made up my mind that he offered to get me for them and they were waiting at the warehouse for me. As we approached the warehouse Frank, meet us at the door. I was a little re-lieved, until Frank said.

"He is here waiting for you."

As Frank said those words, I knew instantly who he was talking about. Ted was not turning me into the Cloaks he call the guy that wanted me because of my fire power. Great I think I would rather face the Cloaks than be part of this guy's gang. We approached that all too familiar door of his room. He hesitated just for a second and flung the doors open. On the couch with his back to the door was the man. Without looking or even moving, he said

"You have her?"

"Yes we do have her." Ted answered with conviction and arrogance in his voice.

The man rose to his feet and turned to face us. He was about the same height as me. His hair was long blond and very straight. His eyes were green almost the same color as grass. He was beautiful. I was watching his eyes as he looked at me. He seemed to be delighted to see me as if we were old friends.

"Hey let her go, you don't need to treat her like she is a slave." He said in that familiar voice that I had heard twice before. "Come here sweet heart let me get a good look at you."

I did as I was told for once but the thought was right there to run in the opposite direction down the hall and out the door. But I knew that would be a waste of time because I would not make it halfway down the hall. It may be possible to get away if I used my talent and set the whole warehouse on fire, and burnt anyone that tried to touch me. But I still didn't know how to control it. What if –

"Sam, Sam."

The sound of my name being called pulled me from my depths of demise. I was so deep in my thoughts that I had not realized I had stopped moving forward. The man stretched out his hand towards me. I glanced at Ted and back at his hand. Ted just nodded at me to take it. I placed my hand on top of his.

"Sam my name is Erik. Please don't be afraid I'm not going to hurt you. You have a special talent that I need for my army. You are the only vampire in the world that has the fire touch. You have the ability to bring all others too their knees and that is exactly what I plan on using you for."

"I don't know what you are talking about." I said trying to play dumb. I quick glance back at Ted for some help but he was preoccupied by something he was holding in his hand.

"You do know what I'm talking about the fire touch, is it or is it not how you burnt that house down a long time ago or even when Ted here first found you?"

Damn how did he know that I had burnt the house down? I had no choice but to confess now. "Yes but I don't know how to use it." I said trying to use a different angle now in hopes that he would think that I was not as useful to him as he originally thought.

"That's ok we will teach you."

"Ok, so what is the purpose of the army?" I asked.

He completely ignored my question and spun me around to face the room. "Everyone I want you to meet Sam she is the newest member of the army. You will protect her at all costs while she is in training. Now you should all go have some fun." He said cheerfully to the crowd that had gathered.

Almost as if it was a queue, the music started beating from down the hall. The crowd surrounded me and I was escorted out of the room. I was stuck in the center of the crowd with no way out. I tried pushing my way back to talk to Erik but the crowd turned me around and pushed me forward. I managed to find Ted through the crowd.

"Ted may I have a word with you?" I spat at him but he did not seem to hear me or he was ignoring me. I tried to shove back against the crowd again to get Ted's attention but some of the other vampires picked me up and started caring me to the big room where the music was playing. A few minutes after being in the room, Ted walked in and I ran to him not really knowing if I wanted to punch him or hug him at this point.

"Ted we need to talk! Is there somewhere we can go?"

"Sam not tonight." He turned and walked away from me. This infuriated me so I followed him.

"But I want to know what is going on what did you get me mixed up in this time?" I asked grabbing his hand to get his attention.

"Sam we will talk later, right now we have some visiting to do."

As before we walked around the room, said hi to everyone, and talked about nothing important, also just like before the smell of human and the sweet smell of their blood filled the air. We picked out a couple of humans and went back to the room this was my chance to try to get some answers out of him.

"Ted, we really need to talk I demand to know what is going on." I tried again.

"After you have a drink, I know the thirst is got to be driving you crazy." He answered back to me.

The thirst was not driving me crazy, the unknown was. But just to satisfy him I drank one person and tried the question again, still no answer other than you need to drink some more. Second person down and I was getting to the point where it really did not matter anymore right now. The blood lust had taken over. I burned through my third and fourth humans in a matter of minutes. I went to stand up a started to fall when strong arms caught me before I smashed through the coffee table.

"Wow I think you have had enough for one night, come I think you should lay down." He helped me over to the bed but he started to walk back to the sofa.

"Hey where are you going? Please don't leave me alone." I begged him.

"Sam I'm going to be right over here if you need me." He said, as he kept walking not even turning to look at me.

"No I need you to hold me. I'm scared." I said trying to get him to lay with me so that he may be more apt to tell me the answers to my question.

"Oh Sam it will be fine." He retorted and sank into the sofa.

"No please just for a few minutes. Please, please, please." I begged again.

"Ok but only for a few minutes." He rose from the sofa and walked back to me. Lying beside me but not touching me.

"Ted, I'm so sorry that I did not tell you the truth about our maker and what happened to him." I said trying to make a mends between us.

"It is ok don't worry about that right now."

"But I really owe you the appalo –"

My lips had gone silent, as they could no longer move under the weight of his lips the more I tried the more he pushed. He kept me in the lip lock long enough that I had forgotten what I was going to say. Dang it I hated to be blood drunk. He pulled his lips away from mine and that is the last thing I remembered. When vampires are blood drunk we don't really sleep but we can't function either. Like when a human drinks too much alcohol their body shuts down and they pass out the only difference is that humans sleep it off vampires do not. To pass the time most vampires daydream and that is what I was doing.

While I had my eyes closed, I could see the Cloaks chasing me through the forest again. There were bodies, not human but vampire bodies everywhere burning and there ear piercing screams were heard throughout the forest. A flash of Ted entered my vision and he was burning too. Then from the corner of my eye, I saw the all too familiar green eyes piercing through the haze and smoke. As I looked into the green eyes, they turned from green to blue and back again; this had to be my brother. But, what was he doing at a vampire war in human form. Than as I look around some more I seen wolves lying dead and burning as well. My eyes fell upon one wolf with silver fur it was Aidan. No, no, no, I screamed and that finally shook me out of my daydream. I sat straight up in the bed and started realizing where I was and started to sob. The tears rolled down my face with no end in sight. Then two arms grabbed me from behind.

"Sam are you ok?" Teds voice broke through to me.

"Yeah I'm fine." I said through sobs. "I just had a bad daydream."

"Do you want to talk about it?" He asked.

"No." I wiped my eyes and laid back down and thought to myself, ok pull yourself together. My thoughts were scattered and I was not sure of anything right now. I could feel Ted staring at me just waiting for me to say something. At this point, I was not going to say anything about what the contents of my daydream where. So just to get the pressure off me I asked. "Would it be possible for me to take a bath or a shower?"

"Of course anything, come I will show you the way." I followed him almost in a trance to the bathroom. The bathroom that was attached to his room and was not like the other bathroom. This one had a huge tub that was set in marble tile and was big enough for three maybe four people to get in. I walked to the tub and started filling it with water. Ted turned and started to walk out the door. I started to pull off my clothing that was incrusted in dirt. Just before he closed the door, I said.

"I have one more request can I get some new clothing?"

"I will have someone go get you something right away." He said without hesitation and started to close the door again but before he could get it closed I had one more request to make remembering what they had dressed me in last time.

"Um....one more thing can you have them get me some jeans and tee shirt."

He laughed

"Sure."

He shut the door, I stripped off the rest of my clothing, and before the tub was even full, I sank into the water. I laid there and waited for the tub to fill all the way to the top then shut the water off. I laid back and then sank my whole body under the bubbly water. I closed my eyes and thought of the field with the beautiful wild flowers growing in it. The lady playing with her daughter and I realized that maybe just maybe it was time for me to settle down with someone we could adopt a live child and turn her on her eighteenth birth-day if that is what she wanted. I wondered if they had any laws about that. I laid there in an almost dream state just thinking about the pleasant things in life. I wondered what it would have been like if I would have gotten married and had children. But, I could still do that if I wanted to the only drawback would be having a living, breathing child in the house and I wondered if I could control myself well enough to not end her life. I was almost certain that I could do it though. I was an old vampire now and had way more control over my-self than what I had been acting like lately. I toyed with the idea in my head of being a mother when I heard the door open and close. I did not want to pull myself from the depths of the water just yet so I remained under. I was hoping that whoever it was would go away and just leave me be in my underwater happiness.

"Sam, are you in there Sam." I did not move or give any indication that I was in the tub under the bub-bly water.

"Sam, Sam." This time his voice was more in a panic. I still did not want to come back to the real world but I knew I had too. Just as I had decided to come up two hands plunged into the water looking for me. When they found me, they slowly pulled me up.

"Sam are you alright? How long have you been under there?" Again with the twenty million questions, and I wished that he would just go away right now.

"I'm not sure." I said sounding disoriented even to myself. Then I wanted to cry but I knew that trying to explain the emotion of wanting to be a mother just would sound foolish to him. He quickly broke me out of that mood by saying.

"I'm not trying to tell you what to do but he is going to be here soon to start your training."

Oh great I thought to myself that is the last thing I wanted to do right now. "Um… yeah I just need to wash my hair. Did you get me the clothing that I asked for?"

"Yup they are right over there on the counter." He turned and pointed to a pile of neatly stacked clothing.

"Thanks, um… one more thing do you mind helping me with my hair?" I asked not really sure why I even asked him to help me but I guess maybe it was my way of reaching out to him.

"Sure I guess I could do that." He replied back sounding a bit puzzled as to why I would ask him to do it.

"I just need you to help me rinse the soap out." I lathered my hair with the soap and scrubbed my scalp with my fingernails. I grabbed the bowl that was sitting next to the tub, turned on the water, and handed the bowl to Ted. As I sat there letting the water rinse the soap out of my hair I couldn't help but to think about when Jaxson and I went to his friends and Lilly helped me wash my hair. Before I was ready for him to be done, he turned the water off.

"Ok the soap is all out." He said after a few short minutes.

"Umm… thanks."

"Well if you are done with me then I am going to leave."

"Yeah I am thanks again."

As he left the room, I got up and reached for my towel. I wrapped it around me and went over to the clothing but just before I could get my clothing on the door flew open and Ted came running in

"Sam, you have to go, you have to go now."

"What, why, what is going on?"

"There has been a breach in our security system and they are coming for you." I was about to ask the question, who but I already knew the answer to that.

"I thought I was safe here." I retorted followed by an electrical stinging charge that went through my body.

"You were safe until they found out you were here they are going through my vampires as we speak it is just a matter of time before they get here."

"How do I get out of here without them seeing me?" I said in a rush of panicked words.

"Don't worry I will help you."

I dropped the towel and started throwing on my clothing as I was running for the door.

"Listen follow me and at all cost if they get to us run as fast and as far as you can." He whispered to me.

"Run to where?"

He didn't answer my question he just opened the door and peeked out in both directions.

"It is all clear lets go." He grabbed my hand and pulled me through the door. We were racing down the hallway. The hallway ended in a room with only one door and no windows just the concrete brick walls.

"Ted I thought you knew where we were going. Now we are stuck with no way out." I yelled at him panic-stricken. The fire blazed with in me and threated to come forward.

He grabbed my hand and led me back to the door. He peaked around the corner and down the hall. He grabbed my hand even tighter then spun me and pushed me back against the wall. I watched as he backed all the way into the farthest corner of the room, and then ran with all of his might towards the brick wall. In one triumphant shot, he punched all the way through the wall and out the other side. I didn't hesitate one little bit, ran for the wall, and went through the hole that he had made. I landed softly on my feet and spotted him at once he beckoned to me to come with him. I ran to his side and we ran through the night to parts un-known. I shot a glance over my shoulder every now and then to see if I saw the Cloaks but there was nothing. The farther away we got from the warehouse the more we slowed our pace but neither one of us willing to give up the run just yet.

CHAPTER 12

The next thing I remember is the site of a house on a hill.

"Is that were we are going?" I asked.

"Yeah this is Erik's house."

How is that possible I thought to myself I thought that vampires were just nomads cursed to walk the earth for eternity with no since of belonging. But I knew that couldn't be right because Jaxson had his own house. Maybe I was just missing something. Have I really forgotten what it was like to sleep in a house or even to live in a house? I guess that just goes along with the sudden urge to want a child even in the midst of the problems. As we approached, the door swung open and Erik emerged from inside of the house.

"Ah…friends you made it safely. It is a pleasure to have you here at my home." He greeted us.

"The Cloaks got wind of her being at the warehouse and came in looking for her. We had no choice but to run." Ted said to Eric making his point clear.

"Yes I know I talked to Frank a little bit ago, he said that you may be coming this way. Please come in you are safe here."

Nothing prepared me for what happened next as I walked up on the porch a little girl with bouncing red curls came running out of the house. She must have been only six or seven at the most.

"Daddy, daddy she squalled."

"Yes Sarah what can I do for you daddy is kind of busy right now." That is when she noticed us standing there.

"Oh sorry it can wait until latter." She turned and ran back in the house and out of site.

"Sorry about that she just gets so excited some times."

We followed him through the door and into the house and sat down at the dining room table. Erik at the head of the table and Ted across the table from me, he cut right to the point.

"Well you will need a place to stay for a while and I would like you to stay here with me. Also we will go hunting together. Sam you have a lot to learn yet about being a vampire and the talents that you possess.

My wife and I are prepared to do whatever it takes to keep you safe."

Just then a figured walked through the doorway it was a women this must be his wife. She was beautiful, long bronze color hair flowing down to just above her buttocks. She was wearing a long teal colored dress that fit her curves in all of the right places. I had to remind myself to look away because it was rude to stare she was that pretty. Erik didn't waste any time and started with introductions.

"Shannon this is her, the girl that is going to help us, this is Sam." He said and gestured towards me.

"Sam this is my lovely wife Shannon. If you need anything, anything at all don't hesitate to let her know or even me for that matter." He paused then looked at the both of us. "Shannon my dear, would you please show Sam around the house?"

"Sure dear. Sam, do you want to come with me?" She said looking at me now.

I really didn't want to go with her but I felt as though I didn't have a choice in the matter. She walked me around the whole house and showed me were everything was like towels and my room. But my thoughts were in another place. My thoughts drifted back to the day that Jaxson was murdered for something that he did not do something that my brother had done in an attempt to save me from dying. How could I still love my brother enough to cause myself the same pain of the in pending death that was surly coming? I knew that there was no way out and nowhere to run, Jaxson and I had tried. I stood there staring into my room but it was a different room and a different time that I saw. I was seeing the room that Jaxson and I had shared. The room where I found out that Jaxson loved me as much as I loved him. I stood there staring and watching the moment unfold in front of my eyes. I wanted to run to him, I wanted to feel his strong arms around me again. Without knowing, I started to drift forward and reach for him.

"Sam." A soft voice came from behind me.

The scene dissipated and he was gone. It was just a room. Nothing more than a small bed and a chair that sat in the corner. I followed her back through the house like a puppy back to the boys that were still sitting at the dining room table. They were not saying anything just staring blankly at the walls. Shannon cleared her throat to let them know that we were there.

"Sam, we need to go hunt Erik is going to go with us and there are a few other vampires that are coming too."

"No, no we can't do that." I yelled as the memories of the last hunting trip came back to me. I fell to the floor and started sobbing. Everything was too surreal again and I felt like this was going to be the death of us all if we went.

"Sam what is wrong? Ted threw his arms around me and squeezed me tight to his chest. "Can we have a minute please?" He asked.

I heard Erik get up out of the chair and the rustle of his jeans pass me and I lost it even more burying my face into Ted's chest. He pulled me to a standing position and just held me close to him for a few minutes. Then he pulled away, put one finger under my chin, and pulled my face up to meet his.

"What is going on?" I managed to pull back the tears and hold steady for a minute and told him exactly how the Cloaks murdered Jaxson including all of the gory details. I also told him about my run in with them later after they had killed Jaxson.

"So you are afraid that this is going to happen to you? Sweetie don't worry we are not going to let anything happen to you. You are the future of the vampires and we are going to protect you. So what do you say how about we go see the city lights and have some fun?" He grabbed my hand and led me away from the dining room and into the family room where Erik and Shannon were waiting for us.

"We are ready to go now." Ted said with confidence and he pulled me along at his side.

I was still shaken and really just wished that we could stay right where we were for now. I hated the idea of going anywhere with the cloaks out there looking for me.

CHAPTER 13

The smell of human entered my nose I could tell we were getting close to a city. We slowed our pace to a more human pace so that we did not stand out. I know that this is not the first big city that I had ever been in but I was still amazed at what I saw. Buildings standing tall against the star and moon lit night. The full moon shimmered off the windows of every building and casting a silvery gray light across the town. As we passed through the streets, I could hear people talking and whispering, babies screaming and the constant humming of the cars engines all over the city. I think if you stayed here too long, the noise would drive you insane. It was so loud I couldn't even hear myself think. I fell behind the rest of my group just a tad as they were in a quick hurry to get somewhere. I wanted to site see a little bit and was not in a hurry at all. We were passing by an ally way when I heard a women whisper.

"Please, please don't kill me. I'm just trying to get home to my children."

"I will kill you if you don't give me every pen-ny you have." A man's voice, full of anger and hatred replied to her begging.

How could this man be so violent? I thought and I really felt sorry for the woman that he was badg-ering. I must have felt so bad about it because the next thing I knew my feet had taken me in the direction of the confrontation. At the scene, I cleared my throat. The man had forced the women on the ground and she was digging through her bag that she was carrying. The man looked up at me but he was not startled.

"Oh look at you. Did you come to save this woman?" He said in a sarcastic voice.

"Well as a matter of fact I did."

"Ok I will deal with you in a minute precious."

"No you will deal with me now." As the words came out of my mouth, the man turned to look at me. He had not realized that I had gotten so close to him and I was already in his face staring him down. The look of shock had come over him, he had no idea how I had gotten to him so quickly.

"Give her the money back and I may consider leaving you alive."

"What are you going to do you are no match for this gun." He raised and pointed the gun at me. As he said that, I made my eyes shift from green to the pale translucent blue and back before the women could see what I had done. The man jumped back away from me and dropped his gun. The gun landed with in a step of my right foot.

"What the hell was that?" He thru the money back at the women because he knew that he was defeated this time. She quickly started picked it up and stuffed it back in her bag.

"Sweetie you should get your things and go, go home to your family." I said and without a word she finished gathered her things quickly and ran out of the ally. When it was all clear I picked up the gun, bent the barrel, and tossed it into the trash. I don't know why he was still standing here, he could have ran at any time. Less work for me as I didn't have to chase him down now I thought and giggled to myself.

"Now as for you I going to let you go this time but if I hear of this again you will be dead. Now go before I change my mind. Oh and always remember that I will be watching."

He found his feet and ran as fast as he could tripping and stumbling over his own feet. As he disappeared, I started to laugh to myself at first then aloud. That was fun I wish I could do it every day. I turned to walk back the way I came when I realized that Ted, Erik and Shannon where all standing at the opening of the ally to the main street waiting for me.

"Sam, are you coming?" They said almost in unison.

"Yeah I just wanted to take care of that little problem." They all busted into laughter. I could not figure out for the life of me what they were laughing at. But I'm going to assume that they all had done what I just did once or twice. Then the laughter stopped abruptly.

"Sam, run, run." They all started shouting at me.

I was watching them as their faces changed from amusement to fear. I glanced over my shoulder and there just inside of the dark shadow from a building was a cloaked figure. I instantly stopped in my tracks and turned to face them. I looked for the signs of any more around but I did not see anyone. The fear rippled through me right down to my core. The fire pulsed through me and was ready to come at a moment's notice.

"I mean you no harm." The cloaked figure said as he stepped out of the darkness and into the silvery moon light. The fire started to burn though my veins as he drifted closer to me. The instinct to run was also triggered but I knew it was too late for that. My hands burst into flames and I was ready to set him on fire. As soon as he seen the flames emanating from my hand he stopped, his advance and pulled the hood off his head.

"Really I mean no harm." He said again moving towards me slowly again.

"Scott, is that you?" I heard Erik say from behind me.

"Erik it has been a long time old friend." He said as he looked past me to Erik. I did not drop my guard though and I stood my ground with my hands burning.

"Sam it is ok, he is not going to hurt you." Erik said and I tried to put out the fire but it just was not going out.

"Does anyone have a bucket of water I can't get the fire to go out?" Everyone erupted into laughter. I didn't think it was funny and it infuriated me that they laughed at me.

"Sam it is ok, you need to relax and the fire will go out. Close your eyes and think of the most beautiful place you have ever been." Ted's voice came from behind me in a very mellow and soothing sound.

I did as he suggested and closed my eyes and pictured the park with all of the beautiful tall trees. I loved to sit at the very top. I thought of the beautiful sunrises and sunsets, then the sweet smell of the wildflowers, honeysuckle, lavender, and lilies.

"Ok love you can open your eyes now."

I really at this point wanted to keep them closed, it reminded me of some of the best times that I have ever had. I opened them anyway and the fire was gone. The cloaked figure named Scott had passed by me and was now in the thaws of talking to Erik. It sounded like they were old friends that had not seen each other for a while by the way they were laughing and talking about the past. I turned and buried my face in Ted's chest. He ran his hand over my head and down my back and just held me close.

"Are you ready to feed?"

"Yeah, can we go now?"

"Erik I'm going to take her to feed, are you guys coming or should we catch up with you later?"

"No we are coming with you."

They said their good bye's to Scott and we were on our way again.

"Sam, are you ok?" Erik asked

"Yeah I'm fine." I said sarcastically. I was still pissed at them for laughing. The only one that I was not mad at was Ted because he helped me.

"Ted you handled that quite well getting her to calm down like that before she hurt someone. I'm very impressed. You never cease to amaze me." Eric said dubiously.

At this point, I was getting mad and wanted to punch him right in the mouth but I knew that would not have done any good. I just kept walking holding Ted's hand. Nothing else was said the rest of the way, it is a good thing too I don't think I could have controlled myself from hitting him. I don't know why I was so angry at him I just was. I really just wanted to punch him.

"Ah…we are here." Broke my concentration of watching the cracks in the sidewalk go by. I looked up from watching the ground to read the sign that said hotel in neon and no vacancy that also glowed in red neon. We walked into the hotel that smelled of stale cigarette smoke and heavy cleaners. No one was sitting at the main desk that we walked by and from the dust that covered it you could tell that no one had sat there in a while. There were two big doors to the right side of the desk. They look as if they were made of solid wood and very heavy. As we passed through a doorway I could hear music coming from somewhere in the building. There was no thumping of the base like at Ted's. It was the soft melody of a piano playing. The further we walked the louder it got but still calming and quiet. To my surprise as we walked through another set of doors into a huge room, it was filled with vampires. The room was an old ballroom. The ceiling painted gold, the floor made of marble and huge marble pillars that ran to the arched ceiling. The points of the arches touched the top of the pillars. The marble was mostly white with black veins running through it. I had seen a few ballrooms way back when I was younger but never anything that looked like this. I was distracted by the beauty and had not realized that I stopped in the doorway until Ted touched my hand and pulled me forward into the room. He found a corner in the darkest part of the room and we sat down. I watched the other vampires dance and mingle with others but I had no desire to do any of that stuff. The doors opened on the far side of the room and the fresh air wafted in the smell of humans. My throat started to burn. I was ready to have a drink and go back to Erik and Shannon's. Ted rose to his feet but did not reach for me.

"Sam, you stay here I will get you a couple."

I did what he asked and waited for him to return with a human for me to drink dry. He brought them over and sat one down beside me and distracted the other one's while I acted like I was going to whisper in her ear, but sunk my teeth into her flesh. The blood hit my tongue it tasted sweet like they had drank a cup of sugar. When she was done, I moved the body out of the way with ease, Ted brought over a male this time, and he sat beside me. I used the same moves with him as I had the women before him. When he was dry, I sat back in my chair and watched as Ted finished his person off. He came and sat beside me again moving the man's body down a few chairs. I watched as other vampires played with their food by dancing, and cooing over them. I was getting a little aggravated though as I watch them killing people slowly just for fun. Ted must have noticed he took my hand and lead me towards the door. He lightly knocked on the door and it opened, we passed through and the doors were locked behind us.

"Where are we going?" I asked and was going to protest but at this point, whatever happened had to be better than sitting here watching vampires play with their food for fun.

"I think I know of a place that you would like."

We ran down the alleyway to the sidewalk. It was beautiful night and the glow of the signs had me mesmerized. We came to a huge building and it looked like you could touch the stars by standing on top of it. Ted dropped my hand, dug his feet and hands into the side of the building, and started to climb. I just stood there and stared after him. I couldn't believe that he was doing that. He looked down at me and said.

"Are you coming?"

This broke my trance like state and I too started the climb. At the top, I could see for miles and miles. All of the houses looked like they were the size of a very small box. The other taller buildings also looked small from here. This was almost as good if not better than the trees in the park. I ran from side to side of the square building taking in everything that I could. Ted threw his arms around me.

"Do you like it? I know it is not the trees in the park but I thought that you might like it."

"I love it!"

I could feel all of the stress from the day rolling off my back. He sat down and pulled me down with him. We sat in silence for a long time. I gazed at the stars and the moon not thinking about anything right now.

"Sam, I'm sorry about earlier I know that was unpleasant for you. You need to relax a little bit though we had the situation under control." He said and that dredged up the memories from earlier and how mad and upset I was because Erik had laughed at me when I asked for a bucket of water to put my flames out. I was getting furious again and didn't want to even think about this right now.

"Ted, please understand that I'm not being rude but can we talk about this later please."

He threw an arm around me again, we just sat there not moving, not talking, and well at least I was not thinking either. I was listing to the city that seemed thousands of feet below. A man walking down the sidewalk talking to a friend, a dog barking in the little neighborhood, sounds of the cars zooming up and down the streets. The screams from a building nearby, but I was mostly blocking them out. This part did not compare to the park where all I could here is the crickets chirping, frogs croaking, and the sounds of little pitter pater feet on the forest floor. I really missed the forest for that part. Everything in my world right now was perfect and nothing was going to end this happy moment in a dim and dark future. The more time that I spent with Ted the less, I thought about Jaxson. I am guessing it is because Ted and I were cast form the same maker and when I was with him it almost felt like I was with Jaxson again. This kept everything in my mind where it should be and kept me from falling apart when Ted put his arms around me or held my hand. I could just stay right here the rest of my vampire life as long as Ted was there holding me.

CHAPTER 14

My mind was replacing the sounds of the city with the sounds of the forest. Ted abruptly stood up and grabbed my hand and pulled me to my feet.

"We have to go Erik and Shannon are in trouble."

My mind went back to the screams for help that I ignored earlier. I had no idea that it would be coming from vampires that were in trouble. I thought that maybe it was the humans that the vampires had been drinking dry. We jumped off the back of the building so that no one would have seen us. When we landed, the cement cracked under our feet but not enough that people would notice it was footprints. We ran in the cover of the Alleyways. The screams were coming from the ballroom where we had been. We ran down the hallway and to the big doors. Ted grabbed one door in each hand and ripped them from their hinges. The first thing we saw was Erik and Shannon in a corner staring in the direction of their attacker. As I follow their gaze, I saw a huge wolf. Lips pulled back over his teeth ears pinned back against his head taking cautious steps forward. Something snapped in my brain about that time the fur was the length and color of Aidan's. Without even thinking, I blurted out.

"Aidan" The wolf flung his head in my direction still snarling. It was Aidan.

"It is ok they are not going to hurt you." I shot a glance at Erik and Shannon and Aidan seemed to calm down a touch.

"Erik, Shannon, Ted can you all excuse us for a minute." Ted started to protest but gave up when I shot him an angered glance. They left the room and Aidan changed from wolf to human.

"What are you doing here? How did you know where to find me? How is my brother? Did my brother come too?" The last question had me glancing around the room looking for him.

"Your brother is the reason that I'm here. He has lost his mind. He is killing the campers." This news took me off guard and my eyes started to fill with tears. Aidan pressed on with what he was here to say though, "We don't know what happened he just snapped, it is so bad that when some of the other wolfs tried to stop him he killed them, without even batting an eye. That is why I'm here no one knows how to stop him. I was hoping that you may know or come back with me to stop him."

"Well we are wasting time standing here yapping about it, let's go." The doors flung open behind me and slammed back against the wall.

"Sam, don't go, you don't have a chance to stop him by yourself. He will kill you too." Erik said to me, practically begging me not to go.

"I don't think he will." I said, turned, and started walking towards the door with Aidan in tow.

"Sam, can you kill him if you need too?" This stopped me dead in my tracks as I thought about that for a second and turned around to face them. "We will help you but you are going to have to be patient. Aidan how did this come about?" Erik said and I stopped to listen to what he had to say because he was right, I don't think I could kill my brother if I had too.

"He came back from a solo patrol, and his eyes looked funny like it was not him anymore. His eyes used to be kind and giving and now they are hard and careless. I have never seen anything like that before. It was like a switch had been triggered."

Ted and Erik exchanged a glance but did not say anything right away the silence was getting awkward and I was about to say something but Erik beat me too it.

"Well let's go back to the house. Aidan you are more than welcome to come with us." Eric said.

I took Aidan's his hand and pulled him along with us. I was not really paying too much attention to anything except for the thoughts in my head. My mind came upon a silly idea but I still wondered if it could happen so I asked.

"Erik, is it possible for a vampire to be possessed?"

"I don't really know, but I may know someone that might know." He said turning to Shannon.

"Shannon, I must go see an old friend." Then he put both hands on each side of her face and kissed her softly. When he released her, he turned to address everyone.

"Ok you guys I'm going to see my old friend. I'm living my lovely wife with you can you please see that she get home safely." We all nodded and watched as he kissed her one more time and was off. I watched her for a minute as the waves of sadness washed over her face. It was almost as though he had never left her side. I walked over and put my arm around her shoulders.

"Don't worry he will be fine. He will be back before you know it. Why don't you tell me how you met Erik" She giggled a little bit then started.

"Well about fifteen years ago I was walking to a friend's house. My hands were full of books that I had borrowed from her and I was returning them. I spotted him on the opposite side of the street leaning up against the drug store wall. He looked like a homeless man standing there his hair was messed, tangled, and just completely un-kept. His clothing had holes and was in tatters. I meet his eyes for a brief second and I was instantly scared by the look in his eyes that said I'm going to kill you if you give me a chance. I dropped my eyes instantly and kept walking. I was spooked and no matter how much I did not want to look behind me I decided that I should, so I glance back to make sure that he was still in the same spot. But, to my surprise he had moved and now was keeping his distance but he was walking behind me. I picked up my pace but did not want to break in to a run because I was a bit of a klutz and tripped over my own two feet all the time. I knew I didn't want to fall and I thought that maybe it was just a coincidence that maybe he need to go this way too. At any rate, at my quickened pace I didn't see the sidewalk was uneven, I tripped, fell and the books went everywhere. I picked myself up from the ground and found that I had scraped my hand but ignored it to pick up the books and keep moving. I glanced to see where he was in relation to where I was, and found that he was picking up a book behind me that I had missed. Oh, man I was scared I thought for sure that this was it for me. Frozen by fear or something entirely different I couldn't make my body move as he stared at me with the pale blue eyes. He slowly held out the book for me to take and I slowly reached my hand out to take it, I was shaking uncontrollably. He instantly looked down at my hand that I had extended. That made me look too and I realized that I had extended the hand that was bleeding from the missing skin that the concrete had claimed. He put his other hand in his pocket, pulled out a white handkerchief, and wrapped it around my hand. I knew then that he was not going to kill me and I relaxed a little. Then I said, hi, my name is Shannon. Thank you for helping me. My voice was still shaky from the fall and the adrenalin of the ordeal. He replied back my name is Erik, and you are very welcome. Our eyes meet for the second time but what I had seen the first time was gone they were full of kindness, love and caring. Then he said, I need to go it was nice meeting you. I replied it was nice meeting you too. At that point, I was not scared anymore and it was almost as if I was in some kind of trance. But, when he walked away and the trance like feeling wore off I noticed the handkerchief still on my hand. I turned and called after him wait here is you handkerchief back. No, no that is ok you keep it he replied without turning around then added I will see you again someday and you can give it back to me then. Then he disappeared around the corner of the building. In a somewhat daze I walked the rest of the way to my friends and told her the whole story. She said, I needed to relax and stop reading so many horror novels. On my walk home from my friend's house, I was expecting or maybe hoping to see him again but I didn't. The days turned into weeks and the weeks turned into a months before I saw him again. I was sitting in my living room staring out of the window holding the book I had just finished reading when I saw him slowly walk by. I jumped up out of the chair and ran for the door with the handkerchief in my pocket. I seemed to always have it with me just in case I saw him again. I ran to the sidewalk and shouted Erik please wait. I flung the gate open and it smacked back against the fence and made it shiver and rattle. He stopped in his tracks and turned to face me. I want to give you your handkerchief back. He replied, no you should keep it you have had it this long. He looked pleased that I still had it after all those months. I insisted that I should give it back. That is when he said how about this, you keep it until our date tomorrow night and if you still want to give it back to me, you can do so then. I don't know why but I was buzzing about his offer of a date. I calmed myself a bit before I answered him and said. Ok then I will hold it until tomorrow night. Um… what time? I asked with my head spinning. Oh let's say around seven he said then he had to go because he was late for lunch with a friend. Ok, I will see you tomorrow at seven I called after him. I watched him as he disappeared around the corner at the end of the block. I went back in the house, grabbed my shoes, and ran over to my friend's house to tell her what happened. She was so excited for me. I left her house, went home, and did all kinds of chores around the house just to pass the time. I knew I need to get some sleep but I just could not make my eyes close. I was excited and nervous. When my body finally gave into sleep, I had a dream about him, me in a white dress and him in a tuxedo standing in front of the preacher. The dream was so peaceful and pleasant that I didn't want to wake up from it but my eyes finally popped open and I glanced at the clock it was six in the afternoon. I jumped out of bed I had so much to do before he picked me up. I need to wash, comb and dry my hair. I need to find some-thing to ware in the vast space of my closest that was full of sundresses, formal dresses and everything in be-tween. Then the thought crossed my mind I had no idea what to wear because I didn't know where he was tak-ing me. I tried on this dress and that dress, narrowing it down to two dresses. I stood there staring at them and then decided that I would go with the dress that was somewhat formal but could also be played down. Next thing was the accessories, and do something with my hair. I found the perfect earrings, necklace that accented the dress. As I was moving on to my hair, I glanced at the clock and it said six fifty. I was going to curl my hair and put it half up and half down but I knew I could not have gotten it done in that short amount of time. So, I settled on pulling half of it back into a bun and left the other half to cover my neck. The last thing that I was going to grab is a jacket in case it was cold. I was on my way too pick up the jacket when the doorbell rang. Coming I shouted in the direction of the door. I grabbed the jacket and headed for the door and I realized that I had forgotten to get shoes. I opened the door but to my surprise, it was not Erik standing there. My heart sunk and any smile that had been on my face was now gone. The tall skinny man standing there said Erik sent me to pick you up mam and he sends his apology that he was not here to pick you up himself. Sure, I just need to get my shoes. I said and slowly walked over to the closest. I was upset that Erik was not picking me up himself.

Anyway, when I walked outside I was expecting to see some kind of car or something to ride in but there was nothing. Please follow me. The man said. I did as he asked. It wasn't a very far walk it was just around the corner and down about a block to the park at the end of the road. There sitting by the smallish pond was Erik sitting on a blanket. In the middle of the blanket was a vase full of red and white roses. The closer we got the more details I could see I also noticed that he had brought dinner too. I was pleased at all of the thought he had put into this date and was happy again. The man that I was walking with announced my arrival and Erik sprang to his feet and gestured for me to join him on the blanket. A dress really had not been a good idea for this kind of date but at least it was long enough that I could sit Indian style and tuck the dress around my legs. We sat there and talked, eating and getting to know each other. I would tell him something about me and he would return with something about him. We went on like that for a long time and found that we had a lot in common with each other. My butt was starting to hurt from sitting on the hard ground I decided to lay back on the blanket and gazing up at the stars still talking and listening. The next thing I knew He was gently shaking me. Shannon, come let me walk you home. The no sleep from the night before had finally caught up with me I guess. Very upset with myself for falling asleep I apologized about a trillion times. Every time I apologized he would say it's ok. So finally, I was tired of apologizing and I offered to make it up to him somehow. Let me cook you dinner or something, I said. He switched it up on me and offered to take me out on another date as long as I promised to get some sleep tonight. When we got to the door of my home, I offered for him to come in but he declined politely and said that we would be doing this again tomorrow night. I went in, closed the door, and went straight to bed. We kept repeating the pattern over and over again but we did go to different places. Then on our five-month anniversary, he proposed to me. Of course, I said yes. We got married about three months later and that is when I found out about him being a vampire. He could not hide it from me anymore. This didn't change how I felt about him though. The only change was I had a decision to make. I could get a divorce and never see him again, become a vampire or stay human and let him watch me grow old and die. The first option was not an option for me so my decision was to stay human or become a vampire. Obviously you can see what I choose and the rest is history."

"That is a lovely story." I said and as luck would have it and before she had time to ask me questions there was the house.

She was excited to be home and took off on a dead run to the house. I kept the same pace not in a hurry to get anywhere. I watched as my friends all ran to the house and went inside. I thought about running to join them but I just really wanted the peace and quiet to myself for a few minutes. I caught a small movement out of the corner of my eye. My head instantly snapped in that direction and I stumbled back two steeps because what I saw was not what I had been expecting. The glowing green eyes of my brothers in wolf form were standing on the edge of the forest. The eyes always drew me in like some kind of homing device but as I looked into his eyes and he stared, back at me I could tell that something was wrong. The eyes did not have the feeling of home in them they had the feeling of run. But never the less I was still mesmerized and wanted to start walking towards him.

Just then, I heard my friends screaming from the porch. "Sam, look out behind you."

I turned to see two wolves that I had never seen before in a crouching position getting ready to jump me like a cat does to its pray. My hands burst into flames ready for the fight. One lunged at me and I lit it on fire. The ball of fire ran off running and yelping through the forest and the other one was being a coward and ran behind him. I turned back in the direction of my brother but he was also gone. Not letting my guard down staring into the forest waiting for the next attack I felt two hands on my shoulders I went to reach for them.

"Whoa Sam its ok it is just me Ted. I think they are gone find your happy place and put the fire out."

I was just about in my happy place when a stick cracked under the weight of something approaching us. My hands still in flames were ready to strike.

"Sam it is ok it is me Erik." Not willing to let my guard down until I seen him just in case it was a trick I kept my hands burning and my eyes zeroed in on where he would exit the forest. If it wasn't him I was ready, but to my relief it was him.

"It is ok, now relax." Ted said in my ear and I closed my eyes and waited for the fire to go out as I relaxed.

"What happened here?" Erik asked and I could hear the panic in his voice.

"The wolves were here." Ted replied to him.

"Is everything ok?" I opened my eyes to see him looking at the house in a fit of panic.

"Yes everyone is fine. They are in the house." Ted said.

"So did you find anything out?" I asked not really caring about anything else right now. I need answers as to what was going on with my brother.

"Yes I found out a lot of information that I will share with you after I get to my family." Erik, Ted and I started walking towards the house. At the porch, I stopped and sat down in one of the puffy lawn chairs still trying to get my bearings and calm down the rest of the way.

"Sam are you going to come in?" Ted asked.

"No I'm going to sit here for a moment. Can you do me one small favor and send Aidan out? I need to talk to him for a minute." He just looked at me curiously for a minute then went in. A few seconds later Aidan came out and sat in one of the puffy chairs too.

"Before you say anything I know." He said cutting my question right to the quick.

"Aidan we need to save him."

We sat there not saying anything just stared blankly off into space. I knew what was wrong with him. I could feel it in my cold dead soul I knew that the Cloaks had gotten to him somehow. He defiantly was not the same wolf or vampire that I left in the park.

CHAPTER 15

"Sam." Erik yelled from inside the house. I got up from the chair and walked into the big family room where everyone was sitting not really saying much of anything and staring at the floor. Erik was sitting in a huge wing back chair with his daughter on his lap they were playing some kind of game. Shannon was sitting in another wing back chair next to them. Ted was sprawled out on the couch staring at the ceiling. The only available setting left was the floor. So Aidan and I sat down on the floor.

"Sam (Erik began) I have mostly bad news for you. It seems that when you turned him into part vampire you made him venerable to the Cloaks. They do have the power to possess other vampire and in cases where they want something but can't obtain it without one of them getting hurt they will possess something close to them. I explained the situation to my friend and he said that the only way is to kill him and that will release the Cloak back to the original body. The only problem is we have to get someone close enough to your brother to kill him. The only other option is to kill you and they will release your brother because they no longer have a use for him and the will they probably kill him anyway. Sorry that this is all doom and gloom for you but it is the only way. I know that you are not going to fight with your brother and I'm sure that you would not be able to kill him so we would have to find the right person to go on a suicide mission."

"NO, no, no I yelled. I made him I will kill him this is all my fault. I'm going to need you to teach me how to fight." I said as the tears streamed down my face.

"Sam, if you were going to kill him how come you did not do it tonight?" The question stirred my thoughts and I jumped up and ran outside. As I sat on the porch weeping over the thought that someone was going to have to give up their life I hated myself for getting us into this mess to begin with. My mind con-cluded that there had to be another way, there just had to be. I went back in the house and demanded Erik to tell me who his source of the information was and how did I know it was not just some kind of trick to kill my half vampire half werewolf brother. I also wondered if this had happened before. Jaxson had told me in my younger days something about a friend that had dealings with werewolves.

"Sam I guess I need to tell you the whole truth about me. Shannon, love, can you take Summer to her room I think that this may be too much for her little ears." Shannon gathered Summer and left the room. He adjusted his self in the chair and began.

"Well a long, long time ago I lived with the Elders in England. I was part of their guard it was my job to stop anyone from being on the grounds. Let me back up for just a minute. I was made a vampire because they could see my brute strength and that I would be a good candidate for the job. They did offer me certain death or I could be a vampire and serve them for eternity. Obviously, I took being a vampire at that point in my life I was not ready to die. So my job as one of the guards was good I was allowed to have as much as I wanted to drink and had a room that I could do whatever it was I wanted to do. But things started to change. They wanted us to go on hunting parties for their food, as they were getting too lazy to do it. More and more stuff was added to our everyday routines. One day out on patrol a man hunting got to close to the boundary line and I was supposed to kill him with no exceptions. Excuse me sir I said to the man you must leave this area as soon as possible. The man said I don't have too I own this land and this is my boundary line too. I decide not to kill the man but take him to the elders and explain the situation. Thinking that they may spare his life because he owned the property but they did not. They were going to kill him but I put myself in the way. I plead with them to wait that I would take him under my wing, and show him the ropes. I also promised them the land that he owned was now theirs. They kicked us out of the big hall and told me that if I wanted him so badly I need to change him myself. I had no idea what I was doing or even how to do it so I asked around and figured it out. I changed him and we became best of friends his name was Jaxson."

This sent a shockwaves right through me. I had no idea that he knew Jaxson. "Sorry to interrupt but are we talking about the same Jaxson that lived by the park were we came from? I pointed at Ted then myself.

"Yes that would be him. Anyway, back to the story. The Elders started demanding more and more killing and destruction as time went on. They were getting out of control. They order Jaxson and I to kill an innocent person that they thought might have seen something. We did the dirty deed but at the same time made a pact to get out of there. We put the plan into action on the third night after killing the innocent. We ran for days only stopping to get a drink here and there. We even ran under the ocean to get here we knew we didn't have time to wait for a boat. When we got here, we were constantly looking over our shoulders to see if anyone had followed us or found us but it was not until years later that we even found another vampire. The vampire that we meet had also been a part of the guard but they now were a part of the small gang that had some special talents like you and the Cloaks. They called themselves the Cloaks obviously; we still call them that today. That is how I know what they are capable of doing.

I needed to explain to you why I want you on my team to begin with. You see you are the only one that has the power of fire no other vampires has it. You are the key to defeating them.

I had no idea that you existed until after Ted had that encounter with you in the city. So I set Ted up to find you and bring you too me before they found you and used you for their evil deeds.

I must confess though I did trick you. The first time that Ted had you I really honestly didn't know that you were laying in the bed but I heard from one of the other vampires that there was a new girl and Ted was showing you around but by the time I came back you were gone. I was mad. Well beyond; mad at him for letting you go. So, we stage a set up hoping that you would come back and you did. So when you came back and heard me yelling at Ted and basically demoting him to just a vampire and that he was not allowed anywhere near the warehouse I knew that you would go running to him. The plan worked perfectly. The only thing that I was not planning on is your brother being bitten and the fact that you would do anything to save him. So, this is a minor speed bump in my road to be the ruler here. But, with your help we can achieve this and be our own group of elders. We will rule all the vampires on this side of the world." He said with a smug smile on his face.

I was so distraught from hearing all of this I ran from the room out the front door, stood in the middle of the front yard, and yelled at the sky. Then dropped to my knees and started crying with my hands over my face. Everything had just pushed me over the edge. I could not keep it together any more. The betrayal of people that I thought loved me and wanted to see me enjoy life had been just one big game for them. How was I ever going to make it through this, I had hit rock bottom. I knew now that if I tried to leave it would just be another hunting party after me. I had no way out except for death, but would that really save my brother? Would I be able to survive long enough to see if he was ok? Just then, I felt a hand on my shoulder and this disrupted my thoughts.

"Go away" I mumbled through the tears running down my hands.

They didn't move or lift their hands from my shoulders. I stared over to see the pale skin of a hand that had been familiar once. I glanced over at the fingers on the front of my shoulder then followed up to the hand and to the arm and jumped a little when I got to his face. The face of my maker and lover staring back at me, Jaxson I gasped.

"Oh Jaxson, I wish you were here I really need you." I sobbed.

"Sam, you must go to see a lady in New Orleans she is the key to save everything."

"But I can't, they will not let me go." Sobbing even harder now knowing that I was speaking the truth and knowing that I was doomed either way I went.

"If there is a will there is a way."

"Ok I will find a way. Can you stay with me for a little bit? I really miss you." I begged hoping that the answer would be yes.

"Sam, I'm sorry I can't stay I need to get home to my true love, she is here with me, and Sam please don't miss me anymore you are wasting your vampire life. There is another that love you more than I ever could. Remember I only chose you because I owed your brother a favor."

My mind could not comprehend what I was hearing. I thought he loved me just as much as I loved him. This tore me apart inside further than I had ever been.

"You have someone else?" The words blurted out of my mouth built with anger.

"Yes, she was my first the one that I loved more than this world, I was happy when the Cloaks killed me. They did me a favor. I have to go I'm sorry, I will not come back ever again." With that, he started to fade away.

"Wait who do I need to contact in New Orleans?" I said trying to make him stay just a little while longer. I was hoping that he would recant what he had just said and things would be back to the way they were before.

"You will know her when you see her." Then he was gone.

I fell to the ground, could not, and did not want to move. My heart, what was left of the cold dead thing inside me had been completely destroyed. I was giving up I didn't care if I got killed any more. Maybe a small piece of me wanted to go with him and maybe just maybe he was telling me a lie. Well at least that is what I wanted to believe. But he had never lied to me before so why would he start now?

I don't know how long I had laid there but I did feel them pick me up and carry me in the house and lay me on a bed. I was devastated and that through my body into some type of coma. I did not see, hear or feel anything for days. My mind trying to talk myself into death but there was a small ray of hope the Lady in New Orleans, but I had no idea how to find her or where I should look for her. How long would that take to find her did I have enough time? If I could find her, would it really be enough to save my brother? Too many question not enough answers. When I was not thinking of those questions my mind kept reflecting back to seeing him and what he had said. It took me a while but my mind finally started to focus on other words other than I have my true love. Something started to stick out. There is another that loves you more than I ever could. The more I dwelled on this the more it was bringing me out of this coma. My left hand twitched and I could feel the weight of something on top of it. I glanced down at my hand to find out what the weight was. It was Aidan's hand and I instantly wondered if he had been there this whole time. I looked up to see Aidan sitting in a chair with his feet propped up on the night table sleeping right next to me. I looked at him, his beauty became apparent to me. His face, hair, arms that any body builder would love to have then onto his neck and chest. I knew at that moment that Jaxson had been talking about Aidan. How come I never seen this before now I wondered, but I knew the reason. That reason was Jaxson and that I thought that we had the love of a lifetime. Either because I was staring at him or the fact that my hand twitched he opened one beautiful green eye. When he noticed that I was staring back, he opened the other eye.

"Sam, are you ok?" I didn't say anything I just nodded my head. The others must have heard him talking and rushed through the door. I was bombarded with

"Sam, are you ok?" From Erik, Shannon and Ted in unison.

"Yeah I'm fine never been better, maybe that is all I need was a little snooze." The room filled with laughter.

"Well we know you must be thirsty so we are planning a trip, let me get everything ready to go, do you think you will be ready to go in a half hour?"

"Yup I'm ready to go now." I went to pull the covers off and realized that I only had my under ware on. "Maybe you guys could give me a minute to put my close back on." I said a little embarrassed.

They all nodded and exited the room. Aidan was the last one remaining but I held onto his hand very tight not wanting to let him go. I needed him more than anything right now. I need to talk to you I mouthed the words at him. Then I wrapped my arms around his neck and started to pull him closer to whisper in his ear. I accidently brushed his neck with my lips and he jumped back. He started to protest but I shook my head no. I tried again this time getting not so close to his neck. I whispered so low that I could barely hear my-self.

"We have to get out of here. I will explain lat-er." I pulled away from his ear and looked him in the eyes. He just nodded. I leaned in and kissed him on the lips just a small peck like you would give your mom before bed. The look in his eyes was that of confusion then I left him standing there. I grabbed my clothing and had them on and out the door in a few seconds. I walked into the kitchen where everyone was standing.

"Are you ready?" I nodded my head

"Well let's go. Is Aidan going to be coming with us?" Shannon asked

"No I don't think so. He really is not into watching all of us drink." I said and made a funny face and everyone laughed.

CHAPTER 16

In the same fashion as last time, we went to the hotel but without incident this time. Ted and I stayed while Erik and Shannon finished up. We left before the party even got started. We also made it home without incident. We all sat in the great big living room where Shannon had picked up a book and started to read. Ted was lounging on the couch. Erik was sitting in his big chair reading a newspaper. Aidan must still have been in that room trying to figure out a way to get us out of this mess or pondering the kiss that I gave him. All at once, an idea popped into my head that may just work to get us out of here.

"Erik, I need you to teach me how to fight."

He lowered the newspaper just enough to look over the top of it at me. "Ok, you got it training starts first thing tomorrow."

"No, I want to start now I'm tired of waiting for tomorrow." I said trying not to sound to aggravated about it. This was part of my plan.

"Ted, would you like to teach Sam some point-ers right now?" Erik asked.

"Um… what no I would rather wait until tomor-row." Ted replied and I could tell that he was not will-ing to give up his spot on the couch.

"Ok so if you two don't want to teach me any-thing right now I will ask Aidan." I jumped to my feet and stormed out of the room. Loud enough for every-one to hear me I said. "Aidan, will you teach me some pointers on fighting right now?" What they could not see is that I mouthed the word lets go this is my plan.

"Sure I would love too." He replied giving me funny looks trying to figure out what I was doing.

We walked to the door and out to the yard. With my back to the house I mouthed, the words pretend fighting to the forest and run. I got into my fighting stance and he change to wolf form. We danced around a little bit, then I jumped on his back, and he threw me about one hundred yards closer to the forest. We kept up this charade until he finally threw me into the forest. He came to meet me and we did it one last time before I motioned that it was time to run. We ran non-stop for two days. Of course, I would carry him when he got tired or when we had to cross-huge canyons. We ran until the ocean restrained us. I knew that I could have kept going but there was no way that Aidan would be able to swim that great distance and he defiantly could not go under water, he still needed to breath air. If only I was a mermaid instead of a vampire.

"Wow! I thought we were never going to stop." He said trying to catch his breath a bit.

"I know we really shouldn't stop now but we have no choice.

"Do you think that we will be ok if we rest for the night?"

"Yeah I think so. They have to be pretty far behind us I think. I'm pretty sure that they would have searched the entire grounds before they would go on this adventure."

"I'm just a little concerned about their tracker, I'm not sure how long it would take for them to get him and then come after us, but you need to rest."

Aidan changed back to wolf and curled up under a nearby pine tree. I wanted to curl up with him but I need to be on guard just in case. As he slept, I was thinking about the Lady that Jaxson had mentioned. I was trying to imagine what she look like. My mind was not coming up with anything particular. But, that thought soon faded away as I sat there and stared at Aidan. Feelings that I had not felt in years were coming back. The feeling of love, this had me smiling. The feeling of lust this put an even bigger smile on my face. I thought back to the time he kissed me. I was so stupid for rejecting him. However, I would no longer reject him because I need him now more than ever. Jaxson had moved on so why not me too. Of course, I wanted to be different and move on with a werewolf. Why is that so different though we are still people, well maybe not people but we are mythical creatures? Why does it have to be so taboo? So far, when I needed him he was there and he has always been there for me so I will always be there for him not matter what. I made the silent pact with myself. I imagined kissing him again but this time with passion and affection. Nevertheless, at the same time I knew that I needed to take it slow because I didn't know how he felt about me. Well I used to know how he felt about me but was not sure if he still felt that way. My mind went on and on about things that didn't matter like the color of the leaves. I noticed him starting to stir and he blinked his eyes a couple of time and raised his head. He was still in that state somewhere between sleeping and awake. But within a few minutes he was awake and changed back to human and sat next to me.

"We need to get moving as soon as you are ready." I said picking at my fingernails and staring down at the ground.

A low growling sound had me on edge for a minute until I realized that it had been Aidan's stomach. "Your, hungry we need to find you something to eat. Is there anything that you would like?"

"Yeah I would like some bacon, eggs, sausage, toast and some pancakes." He said with a laugh.

"Ok then we will find you those things." I said with a screwed up look on my face, the thought of disgusting people food made me want to vomit.

We both rose to our feet and started to walk towards the sounds and smells of a city. As we walked, I wanted to blurt out Aidan I love you but decided that right now was not the time.

As we came into the city, there was a small dinner on the left side of the street. The smell from the dinner made Aidan stomach growl louder.

"Um…do you have any money we could go there and eat?"

"No I don't have any money as it is hard to carry when I change to wolf."

Ok so that plan was busted next best thing was to find someone cooking and go there. I let him lead the way to whatever smelt good to eat. We ended up at a house that was way back in the forest. The house was in a complete state of disrepair. The wood siding had been so neglected that it had turned a grey color and some pieces were even falling off. There was a broken window that was covered by a board and the front door looked as if it was holding the center of the house up. I did a quick sweep around the house and found only one old man that lived here. We knocked on the door and the old man answered.

"Excuse us sir do you have some food to spare?"

The man looked at us and yelled the word. "NO GO AWAY."

I looked at Aidan and he shrugged his shoulder and started to walk away. I was not going to give up that easy though. I knocked on the door again and this time the old man answered with a gun in hand.

"I SAID NO. I'm going to give you until I count to ten to get off my property before I kill you."

"Ok sir, then I guess you are going to have to kill me before I kill you."

I pushed the door open grabbed the man and proceeded to drink him dry. When I was finished, I motioned to Aidan to come in and get something to eat. He sauntered past me to the kitchen. I sat on the old broken down couch and listened as the fork scraped the plate. I imagined him sitting in there licking the plate when he was done I heard the plate being placed in the sink then he appeared in front of me in the living room.

"Sam you didn't have to do that. We could have found another place, besides you can't just go around killing people for the hell of it that makes you just as bad as the elders."

The conversation upset me I was doing it for him not me. However, he was right I could have found someone else. What was the difference if I drank this guy or someone else I still need the blood to survive. A small part of me was angry with him for saying it but that same part was saddened with the fact that he was right. I need to be choosier on who I killed for their blood.

"Sorry, it is just that I knew you wanted this food and I was thirsty too." I apologized for my actions.

"It is ok Sam, we should get going, umm… where are we going exactly you never did say." He said with a laugh.

"We need to go to New Orleans I'm not sure which way we need to go from here but that is the final destination."

"What are we looking for when we get there?"

"We are looking for a lady that can help my brother."

"What does this lady look like?"

"I'm not sure, I will know when I see her." I said with confidence despite the look on his face.

"So let me get this straight we are going on a wild goose chase for some lady that you don't even know if she exists." He said trying not to laugh at me.

"Yup that is what it seems like." I said as sarcastically as I possible muster.

"Well we should get going then." He extended his hand for me to take, I did and he pulled me off the sofa.

"One more question how do you know about this lady that we have to find? How do you know she is real?" He said eyeing me and legitimately wanting to know this time.

This question was the question I didn't want to answer for fear of looking crazy. Nevertheless, I guess it couldn't looking any crazier than going on a wild goose chase.

"Well" I started and swallowed a few times and started again. "That night that I went screaming from the house…Jaxson came to me, he told me about her. I don't think he would steer me in the wrong direction." I was staring at the floor now; I was too embarrassed to look at him.

"So you are going by what a ghost told you?" He was trying not to sound mocking or amused with what I had said. He was actually trying to be genuinely interested this time.

I looked up meeting his gaze and could see in his eyes that this was not funny anymore and he was taking me seriously now. "Yup, it is either this or my brother and I both die." I looked at the floor again and muttered to myself "Or at least one of us does."

Nothing else was said as we walked back to the small city. The first people we came across we asked them if they could tell us how to get to New Orleans. They exchanged a funny glance with each other and kept walking. We came across some more people and asked them, but they too exchanged a strange glance with each other and completely ignored us. We kept walking until we came across a guy that had some sort of large paper on the hood of his car and decided that would be the person to ask.

"Excuse me sir, can you tell us how to get to New Orleans?"

"Oh sure, you need to take this road, that road and some more roads." He said pointing to each of them on the map. When he was finished explaining he looked up at us. He must have seen the confused look in our eyes and that we had still had no idea what he was talking about. "You can ride with me if you would like I'm going close to there, if you don't already have a ride that is." He started looking around for our car and quickly realized that his was the only car around.

"That would be great we would love a ride." Aidan answered without even thinking about it. When his eyes meet mine, I was furious. How was I going to ride in a car with human blood right there, how was I not going to kill him.

Aidan sensing my anger threw his arms around me and whispered in my ear "I won't let you hurt him, I promise." He took me by the hand and led me to the cars back seat. We sat on the passenger of the car with me being right next to the door so that Aidan was closer to him than I was. We all piled in and the air swirled around the cab of the car all I could smell was the man. I wanted to take him right now but knew that I could not or I would never get to New Orleans. I buried my face into Aidan and he wrapped his arms around me and pulled me close. All though I could still smell the man, it was not as bad because it was in intervals. I mostly could only smell Aidan. The sweet fragrance that he gave off smelled a lot like the park. The smell of earth, trees and the wildflowers that grew in the park was mostly what I could smell now. His arms holding me as if I was in the iron cage with steaks pointing at me from every direction.

"So what takes you folks to New Orleans?"

"We are going to visit her mom. She is in the hospital and is very sick." Aidan answered him without hesitation.

"I'm really sorry to hear that. I am coming from a funeral, my dad passed away unexpectedly." The man replied and tried to hide his tears with his voice. But I could tell he was crying just by the slight change in his voice. He sniffled and shook his head in an effort to pull himself together.

"We are sorry to hear that." Aidan replied for the both of us sensing that I was unable to talk. He was mostly right. I was trying to keep myself under control.

"So I didn't catch your names earlier." He said changing the subject.

"I'm Aidan and this is the one the only Sam." Aidan replied and gestured towards me.

"Nice to meet the both of you, I was not looking forward to this drive alone."

"How long do you think it will take to get there?" Aidan asked the question that I was not able to ask on my own.

"Well I really would like to get home in two days but it will most likely be three."

I looked up at Aidan and started to protest but he was not even looking at me.

"How far is it to get to New Orleans?" Aidan asked then looked down at me knowing he satisfied my question.

"Oh, I think that will be about a two days for sure." He said then went on to ask. "What do you guys do for work?"

"Well I'm currently unemployed. And Sam here works as a bank teller."

He acknowledged Aidan with a nod then asked. "Do you have a preference for music?"

"No anything is good we like a little bit of everything."

"You know I didn't catch your name kind sir." Aidan asked.

"My name is Mike." Our driver replied.

"It is nice to meet you Mike and thank you for the ride we greatly appreciate it."

That was the end of their conversation, and the next thing I knew Aidan was sleeping. My head moved with every breath he took in and out, in and out. For once in a long time, I was perfectly happy nothing was going to destroy this moment. I watched the tiny movements of his nose flair and go back down time and time again. His fingers twitched against my back. Ripples of muscles tightening around me then relaxing, it was all like a song that I had never heard before. The car started to come to a stop and his eyes fluttered open. He looked down at me and squeezed me a little.

"Oh good your awake, I'm going to stop at the gas station do you need anything?"

"No we are good." Aidan replied to the man but at the same time, his stomach started to growl again. Your hungry I whispered to him.

"No Sam if you don't eat neither do I." He softly said to me in protest.

"It is different for me." I mouthed too him.

"On second thought I think I would like to get something to eat." He said to Mike. I do not know if it was something on my face that made him change his mind or if his stomach had taken over.

"Oh, ok I will give you some money if you will run in and get us some snacks." Mike said in delight.

"Sure no problem is there anything specific that you would like?" Aidan asked.

"No, whatever you get will be fine."

The man pulled up to the gas pump, handed Aidan some money and got out.

"I will be right back unless you would like to come in with me?"

Trying to be brave, I said. "I would love too."

We both got out and walked into the store Aidan was holding my hand and this made me feel good about my choice. I could smell all of the people in here but it was almost like I could not see them. The only person that I could see was Aidan. He grabbed a few thing some chips, pretzels and drinks. We paid and went back to the car just in time for Mike to be done pumping gas. We all piled back in the car and Aidan gave Mike his drink and snack. I buried my face back into Aidan as quick as I could so that I didn't have to smell Mike's blood. The only thing I could hear was

Aidan chewing and gulping his food and drink. It was almost musical in a since, chew, chew, swish, chew, chew, swish. The smell of the food though was awful it smelled like chemicals and stuff that you should not eat. When he was done, he wrapped me in his arms and held me close. I drifted into oblivion with total disregarded for everything. I was not sleeping but I was daydreaming about all of the things that I would like to do. I was in the most wonderful daydream about a house with a white picket fence when Mike's voice broke through.

"I think we will be stopping soon for the night"

"I plan on staying in a hotel a few miles down the road. Umm… if you guys would like you can stay with me I think I would like the company." Mike said unsure if he should ask or not.

"No, no we will sleep in the car. We don't want to impose too much on your kindness." Aidan said sound slightly apologetic.

"Ok, if that is what you really want to do." Mike replied sounding sad.

They talked more about non-important things. I just tuned them out and pretended that I was sleeping well at least that is what it looked like to Mike but Aidan new better. My mind wondered into nothingness I was not thinking of anything and nothing was popping into my head it was quiet in my mind for once. I stared into Aidan's shirt not really seeing that either. The nothingness was something that I had never experienced before. I was always wondering about this or that. How things worked or how they were made. So, when the car decelerated it took me by surprise and I jumped a tiny bit, not enough for Mike to notice the movement. Aidan however did notice and tighten his grip and looked down at me asking me with his eyes if I was ok. I nodded yes and he relaxed some. We came to a place that said the Holiday Inn. We pulled up in front of the place and Mike got out of the car. He was gone for a few minutes. I sat up in the seat to give Aidan a break from being stuck in the same position for hours.

"How are you doing?" He asked, with the look of concern written all over his face.

"I'm doing ok as long as I am close to you." I said trying not to look at him. I felt a little embarrassed that I had said that.

A small smirk came across his face, the kind of smirk that you do to hide a full-blown smile. Mike got back in the car and we drove around back of the hotel.

"Are you guys sure that you don't want to come in with me?" Mike asked again, hoping that we changed our minds.

"Yes, we are sure but thanks for the offer." Aidan replied for us.

Mike grabbed a bag from the passenger side of the car and got out. He poked his head back in the door and said. "Ok, I will see you in the morning bright and early. He closed the door and we watched as he went inside and closed the hotel door. We waited for a few more minutes before getting out of the car just to make sure he was not going to come back out for any reason.

"Are you thirsty?" Aidan asked me.

"I'm starving after smelling him all day." I said and pointed to his small hotel room.

"Do you want me to go with you or would you rather I stay here?" What did I prefer him to be subjected to that or take the chance of losing him somehow?

"Um… well… I think that if you are ok with it you can come with me but if not I can go alone." I said hoping that he would go with me.

He didn't say a word and just took my hand and we were off stalking the night. The town that we stopped in was a good size so I didn't have a hard time finding a few victims. Yes I said a few, I need to make sure that I was full to ride some more in the car with Mike. Aidan was good about it he would turn away so that he didn't have to see it. When my murder spree was over, we walked around looking at the quit beautiful town. The sidewalks were like walking through a garden, there were all kinds of flowers that lined the sidewalk on both sides, some flowers were tall some were short. Hanging baskets hung from the street lamps. The flowers cascaded over the edges of the baskets and swayed in the light breeze. It was mesmerizing to watch. I wanted to reach out and hold Aidan's hand but was not sure that he would approve of this. I fought the urge and settled for talking.

"So Aidan, I feel like I don't know much about you. Like how did you become a werewolf, or anything else really." I stated in trying to get him to talk about his life but he turned the tables on me and said.

"How about we get back to the car and I will tell you my story in exchange for your story."

What could he possibly want to know about me I wondered? I was pretty sure he already knew my story I was sure my brother had told him. However, maybe he wanted to hear it from me. "Ok then let's go back to the car." I said with a smile.

CHAPTER 17

"Ok as promised here is my story. When I was born, my mom died giving birth to me. So therefore, my father always hated me I was his whipping boy of sorts. Anything and everything that happened on our little farm was my fault. From one of the dairy cows dying to the chickens not laying eggs, when things like this happened my father would beat me as if I was a man. I had bruises and cuts all the time. Nevertheless, nothing compared to one day.

On that warm summer day our one and only horse was dead in its stall. Well the horse was not that old and of course, it was my job to take care of the horse like all of the other farm animals. The other problem was we were not rich by any means, so a new horse would cost my father a small fortune to replace. I didn't want to tell him about the horse but I had no other choice. When I told my father, he went ballistic and beat me so bad that I wished I were dead. I couldn't move or make any sounds my eyes where swollen and I could barely see. He must have thought that I was dead or close to it. In an effort not to be caught and charged for murder he took me out to the forest and left me propped up against a tree to die.

I thought I was taking my last breaths and could see my mom calling to me. I knew it was her from a few photos that I saw over the years. She was dressed all in white with the brightest white light behind her. I could feel myself outside of my body going to her. I was within an arm's reach to touch her when I was slammed back into my body almost like the snap of a rubber band. I could feel the pain of the broken bones and swelling all over again. But there was something new, blood oozing from a gapping cut on my arm. This new cut burned, I mean as if someone had shoved a hot branding iron in it. Then as soon as the burning had started, it stopped. I watched through the small slit of my eyelids as my mom faded away. I still wanted to be with her but all that was left was the trees. (He stopped and seemed like he was replaying the whole thing in his head again. Then after a short break, he started again.)

I could feel some kind of super strength healing all of the broken bones and fusing themselves back together as they popped back into place. Of course, this still hurt but after a second, the pain was gone. The slits in my eyes got wider and wider that too was going away. As all of the pain stopped and I could see, hear and smell even better than before I slowly got to my feet not knowing what to expect but when I got there, I checked to see if everything was in working order and it was. I had never felt better in my whole life. Now I was faced with the decision to go back to the farm or to just walk away. As I stood there motionless thinking about the decision that I had to make I heard a twig pop behind me. I wheeled around ready for anything but what I saw was something totally different. There behind the tree was a wolf staring back at me. I started to stumble backwards thinking that I was in danger. But, as the wolf walked towards me he began to blur and the next thing I knew I was staring at a naked man. I could not believe my eyes. How did a man change into a wolf or how did a wolf change into a man. Then he said it is ok you are with me now. Your brother is the one that rescued me or cursed me however; you want to look at it. I see it as a rescue but some of the others see it as a curse. He explained to me what I was and how things were going to go.

I did go back to the farm but only at night when my father was sleeping. I would leave him things sometimes like bread or something that I found. I know it does not make much sense for me to do those things but it was for my mom not for me but for her. I think that he would have been a different person if she would not have died. I would hear stories about her from time to time, from the locals. They would tell me how she was involved with the community. But, they would always end the conversation with, how much it had messed my father up when she died. One day I had gone to leave him something's but I noticed a funny smell in the air. The smell of death, he had passed in his sleep. I left the things like always, paid my respects and never went back there again.

Your brother and I became close friends; actually, he is the brother that I never had. I had no idea that you even existed until you showed up at the park. That is one thing that he never talked about I don't really know why but it was kind of a need to know bases and apparently I didn't need to know at the time. Then I met you and all hell broke loose."

He finished his story just in time for Mike to come out of the hotel with his bag in hand ready for the day's journey. I guess you will have to tell me your story tomorrow night. He said with a smile. I was will feed and my thirst was completely under control so I didn't bury my head into to Aidan as Mike got into the car, but I pretended to be a sleep though as his scent swirled around the car. Aidan grabbed my hand and held it tight. But I reassured him that I was fine by putting my other hand over his and squeezing it lightly. Mike did his best to be quiet as he entered the car and started the engine. Aidan acted like he awoke for a minute to acknowledge Mike and pretended to fall back asleep, but it was not long before he was sleeping for real. I decided not to pretend I was sleeping and decided to have a conversation with Mike.

"How long will it be until we get there today?" I asked starting the conversation.

"Well from my estimate we should be there in about ten hours." He said dubiously.

"So when you get home is there a special some-one waiting for you?" I asked not sure of what else to say. I maybe a vampire living the life of solitude but I knew I could still have conversations with humans.

"Yup, the most beautiful girl in the world, she is my everything the one person that I would lay my life down for." He said and you could hear her beauty in his voice. He paused and sighed and his mood changed to sadness. "It is just her, we tried to have children but found out that we could not." He sighed again and I could tell that he longed to have them.

"How come she didn't come with you?" I asked trying to change the subject a bit.

"She couldn't get the time off of work to come. She has a very busy and demanding job and it requires her to work a lot. But when I do get to be with her it is like I'm falling in love all over again." He said and I could tell that this lifted his mood.

"Wow that sounds wonderful." I said not knowing what else to say to that.

"What about you too?" Mike asked with a hint of curiosity.

I glanced over at Aidan before I answered. I was not sure if I was ready for him to know how I felt about him. He appeared to be in a deep sleep and I didn't think that there was any danger in letting Mike know how I felt.

"Well we are just starting out in our relationship but I know that he is the one that I would love to be with now. But, I'm not sure how he feels about me. We tried this once before and I pushed him away so I think that he may have some hurt feelings. So I guess in short I'm ready but I'm waiting for him." I didn't give Mike any of the details of what happened that first time. Besides, I would have had to admit that part about him being a werewolf and me a vampire.

"Oh, girl he loves you more than you think he does, he maybe a little scared because of the rejection but he still loves you and wants to be with you. Do you really think that he would be here if he didn't?" He replied without skipping a beat.

I wanted to answer yes he would because of my brother but I really could not go into that part of the facts. "No, I don't' know." I said sounding confused.

"I can see it in his eyes the way that he looks at you and watches you. Trust me he loves you." He replied just as fast as the first time.

Yeah, but Mike had no idea that Aidan was watching me like that to keep me from killing him. Oh well I need a new subject to talk about this one was going to make me say something that I should not say then I would have to kill him anyway. I glanced over at Aidan just to check that he wasn't awake and had not heard our conversation. His eyes were closed and he was still breathing heavy. I have seen him sleep as a wolf but not a human. The closer I looked at him the more beautiful he was.

"So where is home exactly? You said that it was three days away." I asked Mike turning my attention back to him.

"I live in the bottom part of Florida." He replied not giving any other information.

I guess I was so out of touch with the world that I had no idea what else to talk about so I asked Mike to turn on some music. He obliged

The radio came on with a bunch of static. He changed the channel until it came in nice and clear. The song that came on was upbeat but slow and talked about love, and the one and only person in the world. Man I just could not get away from that conversation today. I closed my eyes and pretended to go back to sleep. I tuned out the music until the song changed but the next song was more of the same. I started thinking about Aidan and me, mostly about what kind of life we would have together. Dreaming about a wedding and adopting a child, living in a home instead of some random tree or were ever I spent my time. I felt pressure on my cheek and this startled me but I had to maintain my composure knowing Mike was here too. When I opened my eyes and looked it was Aidan's hand. He was staring at me smiling. The question was there in his eyes he wanted to know what had captured my attention to the point that I was not hearing anything. I could see my face in the mirror and noticed that I was smiling too. Not saying anything I pulled myself close to him and snuggled back into him like yesterday. He stroked my hair with one hand and wrapped the other around me. I could not hide it any more I had to tell him how I felt about him and well if he felt the same way about me that would be awesome but if he didn't that was just going to have to be ok. At least I would know. But, for now all we had to do was ride until we got there. We stopped for gas a few times and Aidan ate some more snacks. Aidan and Mike hit it off really well and talked most of the rest of the trip.

"Well we are here." Mike said.

I had been waiting to hear those words for a while. Mike pulled over on the side of the highway. We were on top of a hill looking down at the city. It was beautiful sight all of the street lights glowing like a million fire flies against the night sky.

"I don't want to go down into town, so would it be ok if I dropped you here?" Mike asked.

"Yes that would be just fine." I replied and hurriedly opened the door to jump out.

We thanked him for letting us ride this far with him and all of his hospitality. Aidan gave him a hug and then he reached for me to hug. I hugged him for a split second. He got back into his car and speed away. We watched as he drove out of site.

CHAPTER 18

We stood there for a moment longer.

"I'll race you" I said to him with a taunting smile on my face.

"Do I get four or two legs?" He questioned back with the same taunting smile that I had given him.

It didn't take us long before we had to stop because we were on the edge of the city. The race was really close, I think he had me by the tip of his nose.

"Well Aidan this is it we have to find the lady but where do we start?" I asked him as he changed back to human form.

"I'm not sure Sam here looks as good as any place that I can see right now. It sure would help if I knew who we were looking for or even a sent would be nice. I could find her that way."

This was it. I had to find this woman, for my brother, for me, and my hopeful future with Aidan. He took my hand and pulled me into the city. We walked aimlessly up and down the streets but no sign of the one that I was looking for. We wondered until dawn then decided that we need to take a break for a little while. I knew that Aidan had to be getting tired and he needs to rest and eat. I too needed some food but it was not the first thing on my mind for the first time in a long time. I was more worried about telling him how I felt about him and finding the women.

He found a restaurant that was getting ready to throw away some good food and begged the man to let him have it. We found a nice quiet place to relax under a beautiful tree that looked to be about four hundred years old. The base of the tree must have been about thirty feet around. The branches hung out far and wide form the base. The tree rested on top of a beautiful green grassy hill overlooking the streets. The tree was surrounded by an old wrought iron fence, that had spikes on the top. The little plot was as big as a city block and it was also landscaped with the most exquis-ite flowers. This little place was a sanctuary away from the hustle and bustle of the busy town. We sat on the ground resting against the old tree.

"So why don't you tell me your story." Aidan said with a mouth full of food.

"Ok I guess it is only fair you told me yours." I said with a sigh and started my story. "Mabel Samantha Fisher is my real name but everyone calls me Sam. I acquired the nickname Sam one day from my father. I am not sure why and I he started calling me Sam and never got around to asking him either. I lived on a plantation with my father, mother, two younger sisters, and one younger brother. We had moved to Georgia from New York when my father had the great idea of starting our own plantation. I mean really it was not a plantation it was just a little farm. Our farmhouse was not extravagant, not like the Smith's house across town. Our home would fit inside theirs three times and still have room left over. The Smith's home is what I would consider a plantation. My sister's and I all shared a room while my younger brother had his own room.

My sister, Sophia was turning eighteen the year I was made a vampire and Jim a very wealthy man was courting her and my family gained a lot after they were married. Rose my youngest sister was sixteen at the time and she too had a beau. I was just lonely old me with no beau and no prospects of one at the time. I was supposed to get married to a man but he died before we got the chance to get married. After that, none of the men fancied me… Maybe it was because I was too old or I was cursed. My younger brother is fifteen that year, and mostly works on the farm he too did not have a special someone just yet, but I did know of a couple of girls that liked him.

Farm life was rough for us. We never seemed to have enough money for things like new material for making clothing or to buy food. We lived off whatever my father could sell at the local general store and what the farm provided. This life was the roughest on my mother. Prior to moving here, she never had to cook or clean. We had people that we paid to do those things for us. She became friends with the closest neighbor Mrs. Plat. I think if it were not for Mrs. Plat, we would have starved to death; my mother could not cook a lick of food. It was either burnt to a crisp, more times than not, or was not cooked all the way through. My Father would eat anything put in front of him without a complaint just to make her feel better about the mandatory move. Over the years though, she did get eminently better and the food became eatable. Making new clothing was also a bit of a challenge for her, but again with the help of Mrs. Plat she started making clothing like it had come from one of those fancy stores in New York.

Even with all of her newfound talents, she still hated it there and wanted to move back to New York. You see when we lived in New York we had an overabundance of money. My Father was a high profile lawyer there and made a decent living. We never understood why he wanted to move so far away and start a farm. There had been many nights that I could hear them arguing through the wall about moving and the plantation. One night my father had enough with the arguing, and flat out told my mother that we are going and that is the end of it. Then he told her to start packing for the trip tomorrow.

As mother pack up our belongings, she would go through fits of anger and sadness and all of the emotions in-between. She would tell her friends that it was unfair and that maybe she should just stay in New York and send everyone away. I knew however, that it was just the anger talking and that she would never leave her children or husband behind.

I could see she absolutely hated farm life. Sometimes I would see her sitting at the little round wooden table with four chairs around it, in a corner of the house. The table was done up with a fancy white cloth over it, and the fancy tea set that my father had bought her one year for her birthday. She would pretend as if she was back in New York having tea with a few of her friends. Sometimes she would even mumble to herself but I could never make out what she was saying.

One day she was taking dinner out of the stove. The pan with the turkey and juices was so heavy she accidently dropped it on the floor. The juice went everywhere but the turkey miraculously stayed in the pan. She sat down on the floor and started to clean up the mess. Then she burst into tears and said I wish your brother were here, I wish my friends where here, I want my old life back I absolutely hate it here. I was sad for her as she said those words and could not help but think about how I could make things better for her. I knelt down and started to help her clean up the mess not saying anything. Even though I wanted to reach out to her and hug her, like she did me when I was sad. I knew that would have made her cry even more, and she still had supper to finish cooking. I knew if I would have hugged her she would have burnt the rest of supper and that would have made her more upset.

The brother that she had mentioned, we did not talk about him. He disappeared one day and never returned, and even the mention of his name made my mother upset and my father angry. We never found his body or had any indication that he was dead so we figured that he had simply just left us behind. You see my older brother and father never seemed to see eye to eye and it seemed to be a constant battle between them. My father wanted things to be done his way or no way and my brother wanted to do things his way. My brother was somewhat of an inventor he was always dreaming up new ways to make life easier and faster so that he would have time left over at the end of the day to court a woman that he liked. Father hated his inventions and always found a flaw with them or would tear them down. This frustrated my brother, and they would not talk for days afterwards.

The girl that my brother had been courting also had disappeared a few days later. The town and her parents thought that she committed suicide somewhere but again the body was never found, despite the searching. This led us to believe that they ran off together to parts unknown.

The whole situation tore my mother apart and she would always tell my father it was his fault and that he should not have been so hard on him. This made my father mad. He thought he was doing what was best for my brother. After my brother was gone, you could tell that he regretted what he had done but now it was un-fixable. This all happened shortly after we had moved to Georgia. As time passed, we just would not mention him and everyone went back to being somewhat happy.

So, the day that my mom had wished that my brother had been there to help I decided to try and brighten her day, and I knew flowers helped so I went out to the field to pick some wild flowers to take home to her in hopes to cheer her up but I never made it home. The wife of one of the elders attacked me and as she was sucking the life out of me, my brother and his pack jumped in to save me. In the process, they killed her. But in the meantime that is when Jaxson saved me or turned me into this monster that I am now." I paused and waited for a moment for the pain to come with the mention of his name but quickly realized the pain that was associated with his name was gone. I went on. "I woke up all by myself thirsty but I didn't know that I would be thirsty for blood so I went to a stream and took a big gulp of water but spit it back out as fast as I had took it in." I did hear Aidan giggle a little bit at that but for the most part, I ignored it and went on. "Jaxson found me and took me in and was trying to teach me the vampire way. This is when I meet my now wolf brother that I didn't know was even alive. Then shortly after that is when they sent the Cloaks looking for me the first time. Jaxson and I ran but it was not far enough, we went hunting but when we went back to his friend's house and was meet by my brother just before we got to the house Jaxson knew something was wrong and sent me away with my brother but not before I seen them kill him. They did come after me and they did catch up to me but for some odd reason they let me live. Something about they were looking for the Elders wife's killer and they knew that it was not me. After that, I went back to Jaxson's house, burnt it to the ground, and traveled around aimlessly for two hundred years refusing to go back to that place or anywhere close because it hurt too much. You see with the little bit of time I had spent with him I had fallen in love with him and still had a lot to learn from him. I finally one day ventured back and that is when I found you and my brother. You already know this part of the story so I'm going to skip ahead to a few days ago. When I ran screaming from the house something happened to me. I saw Jaxson, he is the one that told me I need to come here and look for the Lady you already know that part, but something else happened too. He told me that he was happy with his one true love and that he could now be with her. That is why I was in a coma like state for a few days because I finally had time to get over him and move on with my life. So now, we are here and Aidan I have something very important that I need to tell you. Aidan I'm sorry about before but I have now realized that I love you." There I had said it and now waited for a reaction from him.

"Sam, I know that and I love you too, I have been waiting to tell you that for a long time but I could not take the rejection again like the first time." He said as he looked deep into my eyes confessing his love for me.

"Oh, Aidan I'm so sorry that I hurt you back then but things were not right for me but now I can say that you are the only man in my life."

He drew me in to his chest and laid me down in the grass next to him. I curled around him with one arm around his chest. He played absently with a few strands of hair and we just laid there enjoying being with each other for a moment. I wanted to stay like this all day but knew that this was not going to find the lady that we had come here for.

"Aidan I would love to stay like this all day but I or we must really go and look for the lady she has to be here somewhere." I said softly hoping that I didn't hurt his feelings. It was hurting mine though; I hoped that I was hiding it well.

Aidan yawned. "Ok we should get going before I fall asleep." He sounded so sleepy and content not going anywhere or doing anything right now.

"Maybe you should stay here and sleep I will come back in a little bit to get you." I said thinking about his wellbeing.

"Ok, but sweetie, don't go too far away from me please." He begged. I could hear the worry in his voice mixed with longing for me to stay.

I jumped to my feet and started to run off but realized that I didn't say anything to him, so I turned around and knelt beside him and kissed him with all of the passion that I had.

"I love you and I will be back soon." I softly said.

"I love you too and don't be gone too long."

I walked away felling content, happy and excited that he loved me too, but I also felt saddened because I had to leave him right now. I just confessed my love for him and now I had to try to find someone that would be able to get me out of my death warrant.

I searched a five-mile radius but did not see the lady anywhere. I hurried back to Aidan but when I got there, he was gone. I looked around and there was nobody to be seen for what seemed like miles in any direction. I fell to my knees and felt as though my heart had been ripped from my chest all over again. Where could he have gone or worse yet what if they found us and kidnapped him or something. My mind was spinning circles around what if's when I heard a noise behind me. I jumped to my feet and twirled automatically ready to fight, maim or kill whatever was there. To my surprise it was Aidan, I dropped my guard and jumped on him.

"I thought that you left me or something happened to you." I said in a frantic voice.

"I'm not going anywhere." He replied, and lifted me in the air and kissed me.

"Did you have any luck?" He asked after he had released my lips from his.

"No not at all." I said with a frown.

"Well how about we both go looking."

He grabbed my hand and we headed deeper into the heart of the city. People dressed in all kinds of weird out fits with very vibrant colors. Some were dressed in costumes and were trying to look like vampires, werewolves and zombies. I don't know where they got those looks from but they defiantly were not what real vampires looked like. Every building seemed to have a balcony and almost every balcony someone was standing on it watching the street below as people walked through. All at once, things slowed down for me and I got the first glimpse of her. The Lady that we were looking for, I was frozen in place for a split second and could not seem to speak. I finally got the words out.

"There she is." I tugged on Aidan's hand and started pulling him in the direction of her.

"Where, where is she?" I heard him ask but didn't acknowledge him. He was slowing me down though.

"Sam, slow down you can't run that fast here you need to act normal. He was right but at the same time, I did not really care who saw me. By the time we had gotten to the place that we last seen her she was gone almost as if she had disappeared into thin air. This crowd was getting in my way.

"Damn it, damn it, damn it I mumbled under my breath." However, Aidan heard me.

"It's ok Sam at least you know what she looks like now."

As I thought back to that moment that I had seen her, I could only recall what color her hair was and how long it was. It was curly dark brown and it was halfway down her back. My mind's eye had more details about her. She had tan skin, and her face was beautiful so beautiful that she could have been some kind of superstar. Another thing that I had noticed was she was wearing a brown jacket and jean pants. Nothing else stood out in my head though. No markings of any kind that would defiantly define I had the right person. The image of her face was going to have to work. However, I did not know how my mind knew it was her. Had made up the image or did someone or something put the image in my head.

"How about we stay here for a while maybe she will come back this way." Aidan gestured to a bench resting on the sidewalk under a street lamp.

What are the chances of her coming back this way I thought to myself, why would she, did she live around here? Of course, that made perfect sense let's just sit here and wait. Anger started to build in me. Wait until what, I thought. Until we die, oh yeah that's right I won't die but Aidan on the other hand might. What if she only came this way the one time in her whole life? What if she never came this way again? How long could I wait? Of course, I could wait for forever but how long can my brother wait? The questions kept floating through my mind.

"Umm…Sam I'm going to go get something to eat I'm starving." Aidan said to me after a while of sitting there smelling food.

This whole eating thing was starting to get on my very last nerve. I had to eat or drink too, I mean, but I guess that it was not as irritating as every couple of hours was. I was letting my anger get the best of me. I realized it, and quickly calmed myself.

"Ok, I will be right here when you get back I'm sure." I said back trying not to sound angry or maybe even a tad upset. I could tell he sensed my mood but he didn't say anything else.

I watched him walk away and disappear behind a building. The same time that he disappeared there, she was across the street walking in the opposite direction as earlier. I didn't hesitate this time I jumped to my feet and raced to her but not too fast I really didn't want any gawkers. I approached her from the side.

"Hi Sam I have been expecting you." She said. This took me by surprise, how did she know my name.

"Yes I know it took me a little longer to get here than I wanted but I made it." I said back to her.

"You will be wise to keep your distance I do know what you are and I do know how to kill you." She said with contempt and sternness in her voice.

Ok this was starting to get creepy even for a vampire. She knew my name, what I was and how to kill me if need be. Who the hell was she? Or better yet, what was she?

"You must walk with me. Don't worry about your friend he will be fine without you for a little bit." She said with utmost certainty.

My curiosity got the better of me and I wanted to know the answers to my questions. "Can I ask you a question?" I asked shyly not really knowing what her reply would be.

"Sure." She replied with a smirk on her face.

I think she knew what I was going to ask. I hesitated not sure, if I should even ask now but I really wanted to know the answer. "How do you know about me?"

"Well I talk to spirits all the time and a man came to me his name was Jaxson I think. That is all I will tell you right now there are too may ears on the streets." She looked around wildly for a minute to make sure no one had heard what she said.

Jaxson had cared enough about me to set this whole thing up for me. Thank you Jaxson I said in my head. We kept walking and walking which seemed like forever but it really was only three blocks down the street then to the right. One more block down there on the right hand side of the road was her house. The exterior was blue with bright purple shutters. As we walked up to the door there were some weird things like broken glass hung on strings around the porch. The welcome mat had some kind of symbol on it and there were some grass like things hanging in every window. She pushed the door open and it squeaked very loudly. I wanted to cover my ears but decided that would be rude.

"I'm letting you into my home, I still know how to kill you and I will not hesitate."

She reminded me.

"Jaxson said that you were good spirited and that you would not hurt me but I don't trust any blood sucking demon." She said as a matter of fact.

Wow, that was a little harsh I thought but I didn't say anything. We walked to the back of the house where she sat down in a chair at the kitchen table. She gestured for me to sit down across from her. I slowly pulled out the chair and sat down. As soon as I was seated, she began.

"Sam, I know why you are here and I know what you are seeking from me. What I'm going to give you is very powerful and should not and will not be used to do bad. I will hunt you down and kill you if you do not use what I'm about to give you the way that I tell you too. I know that your brother is in grave danger and that they will kill him to get to you. I can't guarantee that you will be able to save him though because It depends on how strong you are. I don't mean physically I mean mentally. You must know that you are going to have to fight these other demons in the spirit world. You will also need people that you trust on the other side that will protect your body but also be able to kill your body if something goes wrong. You must be balanced if you sway there way for too long you will die they will kill your spirit and take your body as a trophy.

This is extremely dangerous!" She said with a very serious tone to her voice.

I waited for a moment for all that, she had just dealt me to sink into my head before I said anything.

"I can do this for the love of my brother and all things good." I said thinking that is what she wanted to here.

"That is a start but the love of your brother could faultier, then you have nothing to keep you from swaying to one side. Jaxson told me about his death. He also told me that it should have been your brother and not him that was killed.

"What about Aidan he is my rock he has been there for me through this adventure." I say, grasping at straws, trying to come up with something that makes sense.

She retorts with. "Are you going to be able to rely on someone that you barely know to pull you through this?" She crosses her arms in front of herself waiting for me to come up with something.

I was running out of people that I knew. Ted, Erik and Shannon who at the moment are extremely mad at me for disappearing. Not to mention after what happened would they have my back? Things were starting to look grim for me every team member that I could think of could be my greatest down fall. The only person or vampire that was left was me. In that instant I knew that, it didn't matter about the people around me it mattered about me.

"Me, me, me for the love of myself" I said starting at a whisper and gradually getting louder. "That is the only answer ME I have to be strong enough within myself to not let them get inside my head and stick to what I know."

"Bingo, you got it the only person that you have right now is you and you have to be the one. This is what you have to know no one but you can do this it has to be you." She rose from her chair and motioned for me to come with her. She opened a door that lead to another room. We walked in the room and she motioned for me to sit down in a chair as she walked across the room to a cabinet made out of wood. It appeared to be very old; the wood was faded to grayish brown color. She opened the door and pulled two things out. She kept her hands tightly around the two objects, went, and sat in an overstuffed chair on the far side of the room from me. I started the conversation this time

"What can I give you in return for what you are going to give me?" I shyly asked. Knowing that I didn't have any money or anything else of value.

"I'm not asking for anything I just want you to be safe." She said in a soft voice.

I knew that I needed to give her something. It just didn't feel right. My Parents had always taught me that nothing is free. "I don't have money or anything that would help you out in the human world but I do have the gift of forever." I said very slowly not sure that I should offer this to her but it was worth a try.

She eyed me speculatively for a second. "No, I do not wish for eternity." She said. She sounded somewhat sad. Almost like, she did want it but not right now.

I noticed an empty bottle sitting by her. It was a small bottle but it was very pretty it looked like an old perfume bottle. It was shaped like a trapezoid and had a very cute girl figure on the stopper. I slowly walked over to her, grabbed the bottle, and pretended as if I was admiring it. I pulled the top off expecting a perfume smell to emanate from it but there was no smell. It was just an empty bottle maybe it never had anything in it. I didn't think twice and I bit into my wrist wow did that hurt. Nothing ever had hurt me before but apparently biting myself does. I held my wrist over the bottle and let the bottle fill full of my blood. I put the lid on it and handed it to her.

"If you ever change your mind, all you have to do is drink this. But if you never change your mind and you are in the process of dying please, please, please find someone suitable for my blood or if I should die please find someone like me but with maybe less problems and change them for me." I said and I abruptly turned as the tears were coming.

"You don't have to do that. I really don't want anything to do with vampires let alone make one." She said to me

"Ok well let's just make this my dying wish." I said trying to make her take it and not say another word about it.

"Ok Sam, now here is what you must do and I can't stress enough that you have to do right. I'm giving you two vials one has to be given to your brother the other you have to take. This will let your spirit out of your body. So when you get to this point you are going to see your brother and the invading spirit. Now once everyone is in perspective you are going to have to fight for him. You are going to have to kill the other spirits if you fail and do not kill the other spirits the spirits will kill your brother and then you and take over your body and the fire touch."

As she finished talking, she handed me the vials. I took them and looked at them in my hand. I just stared at them. She went on to say.

"Oh and guard that with your life if anyone gets a hold of it they will possess the power to destroy anything they want to. Now onto the next bottle, this has to be given to the other vampire's bodies before you enter the spirit realm. What this does is trap the spirit in your brother and there is no way out for them." She handed me the bottle.

Feeling overwhelmed I went back to the chair, sat, and studied the bottle for a moment along with the vials. One vile was red this was the one that I was supposed to take. The other vile was blue and that one was for my brother. Then the clear bottle was for the other vampire bodies.

"You seem to know a lot about the spirit world do I stand a chance of winning this battle?" I asked not lifting my gaze from the bottle and vials that I held in my hands. My hands were shaking I was a little scared of what she was going to say. I let one tear rolled down my face and drip a red spot on my hand.

"I would not have agreed to help if I knew that you were going to fail." She said trying to build my confidence.

I was not sure if she really had the answer. Something else popped into my head though. It was something she had said previously. I just had to know how she knew.

"How did you know about the fire touch? I mean Jaxson didn't even know about it." I asked. I stared at her waiting for her answer.

"I see a lot of things, Jaxson didn't have to tell me, I have seen it in a vision that is one hell of a gift and I also have seen that you have used it when it was necessary. I have been watching you for a long time now, well at least sense I first met Jaxson some time ago." She said staring back into my eyes and I could not find fault in her statement. "Does he come to you?" She asked me.

"No, not really the last time I talked to him he was happy with his spirit life and had a woman that he loved more than he ever loved me. That is how I found out about you." I said hastily, not really wanting to talk to a stranger about it.

"Yes that is true but he still cares what happens to you." She said.

"How do you know all this stuff? I mean how did you learn it? I mean how to communicate with the dead or undead?" I asked this time.

"It came to me when I was a little girl, you see everyone needs help once in a while dead, alive, spirit or even the undead and that is what I do. On another subject Aidan is the right choice for you he is loving and kind and you will have the life that you dreamed of with him. He loves you too but I must tell you he is scared that you are going to reject him again and if you do, he will be lost forever. So you must make sure he knows that you love him more than your own life. He is also the key to getting your brother to drink his vial.

Now you must go, he is starting to worry about you. You can always come back any time that you would like too I'm sure that I will be seeing you again. It is not in the cards for you to die just yet." She said.

I put the bottles in my pockets and started for the door.

"Umm… one more thing before I go, make sure you take care of that" I said and point to the blood. "Maybe use it someday. And one other thing please don't be afraid to contact me if you need me, if I make it through this that is." I said as I paused with my hand on the door handle.

"You will be fine. Good bye see you soon." She said.

I took one last look around at this room and walked out the door, and whispered a faint. "Good bye."

I walked out to the street and back to where I knew Aidan would be waiting for me. I sucked in a deep breath before turning the last corner around the building and suppressed all of the feelings of doubt that I had in myself I knew that no matter what I had to be strong and make this work.

She was right Aidan was pacing back and forth waiting for me, with the look of worry on his face. When he turned the last time and seen me standing across the street a smile lit up his face, he was truly happy to see me. The next thing I knew his arms were around me.

"I thought that you might have left me or something happened to you. I was getting ready to start looking for you." He started rambling and I hushed him with a kiss.

"Oh Aidan don't worry I'm here now. The Lady came back as soon as you rounded the corner in search of food. So, you know that I had to follow her. I have a lot to tell you but here is not the place to talk about it. We need to get going anyway. On the way back I want to take our time a little bit, we have to fortify a plan that is solid and fool proof. We only get one chance at this."

I grabbed his hand and he grabbed mine. We started walking out of the city and back to the forest were we could run and be free of the public eye. Even though we were running, I still wanted to take our time because even though the lady said that I would make it I still was unsure and I wanted to spend as much time as I could with Aidan before I embarked on the looming events ahead of me. As soon as I was comfortable and were we were deep in the forest were no one ventured I slowed my pace. As I came to a stop by a stream so did Aidan. He changed from Wolf to human.

"What are you doing?" Aidan said, sounding extremely nervous.

"Aidan I… I need to talk to you." I said having a hard time getting the words out. I knew what I had to tell him and it was not going to be easy for him to swallow.

I spotted the perfect place to sit. An old fallen log that looked as if it had been used as a bench before.

"Aidan this is going to be very risky for everyone involved. There is a chance that I might not make it back to you and I need you to know that I love you with all I have. I have loved you since the day I met you but I was too afraid that I could not live up to your expectations and Jaxson was holding me back. Aidan I want to make a life with you, I want to be your one and only and I want you to be my one and only." As I said these words to him a few tears ran down my face.

He put his arms around me and whispered in my ear. "Sam, I want the same thing's and I see now that you truly love me. I was a little scared that you would change your mind and I just did not want to get hurt again. Sam will you marry me? I know it is so sudden and if you need time to think about it than take your time." He said and I think my mouth fell open in shock. But I quickly gathered myself.

"No Aidan, I don't need time. Yes I will marry you and it is truly what I want." I said through my tears of joy.

"Sam you made me the happiest man alive." He scooped me up in a bear hug and kissed me.

We both cried a little bit there in the moon light and shared more kisses of our new life together. As my lips touched, his it was tiny electric shock running through my body. The closer I got to him the more I loved him with every breath in and out.

"Do you think we could rest for a little while? I'm exhausted." He asked.

"Sure." I simply said.

CHAPTER 19

I sunk down to the ground resting my back against the tree that we had been sitting on. He changed to wolf and curled up into a ball under a pine tree. He was so amazing to watch in either wolf or human form. I sat there and stared at him for a long time, will at least until I felt it was rude to stare. I closed my eyes and let the musical sounds of the forest fill my head. The babbling stream, the slight breeze through the trees rustling the leaves, the song of a song bird in the distance everything was in place now all I had to do was kill some spirits and get out without killing myself or someone else. My mind went over and over what the lady had said. I first had to find the bodies of the spirits. Then I had to make their bodies drink the potion in the bottle. Then I needed people around my body that would not hesitate to kill me. My brother then needs to drink his vial and I needed to drink mine. Then I had to fight for my life and my brother. This was the thing I was scared of the most. What if I lose and they get my body what would they do with it? Of course, the lady had already told me that they would have the power. But, would they use it for evil? I too already knew the answer to this as well, and the answer was yes. I'm sure they would rule the world somehow but what were they going to do burn everything to the ground humans included. Then I thought about other people that I knew and Mike that gave us a ride. What about all the other vampires I wondered? If I didn't make it they would surly suffer, like the story that Erik told. I had one chance at this. My mind flashed back to what she said; only you can win. Why was I the only one that could go in? As my mind kept wandering through the many facets of why, how come and what if's. I heard a noise; a branch breaking in the distance, my eyes snapped open and I took in a deep breath. I smelled humans but what were they doing this deep into the forest. They must be lost I thought but then I could smell something else as well. It didn't smell human, vampire or werewolf. I could not pin point what the smell was. I panicked and immediately knelt down beside Aidan and whispered in his ear.

"Aidan we have to go there is something out here."

His eyes snapped open and he was instantly to his feet with his nose to the wind. He looked at me and turned in the opposite direction and we started to run. I knew he could smell the human but also knew he could smell whatever else was with the humans. I don't think he knew the other scent either judging by the way he immediately started to run. We were not trying to stick around and find out either. We ran far enough that neither one of us could smell it anymore and stopped and Aidan could change to human.

"Have you ever smelt that before?" He asked me his eyes wildly looking around.

"No but it seemed as though it was trying to cover its own scent with the humans scent." I said pausing listing intently for any signs of movement. "I think we are safe now if you want to try and go back to sleep."

"No, sweetie I'm ok for now. How about we just walk and talk for a while beside you need to tell me what the lady said." He said and reached for my hand. I took his and proceeded to tell him the whole story without leaving anything out.

"We need to make a plan and everything has to go right on all accounts or I, (I choked on the words.) or well die." I said ending all that I needed to tell him. "You don't happen to know where they might have stashed the Cloaks bodies do you?" I asked trying to make light of the situation.

"No I wish I did though. That would be so helpful. We are going to need help we need to get Ted, Erik and Shannon on our side. But, we need to make it clear that we have to do things our way but there too lies a problem they don't really care what happens to you they only care about their plans for the future. So maybe we need to make new friends that we know would stand with us and not for their own purposes." He said tying to help.

The truth is though we do not really have anyone else that I knew. How could we trust people we didn't know to do the right thing.

"I really don't know anyone that I can trust at this point. I don't know how deep they have gotten there hooks into the rest of the pack. Sam this is going to be very tricky to pull this off." He said mirroring the questions in my mind.

"I know that is why I'm not in a hurry to get back there yet and I want to spend as much time with you as possible. If I'm going to die I want to die happy." I say trying to fight off the tears that were coming.

"But you're not going to die! You can't you have too much life to give yet." He broke down in tears and started crying as he realized that there was a real danger that I could die. I wrapped my arms around him and just held him close. We sank to the ground and leaned into each other with our arms wrapped tightly around each other. We cried for a few minutes and I pulled us together.

"Sweetie everything is going to be ok though as long as the fool proof plans that we are working on works." I said and pulled his face to mine and kissed him. He kissed me back and refused to let me go. My whole body felt tingly. I was ready and so was he. The sensations of his kisses and hands on my body lasted for hours, as he lay sleeping. I cuddled up on his chest and in that moment I realized that, I had to make it through this somehow someway I have come too far to give up now. As Aidan slept, I made no attempt to lay out any plans for the upcoming battle the only thing my mind could concentrate on right now was a house with a white picket fence a little girl standing in the middle of the green grass. This little girl had the face of a doll with red curly hair. Not just any red but her hair looked like a beautiful red rose that bloomed on her head. Then there was the wedding. I could see myself standing there in front of my brother and all of the wolves plus Ted, Erik and Shannon. I would be standing there in a Beautiful white satin gown that hugged my hourglass shape in all the right places, and only revealing a little bit of skin. The gown was mostly plain with just a few accent pearls and some sequence nothing extravagant. We were holding hands and the minister said I now pronounce you man and wife you may kiss the bride. As we kissed, everyone erupted into cheers. Then there was the wedding night if he was not too tired but lying in an actual bed would be great. Then we could move on to our life I think that I would like to go to school so that I can get a good job and make money so that we could have a house, cars and anything else we wanted. Of course, there was the alternative to working and that was just killing or threating someone within inch of their life to get what we wanted but I did not want to be that monster I wanted to do stuff like regular people live like regular people. As I lay there with all of these thoughts in my head, I knew what I wanted out of this life now and I was going to do whatever it was going to take to make it thru this and come out on top. I wasn't doing it for my brother, Aidan or anyone else for that matter it all boiled down to me I was doing it for me. The future was mine and mine alone and I was going to make this dream come true. This also too gave me inner peace and I knew that I was undoubtedly happy with myself.

Aidan started to shift under me and I knew that he would be waking up soon this too made me happy. I watched as his eyes fluttered open and closed a couple of times. Then he looked at me and smiled. I returned his smile. He pulled me in close again and just held me there for a few moments.

"I thought that I might have been dreaming about last night but nope it was real. Sam I love you." He said, whispering.

"Oh Aidan, I love you too." I exclaimed, I was happy about everything right now.

As we laid there watching the first rays of light hit the ground and feeling the warmth of the sun on our faces we knew that it was time to get moving but neither one of us wanted to move.

"Aidan we must get going we have to get to Ted and Erik they must help us if this is going to work." I said after a short period of time.

"I know but I really don't want to give this moment up I want to stay right here forever and not worry about the future right now. I want to be selfish and keep you with me safe and sound. But I know that they will find us eventually and we can't run forever." He said and you could hear the sincerity in his voice.

Just then to lighten the mood Aidan stomach growled. I giggled at the sound.

"Ok well I guess my stomach is telling me it is time to get going. How are you doing on needing something to drink?" He asked giggling to himself.

"I'm good right now but by tonight I may need some." I said concealing my giggles. I was thinking it was kind of funny to me neither one of us would say blood nor human to drink, giggles erupting inside my head. I helped him to his feet and we were off running towards the next town.

We reached town, got Aidan something to eat, and kept going in the direction of Erik's house. We were lost in this vast forest coming across small town here and there but nothing had smelt familiar yet. However, we soon got our first smell of the familiar city where Ted and I climbed the huge building and sat on top. Therefore, I knew that we were getting close and we didn't have too much more time together. Not quite wanting to let go of the last few days I decided to be selfish for one more night.

"Aidan, I really would like to stay here for the night. I want one more night to spend with you before, well you know." I said not wanting to say anything more than that. Most importantly I didn't want to upset the mood.

"Sam, I'm going to be honest here I don't really want to go back at all. I finally found the women of my dreams and want to be with her forever. I would love to spend another night with you. In fact, Sam he said as he got down on one knee. I love you, I want to be with you forever, and I know now that you feel the same way about me. So Samantha will you marry me tonight, right now?" He asked.

My mind blanked out for a second from shock of his words. It took me a minute to get my voice to respond to answer yes to him. I had been waiting for this moment for few hundred years and now it has finally happened. But, in the same moment of sunshine there was the ominous dark cloud hanging in the distance just waiting for the chance to rain on a wonderful day.

"Aidan are you sure you want to do this right now? I mean what if things don't go so good and the outcome is not good?" I said, my rational mind screaming yes just do it.

"Sam, you have to believe in yourself that things are going to go right and that everything is going to work out perfect. That is what I believe and nothing or no one is going to stop it." He said with confidence and a faint smile playing on his lips. His faint smile turned into a huge smile. And he said. "So what do you say, I know a person that would marry us right now." He looked like a Cheshire cat grinning ear to ear. I saw a hint of worry in his eyes. Worried that I'm going to say no.

"Ok let's do it." I said. He grabbed my hand and led us to his friend.

When we arrived the house was quiet. There porch light was on and one of the lights in the house shown through the window. The light shining through the window was very dim and appeared that it could have been a night light. Aidan knocked softly on the door. A man about six foot tall, sandy blond hair and blue eyes answered the door sleepily. However, his sleepiness gave way to excitement when he saw who it was.

"Aidan it has been years since I saw you last, what can I do for you?" The man asked.

"Well Jim I need you to officially marry us right now." He said and pulled me up to meet Jim. Jim had not noticed me before this.

"What the rush is she pregnant or something?" He said, making a joke out of the situation. Aidan let out a bellowing laugh and I just stared at the floor because I did not think it was funny.

"No nothing like that we just want to get married right now." He said after the laughter died down.

"Ok well do you want to do it right here or would you like to at least stand in the backyard?" Jim asked.

"Nope right here is fine." Aidan said.

I nodded in agreement. Jim said some words but I was only half listening it was like I was in some kind of sped up dream. Everything was moving so fast that my mind almost could not comprehend the fact that I was getting married. The next thing I knew Jim asked me do you take this man. Without hesitation, I answered yes. The next words that I heard was I now pronounce you husband and wife you may kiss your bride. Aidan pulled me in close and wrapped his arms around. Our lips touched and tingles ran up and down my spine. He released me all too soon, took my hand, and led me away from Jim and the scene of his front porch. When we were out of sight of every one, he pulled me in close again and kissed me.

"So how does it fell to be Mrs. Aidan Fox?" He asked.

The name took me by surprise because before this moment I never knew his last name or rather my last name.

It took me a short second to reply. "Good," is all I could manage to say.

He took my hand again and we walked for a little while not saying much of anything to each other. The day was wearing on me and I was coming to grips with the fact that my last name was that of the man that I loved and adored. As I settled into my new name and things started to come back to reality a bit. The more that it became real in my mind the more I realized that I wanted this more than anything. This is what I had been dreaming of for years upon years.

I pulled Aidan to a stop and turned to face him as my emotions took over. "Aidan I love you, I know that we just got married but I was wondering if we make it through this can we do a real wedding with family and friends?" I asked not sure what he would say but I really wanted to make this official to my brother (if I could save him) and his werewolf pack. I wanted a real wedding where I was dressed in white and walked down the aisle.

"Oh course anything that you want is yours. I love you more than you will ever realize." He paused as tears welled up in his eyes. "It is tearing me apart that we have this impending battle and there is nothing I can do to help you I wish I could take your place." He said. He pulled me in close and tucked me into his chest. I think he was trying to hide his tears but I could feel them drip into my hair.

"Aidan, please honey, let's not talk about that right now we have a whole day to our self's and that is it. Tomorrow is going to be back to reality." I said trying to get him to stop crying.

He held me for a few more moments; he sighed and gathered his tears, then said.

"Ok Mrs. Fox what would you like to do today?"

"Well, Mr. Fox, I would love to consummate our marriage with you, maybe all day." I said and smiled a devilish smile at him.

"Well, Mrs. Fox, I'm young and strong but I'm not quite as strong as you. I do not have the endurance that you have. Besides, aren't you getting hungry? I know I need some food before that takes place. I'm starving." He said, even though his expression said come on let us do it right here and now. I think he was also trying to be funny so I giggled a little at his reply.

"Well Mr. Fox I think we should get you something to eat then. I wouldn't want to starve you to death." I said through more giggles.

He reached for my hands and pulled me close to him. He leaned in for a kiss and I tilted my head back and closed my eyes.

CHAPTER 20

In town, I found a man that was walking down an alley and decided that he would be the blood donor tonight. I attacked him and drank him dry then took his wallet and took all the money that was in it. This was a new one for me because I normally did not care about the money, just the drink. I had Aidan now though and he deserved not to have to eat out of a garbage can. We walked to the nearest place to eat went in and sat down in a booth next to a window. Both of us sitting on the same side, in cozy little corner of the dinner. Aidan picked up the menu and began perusing through it. I watched as the waitress ran around in circles getting people there food, drinks and the bill. The waitress came over to take Aidan's order. She started hitting on him and I did not like it at all. I was ready to end her but something inside me said no you do not want to do that.

I settled for saying "Could you please stop flirting with my husband?" I said in a very angry voice. She must had got the hint because she got huffy and walked away from the table.

"What was that all about?" Aidan asked me when she left.

"I didn't appreciate her flirting with you. If I had my way she would have had her throat ripped out." I said defensively and playful at the same time.

"I like the fact that you chose the non-violent route, I'm so proud." He said in a joking tone. Then we both laughed and shared a kiss.

As we waited for his food, I watch out the window as the people of the town walked up and down the streets. It was perplexing to me, that they did not even know that they all could be in danger of a vampire lurking. Just waiting for the right moment to lure them in and kill them before they even had a chance.

A tiny movement across the road caught my attention. In the dark shadows of an alley between two five story building and a place where the morning sun had not touched yet. I caught a glimpse of the man that I had run into before the dark cloaked man. I think that he may have recognized me as well because I saw him stretch out one hand and beckon to me. Not taking my eyes off him for even a second, I said.

"Aidan I think that we need to get your food to go and get as far away from here as possible."

"Sam, what do you mean? Is this a…" He said, he must have noticed that I was not looking at him as he trailed off.

"Look over here in this direction that I'm looking in." I said without pointing at him.

"Oh I see, and who is that?" Aidan asked, but he had no emotions attached to his voice.

"I ran into him a while back with Ted, Erik and Shannon. I am not sure that I trust him. He wants me to come over there but I think that would be a mistake." I say still not taking my eyes off him.

"Ok let me get my food and pay for it." He says and I hear him call the waitress and tell her that he needs his food to go and the bill.

I was still watching the man as Aidan got his food and paid. We exited the dinner and started to walk in the opposite direction of the man. As we walked, I could feel the cloaked man's presents behind us and this made me tense. I knew what I had to do.

"Aidan, whatever happens run far away from here and never look back, I love you." I said then I planted my feet on the sidewalk and turned to face the man. I stood in front of Aidan and put him as far behind me as possible.

"What do you want?" I said with a growl letting him know that I was not afraid to kill him.

"Well there is something that you should know and I think that it would be best not to talk about it here on the street." He said in a non-threating tone.

"How do I know that this is not some kind of trick?" I growled back at him.

"You don't, but I know about what is going on and have some advice for you." He said and offered his hand for me to take.

"I have all the advice that I need thank you." I spat back at him then I started to walk backwards to-wards Aidan not taking my eyes off of him. He made no effort to come towards me. Then he said.

"Ok well I guess you are not interested in find-ing the Cloaks then."

Then he turned and started to walk away I knew that this is something that I needed to know and I hoped that I was not making a mistake in saying "ok you have my attention, what do you know?"

"Come let's talk. He can come too you have my word that I will not hurt either of you." He said then he turned and started walking back towards the alley.

We followed a few paces behind him. He led us to an abandoned building and he went inside. I hesitated for a moment thinking about how much danger that I had just put Aidan and I in.

"Maybe you should wait here?" I turned to face Aidan. He had no hint of doubt or fear on his face or fear.

"No we are a team wherever you go I go." He retorted and I knew that he was not going to let me do this by myself.

"If something happens I don't know if I will be able to protect you." I said.

"Sam, nothing is going to happen everything will be fine besides I think I can hold my own pretty well." He said back to me, eying me speculatively, and then he said. "I am wolf remember, I could tear you to shreds if I wanted to."

I pulled him in close, gave him a kiss, and turned and walked into the building, with Aidan right behind me. Fear was swelling up in my throat and my veins started to burn. Come on Sam keep it together everything is going to be fine. I said over and over again in my head. As we approached the top of the stairs, the man was standing there.

"I thought you might have changed your mind." He said with a crooked grin. He led us down the hallway to a door and he pushed it open.

"Please come in." He said

"Is this were you live?" I asked trying to make small chatter while I assessed the situation.

"Yes this has been my home for a few years now." He replied, and then gestured towards a table and chairs for us to sit at. The table was nothing more than a metal frame with a square board on top. The chairs were made of wood and creaked under our weight.

Once we all were seated, he said. "I brought you here for a couple of reasons. First and foremost you, know they are worried about you. They really do not care why you left they just want you back. Secondly I know where to find the Cloaks."

"Can I ask you a question? How did you know that I was looking for the Cloaks?" I asked not hesitating.

"When I talked to Erik he told me that he thought that you might have gone after them. I do not really care where you went or why. I am not interested in that. The only thing that I am interested in is defeating the Cloaks. If they win, the battle then that will mean that the world as we know it will come to an end. The elders would have finally taken over here and we would have to abide by their rules. Sam, you are the only hope of the vampire world right now. If you fail then the rest of us will be enslaved to the elders. Some of us possibly eliminated if we do not follow their rule. I have waited a long time for this to happen when we could finally be free from the elders and not have to worry about when they are going to come. Now the reason that I brought you here is to talk about the Cloaks. They are in hiding waiting for you to come back. They know that they have something that you want back so they are waiting for you. In my scouts of the area, I have found one of them sitting by a tree on the far side of the park. From what I could tell, it did not move but I did not get close enough to it to see why. Nevertheless, it has been sitting there for weeks now, in the same position every day. The other two I have not found yet but will soon. But I have watched enough to know that there is a pattern. Two wolfs are always around only when the lone wolf is gone. I have also noticed that the one lone wolf comes every day and will lie down beside it and sleep. But the patterns are irregular with no rhyme or reason. I think they are protecting it but I really am baffled as to why it just sits there."

I glance over at Aidan. I wanted to see if he had any input. He just blankly stared back at me not giving anything away. I knew now that I had them right where I wanted them. I also knew that the wolves were guarding the body. The only problem that I saw right now was that we did not know where the other ones were.

"So how do you think we can find the other Cloaks?" I ask trying to give myself a little time to formulate the plan.

"I'm not sure." He replied.

"Do you think that you could help us out and find the other two Cloaks? I have to know where all of them are to make my plan work." I say, not giving away any details of the plan just yet.

"Yeah, I think I can help find them." He said, as a look of determination crossed his face.

"I know that this may seem a little rude but I don't remember your name. Oh, and I apologize for trying to kill you last time." I say trying to lighten the mood a bit.

"Apology accepted. My name is Scott." He said with a smirk and a little bit of laughter.

"Scott this is Aidan." I said and gestured to Aidan with my hand. I wanted to introduce Aidan as my husband but decided that was better left for some other time. He nodded towards Aidan and politely smiled. "Well Scott we should get going I really need to get back to Ted, Erik and Shannon." I said but this really was not my plan tonight anyway.

"Sam, I have some more news to tell you, Ted took off after you. The last I heard the wolves captured him. I heard that he may be somewhere in the park but don't know where." Scott said

This was not good news for me this complicated things a little. However, this was just a slight kink in the plans. The more I knew how to find the Cloaks the better off I was going to be. Besides, I was not really a fan of Ted but I did not wish him harm. However, with Ted not around I needed to make some kind of attempt at a partnership.

"Scott I know that we are all fighting for the right to be free. I am trusting and hoping that you will help me with this fight." I said and I eyed him for any hint of weariness. There was nothing in his face that said he would run from the fight.

Without hesitation, he said. "Of course I will and it would be an honor to fight with someone that has your talent. I am going to assemble a small army to help take them down in two days' time. If you know or find anyone that will help that would be a plus."

He was already planning war with them. This was astounding and heart wrenching to hear. I never thought in a million years that other vampires would try an upheaval against the Cloaks. I almost felt sorry for them because without the stuff in my pocket and me they would lose. They all would die. My hand rested over the pocket with the bottle and vials in it. I must have been deep in thought because when Scott cleared his throat it startled me a bit.

"Scott it is very important that I know were the other two Cloaks are I need to know this information ASAP. I will be staying at Erik's and Shannon's house where we should be safe. I said emphasizing the words most important, Two Cloaks, need to know, and ASAP.

"I'm on it and I should have some answers for you by tomorrow evening." He replied back immediately.

"We are going to get going and let you work." I say wanting to get away from all this for a little while. I also wanted to be alone with Aidan.

"You and your husband can stay here if you would like while I'm gone." He said with a shit-eating grin on his face.

I think my jaw hit the floor and it took me a minute to pick it up off the floor.

"How did you know?" I said slowly still flabbergasted that he knew.

"I hear and see a lot of thing. But don't worry I won't say anything to anyone." He said with a reassuring smile.

"Thank you, I will tell everyone but not until it is over." I say still trying to figure out how he knew.

"Well then I will see you tomorrow evening. You kids have fun." He said with a snicker then he was gone.

"Well are you ready to go?" Aidan asked me.

"Yeah let's go I don't want to spend the night here. I was hoping for something a little more romantic than an old dirty abandoned place with no bed or anything for my husband to sleep on." I said and gave him a smile and he returned my smile with a kiss.

The words husband still sounded a little funny inside my head. I knew that it would take some getting used to. He grabbed my hand and led us out of the building. We found a secluded place away from everyone and untouchable by humans. We laid under the stars on a blanket that we had grabbed off of a close line. We did consummate our marriage and it was the most wonderful feelings that I have ever experienced. Aidan was so tired that he fell asleep in the middle of me talking to him. I watched the stars curled up next to his naked body. I was so tempting to touch him all over and wake him up for another round but I decided to let him sleep. The time seemed to fly by and the next thing I knew the sun was coming up. I watched the sunrise in the sky and it began to beat down on Aidan. He started stirring beside me.

"Aidan sweetheart we need to get going." I said, rubbing on him and trying to coerce him to open his eyes. I could see he was fighting it though even though the sun was hot.

"No, no please lay with me for a few minutes more." He said and grabbed my hand and locked his fingers with mine.

I held still not wanting to go either but I knew that we also needed to get to Erik and Shannon's. We need to get there soon too because I need to make amends with them before we could keep going forward with the plan. We lay there only for a few minutes more really just long enough for Aidan to finish waking up. We slowly got to our feet, put on our clothing, and started in the direction of Erik and Shannon's house. We were leaving all peace and happiness behind knowing that I had a dangerous job to do, one that if I screw up everyone will die including Aiden. Ever since the day that I talked to that Voodoo lady, I knew these final days were coming. The waves of fear would wash through me time and time again but I put on a front for Aiden's sake so that he would not know of my emotional state except for happiness. Honestly, I guess I did this because I wanted him to remember me this way. If I had to tell the truth, I was scared to death that I was going to fail. I was really feeling it now because in less than twenty-four hours I would either die or live.

As we walked, we held hands and talked about the weather, which was sunny with a few puffy white clouds here and there. The closer we got to the house the more nervous I got. I was about to break and I knew I needed a distraction. I pulled on Aiden's hand and spun him towards me. I locked my lips with his and held him close I think he may have complained a little bit about not being able to breath.

"Aiden no matter what happens now just know that I love you very much." I say with my lips still on his.

"And I love you too. Nothing is going to change that." He said back through my lips.

My heart melted a little bit and I wanted to say let us just move away and never come back and hopefully this whole thing would sort it's self out. However, I knew that was not an option. I was content to stay right here and never let him go, but he grabbed my hand and pulled me towards that house. As we broke from the forest that surrounded the house the tension inside me grew.

"Aiden I…" I started to say but he cut me off.

"It will be fine."

We approached the stairs and the door but something felt odd to me. They had to know that I was here and I half expected to be greeted on the lawn.

"Aiden something feels wrong. We should go." I said and started to pull him away from the door but I was too late. The door flew open to reveal Shannon standing there. Something was wrong though she looked worried and scared. It seemed like she wanted to say something but did not. So, I started.

"Shannon, I'm…" I trailed off as I noticed a person that I did not recognize in the background. I grabbed Aiden's hand and pulled him behind me slightly. Shannon realized my gaze and looked over my shoulder but she was not looking at Aiden she was looking behind him. I snapped my head back to see what she was looking at and there on the edge of the forest was a wolf.

"Aiden we have to go it is a trap!"

Aiden immediately shifted to wolf form. I heard a bark behind me and knew that we did not have much time to make a break for it. As I jumped down from the porch I looked, left then to my right looking for an escape but everywhere I looked there was a wolf. I jumped to the roof quickly and came to the realization that we were surrounded. I jumped back to Aiden's side and gave him the bad news. Aiden this is not how it is supposed to happen. Just then as if an angel sent from heaven I seen Scott then I saw others slowly creeping up behind the wolves. When the wolves realized that, they were starting to be out numbered they turned and ran. The only remaining problem was who was in the house. As I turned and peered through the door there in the mirror, I could see a face that was very familiar to me and I knew that I could not go in. It was my brother sitting in Erik's chair. I turned to Aiden.

"He is in there… we must go."

I took one last glance at the face in the mirror and as I did, he must have noticed because his head snapped up and looked back at me through the mirror. For the first time seeing him in human form sense this all started, I seen his eyes were blood red. For me being a vampire and not scaring very easy, this however, scared me far worse than anything did so far. The fire that burned behind those eyes were filled with so much hate, they were not the eyes that used to be enchanting to me they were the eyes of a mindless killer. Aiden nudged me just then to get my attention. He knew what I was seeing and knew that he needed to get me out of here. This was not the plan, and we needed to stick to the plan. Scott was now on the edge of the forest and gestured to us to follow him. I turned and glanced back through the mirror and those eyes not of my brother but something else were still peering back at me. I turned away from them and Aiden and I ran to Scott.

"Did you know about this?" I asked Scott but he did not answer he just turned and started running into the forest. As we ran, the other vampires fell in behind us one by one. I caught up with Scott and asked again.

"Scott, did you know about that?" I asked cool and calm this time.

"Yeah, I knew about it. I have been watching and shortly after you left they took over the house and everyone in it." He said trying to sound nonchalant.

"Why didn't you tell me? We could have been killed!" I spat back at him. I was furious with him. He had better have a good reason why he sent me into danger I thought or I will kill him right here and now.

"Sam, I wanted you to see what you are fighting for, and if I would have told you, you would not have gone there." He said.

"Your right that could have been suicide for us, if that would have gone poorly the whole world now would be in danger." I spat back at him still heated.

"Sam, I assure you I knew the risk, but I need the distraction." He said and this cooled me down a bit.

"Ok well please don't do that again you could have compromised everything." I said with a hint of madness still playing with the edge of my words.

I could feel the eyes upon me staring at me as if they were waiting for a speech of some kind. I glanced at Aidan and he met my gaze and shrugged his shoulders. I collected my thoughts and turned to face the waiting crowd of vampires.

"Um…I'm not sure what I should or should not tell you. Some of this battle is mental and some is going to be physical." I said took a breath and one of the vampires saved me by saying.

"We don't need specifics of how that battle is fought we just need to know what each one of us should do." The crowd agreed.

"Well ok then I will let you know after I have a talk with these two men and we get a strategy together." I said and pointed at Aidan and Scott.

"What about the wolf how do we know that he is not a spy for the other side?" Another vampire spoke up and was eying Aidan like he was a trader.

"Um… ok that is kind of complicated…" I trailed off not sure what to say when Aidan said.

"We are married and I would never betray my wife no matter what the cost. Some of the women vampires sighed and the men groaned. As no other question came, I turned to Scott.

"Well let's talk about the strategy and how they can help the cause. Oh and Scott I need to tell you everything about this this time." I said and gave him a small I am sorry smirk.

I picked a site away from the other vampires so that they could not hear all the details that they did not need to be burdened with.

"First and foremost do you know where the other two Cloaks are?" I asked before saying anything else.

"Yes one lies to the northeast of the first one and the other one is to the southeast forming a triangle." He said.

I was satisfied with his answer and started the story about what Jaxson had told me to do. As I finished talking, I pulled the bottle and vials from my pocket tightly secured them in my palm with my other hand cupped around them as well. As the last words came out of my mouth, I was staring at my hands and could feel the eyes upon me. I drew in a deep breath even though I did not need to but, I knew this was going to sound like hogwash to him. In a last ditch effort to make him believe me I showed him the bottle and the vials he started laughing.

"I didn't know vampires could get drunk." He said through his laughter.

"No Scott please hear me out I know that this sounds funny. When we were here the first time an old friend Jaxson came and visited me." I restated that fact hoping that would calm his laughter but it did not.

The look of scorn and shame fell over his face but I kept pushing forward telling him the story again.

"He told me how to defeat them and it involved going to see a voodoo lady in New Orleans. I did as I was told and came back with this bottle and two vials. The problem now is getting it to the vampires and my brother. This bottle needs to be divided between the three bodies and given simultaneously. This is going to be you and your army's task." I said telling him my strategy. I paused to see if he had anything to say but he was silent. "I don't care how you do it as long as all three are done at the same time if one fails I'm not sure what will happen. Now as for me this one is for me and this one is for my brother and this has to be given to him after you and the army has given this bottle." I shook the bottle at him.

"Sam, how do you plan on getting your brother to drink that?" He asked sarcastically.

"I'm not sure as of yet, this is where Aidan comes in." I turned towards Aidan and said. "I need to know more about my brother wolf side or anything that will help me to get him to take this." I held up the vial of stuff and looked at it.

The purple liquid inside gave me an idea. My brother was half vampire and I could disguise it in blood or make it a final toast to me but would the possessing vampire go along with this? This was something that I was going to have to wait and see. If this plan does not work, I do not know what I am going to do.

"What about the other vile?" Scott asked

"That one is mine, so that I can enter the spirit world and battle to the death. While I am out of my body, Aidan will be taking care of it. However I ask that if something happens and I lose you must kill my body." I said pausing and waiting for a reply but all I got was a head nod. So I went on to say. "One more thing after the bottle has been given you must keep an eye on the Cloaks. I am not sure what happens once I defeat them. They may come back and require a steak at that time but not before then. This is going to be tricky to pull off."

Scott all of a sudden erupted into laughter and said. "Are you joking, did you fall down and bump your head? This has to be the most absurd thing I have ever heard. How do you expect me to have these vampires fight for something that is crazy? Voodoo does not exist and you are full of crap, I'm sorry I don't think we can help you on your suicide mission."

He went on ranting and raving at me. I kept saying repeatedly in my mind Jaxson I need your help. Please help me I begged silently.

"Sam, umm…." Scott had stopped in his tracks with his ranting and raving. I looked up at him and he just stared past me.

"Jaxson, is that really you?" Scott said almost in audible.

"Ah, Scott my old friend, yes it is I. Please listen to her she is telling you the truth." Then just as fast as he appeared, he disappeared. I only saw a glimpse of him out of the corner of my eye.

"Ok, you have my attention now." Scott said after a few moments trying to gather his wits. "I know that they are not going to believe me though." He said still staring at where Jaxson had appeared.

"Well all you need to do is get them to do what is asked. Maybe we can make up some other reason that we need to give out this." I said and held up the bottle and shook it back and forth at him.

"Sam, I will think of something to tell them without telling them about the voodoo." He said still in a state of shock.

"Scott you know it is imperative that I win this battle, because if I lose the whole world loses." I say trying to make it crystal clear my intent.

He flashed a quick smile at me, and then started to walk away without saying another word. As he walked past me, he stopped for a moment like he was going to say something but then just started walking again. Aidan reached over and grabbed my hand. He spun me to his face and kissed me. We started to walk towards that rest of the vampires when I heard Aidan's stomach growl.

"Oh my you must be starving I forget that you have to eat every so many hours. We must find you food." I said feeling bad that I kept forgetting about his needs.

"Sam I don't think that we should be wandering around on our own. They know that we are here. I'm sure they have scouts out looking for us." He said and glanced all around us and sniffed the air checking for any signs of the other wolfs.

"You need to eat I need you strong for tomorrow. You need to be at your best." I say pausing as an idea came to me. "Let's just go see if anyone else wants to go."

As we drew closer and closer to the rest of the vampires, we could hear the low grumbling and whispers. Nothing of significant though, as everyone was discussing other matters about who they drank last night or last week, the weather and everything except the coming battle. We stopped on one edge of the huddle and I cleared my throat but no one stopped to look. Scott must have noticed us just then and he raised his hand and cleared his throat very loudly. Everyone seemed to notice him…Figures I thought.

"Sam has something that she would like to say." He said and pointed towards me.

"Actually it is just an invitation. Aidan is hungry and I need to take him somewhere to get him some food. Does anyone want to go with us?" I say eyeing everyone and practically begging them to come with my eyes.

"Sam, hi I'm James, I can speak for most of the people here and when we are committed to something we all go together so we are all in besides we all could use a hunt anyway." He said and extends a hand towards me in a gesture of friendliness. "Not to mention we have to protect you at all costs to win this battle"

Scott motioned with his hand and said. "Come I know of a dinner that would love to have us." Then he turned and led the way. Aidan and I were shuffled into the middle of the group, and protected on all sides.

CHAPTER 21

We all filled up on blood and of course, Aidan ate people food. Everyone was happy, dancing, and joking with each other. Me on the other hand I sat there and just stared into the abyss not really seeing anything. Scott waved at me though and this caught my attention. He mouthed the words it is time. Everything instantly went into slow motion. There was so much riding on this and it was all on me.

Aidan grabbed my hand and said. "Sam, every-thing is going to be fine." He pulled gently on my hand and we rose from the table and joined the rest of the vampires.

Scott asked everyone if they were clear on what they had to do. Scott held up three vials and asked James and Sean to come speak with him. I do not know what he said to them but I am sure that it was about the delivery process of the vials.

When he was done talking to them, he sauntered over to me. "Sam, you are going to hear two whistles when James and Sean are into position. Then you will hear a third one for the delivery of the vials, after that it is all you." He said and flashed me a small smile trying to hide the worry in his eyes.

"Can you excuse me for a minute?" It had just dawned on me how to get my brother to drink his vile. Actually, the old bum gave me an idea. I knocked him out and took his small bottle of alcohol out of his pocket. I emptied it out and refilled it with the vial that my brother needed to drink. I slung the bum over my shoulder and proclaimed that I was ready.

Running through the forest towards the park that I called home for a while, I could feel the fire starting to lick at my veins and wanting to burst into flames. I barely held them back by telling myself not to burn up the bum. The group started to split off in different directions with Scott, James and Sean in the lead of the three groups. This left Aidan and I alone waiting on our signals. Scott had watched and found a pattern and knew my brother would be in the park. However, this was going to go I needed this moment to leave no unfinished business considering that I may not come back.

I took Aidan's hands in mine and snuggled into him. "Aidan, I love you, I just want you to know that and I'm glad that I met you and if I don't come back please know that these last few days have been the best of my life." I looked up into to his eyes and could see the pain of losing me.

He touched my face so lightly you would think that I am breakable. "Sam doesn't say that you are going to come back to me. I know you are." Then he placed his lips on mine and we kissed and held each other.

"Come on you too this is not the end." I heard a voice from behind me. This startled me I thought everyone had left. I turned and was ready to explode into flames. That is when I saw him.

"Jaxson, what are you doing here? I thought that you were never going to come back and talk to me." I spat at him still trying to calm myself, even though I had seen him a day ago.

"About that, I'm sorry for making you that sad but I didn't want you to spend the rest of your life pining away for me. Sam I really did and do love you, and you are the one that made my cold dead heart thump when I was here. I see that you are happy now and that is all that matters." He said and gestured at Aidan and me and gave us slight smile.

"Thank you Jaxson I really appreciate the kind words. I was pining away for you but when you came to me that night and pushed me to get over you that was the best thing you have ever done for me." I said and returned a huge smile.

"One more thing before I leave, you are going to win this thing. Oh and great idea to bring the human that is going to help you." He said and we heard the first whistle. "I know that is your signal. I made you because I knew that you would do great things with your vampire self. Good bye Sam I love you." He said as the second whistle broke through the forest. He started to disappear.

"Jaxson thank you and love you too, but as friends." I said with a smile and grabbed Aidan's hand.

He smiled at me and then was gone. The third whistled when out through the trees.

"Aidan I love you forever." I reached up and kissed him. My time for good-bye's was over and I had to go. I slung the bum on my shoulder and bottles in my pocket and ran towards the forest where I would find my brother. I heard Aidan say, "I love you too." Then he let out a howl. The only question in my mind right now was how do I find my Brother. This ended up not being an issue as I crossed the border and heard the pitter pater of wolf feet behind me.

"I come to make peace, I just need to talk to my brother, and I am surrendering." I said as clear and calm as I could manage. Even though this was not real I was not surrendering I still felt as if I was.

With one wolf ahead of me and the rest behind me, we ran together like old times. Then they started backing off a bit and the led wolf slowed to a walk. The next thing I knew I was face to face with the glowing red eyes of my brother.

"Sam I thought that you would never come back to me. I have missed you sister." He gestured for a hug but I refused.

"I have missed you as well Brother, let's cut to the chase though. I know that you are not really my brother and that you only want to kill me and that is fine but before that happens I was hoping that we could share a drink and I could say good bye to my brother." I said looking at my brother but knowing that I was talking to one of the cloaks.

"You are a wise one aren't you my child, it is too bad that I have to kill you. I wish you would just join us." A voice not belonging to my brother came from him.

"Sorry I don't believe in your antics. And I refuse too." I said sounding a little harsh.

I bent down and pierced the bum's skin with one fang. And let the blood drain into the bottle. As I did, I collected my wits and asked again this time a little less gruff. "So may I please talk to my brother for a few minutes?"

"Sure, you can but I will be watching." She said with laughter.

When I looked back at my brother's face, I saw the green piercing eyes that had been there before. I knew then that it was truly my brother who I was speaking to. "I love you and I'm sorry that I got you in this mess. I know that I'm going to die now and would like to share my last drink with you."

I held the bottle out to him so he could take the first drink. He took it and put it to his lips and took a sip then handed me the bottle. I pretended to take a drink. You should drink the rest of this one brother as I filled up before I came. I nodded and he took the bottle again. I pulled my bottle out of my pocket and held it behind my back until he had the bottle up to his lips and head tilted back. By the time, I got to the end of the bottle he had already fallen to the ground staring in my direction. His eyes were stuck between the red of the vampire and the green of the wolf.

I opened my eyes and was in another world. This world was all white, the floor, the walls and the ceiling. The only color in this room was the black figures that stood out against the white background. I looked down at myself and realized that they could see me just as well as I could see them. I was all black as well.

"I have come for you. There is no way out." I say almost in a whisper.

The figures turned, and the only thing in their black figures was the red glowing floating eyes that I had seen long ago. I also noticed then that there was another figure that did not turn around and the three figures in front of it seemed to be trying to hide it or protect it.

"Finally, Sam, it has come to this. All you have to do is join us and you may go on living in tacked along with you brother all you have to do is be like us." The figure in the middle said. I flashed back to the time in the forest and could picture her face again. This sent a shiver down my spine.

"You lie," I shouted. "It will never be the same."

Just then, the fourth figure turned around to face me. The glowing green eyes that were like a magnet were shinning though and floating inside the dark figure.

"Sister, don't you want to live with me forever in this wonderful place? All you have to do is join us and we will live in peace forever." He said.

I had not realized that my feet had started to pull me forward towards the warm embrace of my brother and for the love of the family. I had no idea that I was getting too close to them.

"Sam, Sam, Sam snap out of it refuse the eyes. Come on Sam you have to look away, LOOK AWAY!

Sam you can do it you are stronger than this. Look at me I'm here, I'm right here I still love you."

My brain finally registered the last four words. I looked to my left nothing, I look to my right and there stood Jaxson.

"How can you be here?" I asked but then quickly realized where I was "Never mind, that does not matter right now." I said.

I looked back in front of me and notice one of the figures was missing I panicked and started looking around. I finally spotted the figure some distance away from everyone. The green glowing eyes were gone but I still faced the red glowing eyes of the other three. Why had my brother turned away and back away so far? I wondered but didn't have time to dwell on it. I could feel the fire in my veins now. I glanced down at my hands to see them a blaze. One of Cloaks crouched low to the ground getting ready to spring. I ran towards them now not thinking just letting my body do what it thought was right. The next thing I knew two of them were laying on the ground in a pile of ash. The third had escaped my fury and was standing by my brother. I turned my gaze on them, the face of my brother the bad brother was staring back at me now. Somehow, she had gotten in his head and he now was approaching me in a manor to attack.

"Brother please, please come back to me." I begged but there was no change. I tried again but a different approach. "I need you to come back and fight with me, we have to defeat them. I am your sister we share the same blood. You have to realize what you are doing please." I begged repeatedly. Nothing was working he still was approaching and was with in two steps of me now. I did not want to fight him; I did not want to potentially kill him. For the first time I realized that, I might have to kill him for the greater good of all the people of the world and my new family waiting for me. The fire began to rage out of control this time, consuming my whole body. I looked up to see the glowing eyes again but this time something was different it was the glowing green eyes that I loved and I felt for the first time I was not alone and everything was going to work out. Then a flicker of red came across his eyes and I knew that it was a trick. My brain processed the scenarios fast and I knew that I was going to have to use my brother to get close enough to kill that bitch. I glanced up at him with the loving eyes of his sister. I had let the flames go out for the time being I knew that I did not want to hurt him. He grabbed me by the arm and started walking me towards the final call if you will. This was going to be easier than I thought.

"Sam, it is nice to see you again." She said and I could see her face now.

"I can't really say that it is nice to see you." I replied as rude as I could muster.

"I'm going to give you one more chance to be-come like us. Now that you killed two of my friends, I need their replacements. You and your brother would do the job well I think. I was really close to her now but I needed to be within touching distance. Maybe I could talk my way closer to her.

"Why should we?" I asked.

"Because if you don't you will die." She replied as a matter of factly.

"What do I have to do to become your helper?" I said hanging my head a bit trying to act like I was go-ing to give in.

"Now that is more like the questions you need to ask. What you need to do is drink from me and I from you. Then you from your brother and me from your brother then we will be all bonded by each other's blood." She said.

"Well let's get on with it then." I said in a small voice of defeat.

Things were going in my favor so far. My brother released his hold on me and gave me a little shove towards her. My veins were burning I was ready but I had to control this no matter what. I got closer and closer. She stuck out her arm for me to drink from; it was pale and extremely bony. It looked like a skeleton arm wrapped in some kind of very thin paper. I went for her arm and acted as if I tripped over my own feet and right into her knocking us both to the ground and at the same time that my body hit hers I burst into flames. She started screaming and yelled for my brother to get me off her but he could not figure out how the do it without catching on fire his self.

A sharp pain through my back almost made the flames go out but I forced them to keep burning. I turned my head to see what had penetrated my back. All I could see was skeletal bones of an arm sticking out of my back. All the flesh on this arm was gone. She shoved her hand through my left side now. I pulled away from her now, slumped off to one side, and rolled onto my back and the flames went out. My brother was standing there with a look of confusion on his face. Looking at me and looking back at her. I looked over at her as her body turned to ash. I closed my eyes knowing that everything was good now and that I could die in peace.

"Sam, Sam, Sam, don't you leave me now, you did it, you really did it." I tried to open my eyes but they would not open. I could hear Aidan talking to me and I wanted to tell him that I was dying but I could not make any part of my bodywork.

"Sam, honey, please come back to me." I heard him beg but then everything went to black. In the middle of the blackness, I saw a women dressed all in white.

"Sam it is ok now, you won, you can go home everything and everyone is safe." She said I blinked my eyes a few times and everything became clear.

"Mom, oh Mom, where do I go?" I said as tears started streaming from my eyes.

"Come take my hand and I will lead you home." She said and stretched her hand out for me to take.

I reached for her hand. "Mom, where is home?" I asked as she helped me to my feet.

She looked at me tenderly, embraced me, and whispered in my ear. "Home is with me in heaven."

I did not know what to say or do but was enjoying her embrace. Something I had waited for since being turned into a vampire. I could be with my mom forever and finally die like I was supposed to. Something though started deep down inside me starting to nag at me.

"Mom, Is my brother there?" I asked, I was not sure if he had made it out or not.

"Your younger brother is there but your older brother is back on earth." She said.

Right then and there, I knew that I could not go with her. I had to be with my brother. Then there was Aidan, I could not leave him right now.

I slipped out of her embrace and said. "I'm sorry mom I'm not ready to go with you just yet. I want to be with Aidan and my brother. I have a commitment to them.

"Ok Sam I will send you home this time but next time I will have to keep you." She said then disappeared. I watched as she faded into the white room. When she was gone, my eyes closed and I felt like I was free falling into the abyss again.

"Sam, please come home to me." The sweetest voice I had ever heard in my life said. I felt a tear hit my cheek. I wanted to open my eyes but could not just yet. I heard Aidan erupt with the joyous sounds of his best friend back to normal. "Is that you, is that really you." I heard him say.

"Yes, any sign from my sister?" I heard my bother ask.

"No she is not responding yet." Aidan replied to my brother.

"Aidan, I don't know if she is coming back she took a couple of good hits. I was sent back before I knew if she was ok or not." I heard my brother say to Aidan.

All I could hear now was the soft sobs of Aidan and tears hitting my check, rolling down, and hit my hand. I could feel there was a hand tightly wrapped around mine. He put his lips to mine, kissed me softly, and whispered. "Sam, I love you please come back to me."

I wanted to cry to and without a doubt knew that I needed to do something. I had to open my eyes or twitch a finger. I had to let them know that I made it back too. I pushed myself to my vampire limit to let out a very light moan.

"Oh, Sam." Aidan said and started to cry again.

"Aidan try giving her some blood maybe that would help." I heard my brother say.

I could feel the trickle of blood hit my lips and slide down my throat.

"How much should I give her?" Aidan asked.

This was really not doing anything for me though. It lacked something I needed to gain my strength.

"Here let me try." My brother said. His blood hit my lips I could feel all my internal wounds healing. I finally could open my eyes. I gazed into my brother's eyes as he pulled his arm away. Aidan pushed him out of the way and scooped me up in his arms.

"Sam, oh Sam, I thought that you were not coming back. I was so worried." He said as tears started flowing down his face. I put one finger on his mouth in order to shush him up and just planted one big kiss on him.

"I love you." I whispered as I regained my voice. "You are my reason that I came back. Then I noticed that we had an audience and gave him a quick little peck and whispered. "We will continue this later."

I slowly got to my feet with Aidan's help. I was not sure what kind of shape my body was in but everything seemed to be in order except for a twinge of pain in my back. As I rose to my feet, everyone clapped and yelled in approval of the won battle.

"Thank you all for the help and the support I could have not done this without you." I said and put one arm over Aidan's shoulder for support.

With the help of Aidan we slowly walked through the crowd were everyone wanted to either shake my hand or hug me. I just wanted to get out of here. When we got to the back of the crowd, there was my so-called friend's Eric, Shannon and Ted. Tears streamed down their faces, staining there clothing.

"Oh, Sam, we are so proud of you and we hope that you can forgive us we thought that we could help you." Eric said.

"Don't worry no hard feelings." I said.

Ted approached me and threw his arms around me like we had been together the whole time. I heard and instant snarl from behind me.

"Ted, you should release me now. I am with Aidan forever." I said.

He released me, stuck out his hand to Aidan, and said. "I guess the best man won."

Aidan lit up with a smile and said. "Why yes I did."

Aidan put his arms around me and pulled me back against his chest. I exchanged one more glance with them Eric, Shannon and Ted.

"Sorry guys I would love to chat more but right now I really am in need of some blood. So I will see you around." I turned and grabbed Aidan's hand and we walked away.

Out of sight of everyone and in a secluded place, I pulled Aidan to the ground with me. I only had one thing on my mind right now. The blood that my brother had given me was enough to sustain me for a little bit. I would hunt after Aidan and I had some relations.

I never did see Eric, Shannon and Ted again after that day. Of course, I did not seek them out either. I would hear now and again, what they were up to but for the most part, I did not really care unless they were going to cause trouble.

My brother and I had the best relationship we ever had. He was my best friend and we would go hunting together. Obviously, Aidan did not mind because he knew that I was safe. My brother and I had become to be an unstoppable team. The Elders had sent a few more drones after me but they were no were near what the cloaks had been. I guess in a way we became the rulers of the United States.

Aidan and I, well we got married again with all our friends and bought a house and adopted a child. Yes, she is a living breathing child and when she becomes old, enough we will turn her but she will always have the option. I wonder what she will choose to stay human or become wolf or vampire?